Winter

Also by Vina Jackson

Eighty Days Yellow
Eighty Days Blue
Eighty Days Red
Eighty Days Amber
Eighty Days White
Mistress of Night and Dawn

THE PLEASURE QUARTET
Autumn

Winter
The Pleasure Quartet

VINA JACKSON

OPEN ROAD ROAD

INTEGRATED MEDIA

NEW YORK

Cover design by Simon & Schuster UK Art Department

978-1-4976-9869-7

Published in 2015 by Open Road Integrated Media, Inc.
345 Hudson Street
New York, NY 10014
www.openroadmedia.com

Winter

1

Down and Naked in London

The music was loud. The club in almost total darkness. Her throat was dry and she needed another drink.

Heading for the counter her attention was distracted by the on/off flash of the strobe lights crisscrossing the floor.

A familiar face. A hand on a woman's waist. A couple kissing.

She didn't need any more light to recognise the two.

Olen. And Simone.

Giselle was on the verge of tears.

She rushed across the slippery paving stones towards the canal and, in pitch darkness, carefully negotiated the narrow wooden bridge of the lock. In the distance, fast approaching thunder rumbled.

The rain began to fall as she reached the cobbled surface of the left quay. She'd visited Camden Market a number of times before, but it had always been in daytime when it was teeming with life and noise. At night, the place felt desolate and eerie, a ghost town film set.

Her heart felt heavy in her chest, freefalling towards the pit of her stomach. Her whole body ached with pain, a terrible weight burdening her shoulders although there was nothing actually physical about it. The discomfort went deeper, as if her soul were being wrenched apart.

It was slippery and she slowed down.

She wished she could be anywhere but in London right now. Back home in Paris, or — a stray thought that just flitted across her mind — Orléans, though she'd never really known the town of her birth well and relied on suspect early childhood memories of more idyllic times. Or, on a note of pure whimsy, maybe she could flee to her imagined New Orleans in America? A place she had never visited but that existed, teeming with life and voodoo magic in her bookish imagination. Just like a character in the Anne Rice vampire novels she enjoyed reading. As that random and illogical thought struggled to break through, she also realised it had been a long time since the city by the Mississippi had even dawned on her consciousness. Why now of all times?

'Giselle!'

She turned round.

'Please, can we talk?'

It was Olen.

Her first instinct was to run. But something held her back and she waited for him to catch up with her, standing by the canal's bank where it began its shallow ascent to Camden High Street, where she'd hoped to catch a bus and flee the growing storm. Already Giselle's hair was plastered down her face and collar.

He looked even more dishevelled than ever, his thin white T-shirt and skinny jeans wrapped tight around his long and sturdy frame, the jungle of curls in his black hair ironed out flat by the now pouring rain, all his self-confidence washed away, a sorry figure indeed.

He reached her.

'Thanks for waiting,' he said.

All of a sudden, Giselle felt so angry and wanted to punish him for humiliating her so publicly. She remained silent, wiped the persistent trail of tears and raindrops from her cheeks.

He was looking at her with puppy-dog eyes, silently begging for her forgiveness, she guessed. Cut down to size. Shrinking in stature by the second under the lashings of the storm.

Giselle had realised one thing at the moment that she witnessed her boyfriend kissing her friend.

That she wasn't in love with Olen.

The pain of this discovery had been like a knife wound.

She didn't care about him in the slightest. All this time, she had been lying to herself, in love with the idea of actually having a boyfriend. In love with the idea that someone like Olen – handsome, safely exotic – would fall for her. And what kind of fool did that make Giselle?

'What can I say?' Olen asked.

'Nothing.'

And her anger began to fade, to be replaced with pity. Not for herself, but for him. She still liked Olen, she supposed, even if she didn't love him.

And now she must somehow explain why it was that she no longer cared about the fact that he had been making out with another girl.

Yet, she still felt so upset about the whole thing. Lost. Confused. Giselle cared greatly about the fact that she was in a relationship with a boy she didn't love. It was as if some part of her identity had fallen away and she now had to come to terms with the idea that she wasn't who she had thought she was, but some other person altogether.

She supposed she ought to just storm off, but couldn't muster the energy.

An uneasy silence ensued as the rain continued to fall and they stood facing each other, both lost for words. The late night traffic was sparse.

'I'm sorry,' Olen said, his eyes cast downwards as he shuffled from foot to foot.

'You should be ...'

She stumbled for the right words.

'Can we talk about it?' he suggested.

With an angry sweep of the hand, Giselle indicated the weather and shrugged her shoulders.

'I don't think this is either the time or the place.'

'There must be a bar, a café somewhere?'

Giselle glanced across at the road and the nearby hump of the bridge. In the distance the orange light of a cab shimmered and she was seriously tempted to hail it and rush home. But she also knew she couldn't really afford a taxi. If she wasted her money on one, she would probably have to survive on baked beans and toast for the rest of the week, until the next instalment of her meagre allowance reached her account. On the other hand she was getting wetter and wetter here and the lengthy walk to the nearest Tube station would just end up making matters worse. And there was no way she could run the risk of catching a bad cold, what with the half-term exams just a week away.

'We need to get inside ...' she said.

Olen was a year ahead of her at ballet school and settled in London for the long term, no longer weighed down by the pressure of exams. She'd watched him perform several times and he was undeniably one of the stars of their group.

Lithe, elegant and quietly assured, he would glide across the wooden floor of the studio, making the dance look so easy, the graceful flow of his body and his interaction with other dancers seemingly free of technique, a natural. Unlike her, for whom everything was an effort. If only he had been as self-assured in bed.

'Where do you want to go?' he asked her.

'Anywhere but here.'

The black cab cruised up the High Street and was now just a few yards away from them, as Olen raised his left arm to attract its attention. She knew his father ran a major shipping company in Denmark and, unlike her, he could well afford to take taxis. He didn't even have to rely on a grant.

The cab swerved towards the kerb where they were standing and came to a halt. They rushed towards its door and Olen held it open for her as she slipped in, a wave of stale warmth washing over her as she dropped down onto the leather seat. Olen jumped in behind her and slammed the door shut.

'Where to, kids?' the driver asked.

In her present mood, Giselle had no wish to return to her minuscule loft room in Dalston and its constant reminders of unattainable dreams and fractured ambitions. And the small leak in the ceiling that the landlord couldn't be bothered to have repaired and the unreliable hot water supply which made every shower a new perilous adventure.

She looked Olen in the eye. He was waiting for her response.

'Yours?' she suggested. 'But maybe we can have a drink somewhere first? Clear the air?' She knew it was totally wrong in the circumstances to go to his place, a large, airy room at least three times the size of hers that he rented on the third floor of a Kensington mansion that was owned by the school and miles beyond her budget. The words stuck in her throat.

Olen instructed the driver to take them to Notting Hill. Waiting for a night bus cutting its way through the rain to overtake them first, the car drew away from the kerb and then took a right turn below the railway bridge. Giselle realised she could have taken the bus, which was heading towards East London. It was too late now. Had she done the wrong thing? She felt Olen's hand alight on her knee, in search of reassurance or forgiveness, or both, and she berated herself for not having had the strength of mind to storm off and just abandon him in the pouring rain. The cab was swallowed by the night and headed south.

'You don't even care, do you?' he said to her, dismally, as they sipped their drinks in one of the red-leather-covered booths at the Electric Diner.

Ignoring the late hour and her better judgement Giselle had ordered a coffee, hoping the caffeine would straighten out her thoughts.

She had been careful to let Olen slide into the booth first, so she could sit on the opposite side, and now she had a perfect view of his top lip, coated with a thin crust of dried cream and cocoa powder from his hot chocolate which had been served with tiny marshmallows floating on top of a layer of froth. The milk moustache didn't make him look kissable the way such situations did in the movies. Giselle resisted the urge to lean forward and wipe the film of grime from his mouth. She had already decided he looked like a little boy, and had no wish to feel like his mother.

Giselle sipped her espresso and thought about how best to respond. It was an impossible question. Either way, she lost.

She smoothed her damp hair back from her face, careful to avoid dragging the sleeves of her cream silk blouse across the sticky tabletop. The other female patrons were dressed more casually, in denim jeans or miniskirts and neon-coloured tops with sneakers, their teased hair and heavy eyeshadow totally at odds with Giselle's bare face. She didn't wear make-up, and was aware that her cheeks were now drained of colour, and her thick dark brows gave her a permanently serious look that made her seem unap-proachable at the best of times. Her brunette hair had never been dyed, and when it wasn't sopping wet curved around her face in a chic bob, with a blunt fringe that covered her forehead.

Even in Notting Hill she didn't fit in, and worse, to Giselle's mind, she stood out. She was taller than Olen. Only by an inch or so, in flat shoes, but that was enough. And he was by no means short. She had to sit at an angle in the booth so that she could stretch her legs out under the table and avoid tangling with his.

In her cream blouse and neatly cut, short – but not too short – formal black skirt and patent leather flat shoes, Giselle looked, well – French. She wore sheer, nude stockings and a suspender belt to keep the chill off her legs and she knew that this too, was unusual. Most English girls her age wore thick, opaque tights against bright colours that she considered garish, and tightly fitting or low-cut tops that showed off their bosoms.

She supposed that all of this was what had made Olen interested in her. She might have been a bit aloof, but she wasn't stumbling out of clubs at three in the morning with her breasts on display no matter what the weather. Giselle at least looked like the sort of girl who could be introduced to one's parents. Olen had once called her 'classy'.

Giselle pressed her lips together, and decided that she owed him the truth. Besides which, she couldn't think of a suitable lie.

'No,' she finally answered, 'I suppose I don't.'

Her heart felt lighter now that she had spoken the words aloud.

Olen spluttered. Specks of hot chocolate flew from his mouth. He wiped his nose with the back of his cuff.

'But do you care about me?' she asked him.

'Well, of course I do,' he huffed.

'Didn't seem like it tonight,' Giselle snapped, testily. 'When you had your tongue down Simone's throat.'

'Look . . . I'm sorry. I don't know what else to say. It just happened. It didn't mean anything. We'd been drinking, and . . .' He reached across the table, aiming to take her hand in his, but Giselle snatched her palm away before he could reach it.

'At least have the courage not to blame it on alcohol,' Giselle rebuked him. 'Accept some responsibility. You cheated on me.'

'Well, I think that's taking it a bit too far. I'm not saying it wasn't wrong, but it was just a kiss.' His voice was sullen, like a teenager caught red-handed but still in denial. In fact, Olen was still a teenager, though nearly twenty to Giselle's almost nineteen.

She refused to raise her voice, so instead hissed at him.

'You cheated on me!'

Inwardly, Giselle was inclined to agree with Olen. She was French, after all, and believed that a kiss was just a kiss. In the scheme of things, it didn't matter much to her. But she was enjoying watching him squirm. She felt a rush of power over him in that moment, as if because she had caught him out, he was now a captive to whatever punishment she saw fit to mete out. Giselle liked playing God.

The bulb in the light fitting that hung above them was beginning to fail, and buzzed like a mosquito hovering just out of reach. A waiter appeared to fit a new lamp into the socket and take away their now empty cups and saucers.

He was thickset, blond haired and broad shouldered, and moved with a clumsy but overpowering sensuality, like a rugby player who would be better suited to digging ditches on his days off rather than carrying tea trays. The polar opposite to Olen's dark-haired, polished grace.

Giselle caught a waft of the waiter's scent – sweat and musk – a manly odour that caused her thighs to clench involuntarily, and drew her attention to the faint scratch of the lace stocking tops and silk suspender belt shifting against her skin.

'Can you forgive me?' Olen asked her.

'I suppose so,' she said. 'We have to take classes together, so I must.'

Olen nodded imperceptibly. His narrow shoulders slumped a little in relief.

They had both studied ballet in their respective home countries, neither feeling that they fitted in particularly. Giselle the tallest girl in her class, and alongside a bunch of pretty, petite French girls, the only one who could be considered remotely Amazonian; Olen who sometimes felt that he was the only raven-haired, brown-eyed Dane of average height in Copenhagen.

They now studied at the same elite ballet academy in West London. Giselle, always searching for adventure, yearning for the glamour and excitement of a move abroad and finding a compromise with her parents who wanted her to be within visiting distance of home. Olen, ever practical, seeking to improve his English in case he should ever need it for business, when his dancing career – if he was fortunate enough to make dancing a career – came to an end.

Olen had learned some French in school and had used this as an excuse to get nearer to Giselle on the pretence of practising his language skills. She'd been flattered, and a little lonely, and she enjoyed his company and attention, and the chance to speak her native language. Having a boy-friend gave her some kind of power over the other girls. A firm footing in the social hierarchy, normalcy. They'd been dating for several terms.

And now, this.

Giselle felt that the conversation had come to an end. What more was there to say? And yet, they couldn't sit there awkwardly opposite one another forever.

She cleared her throat.

'It is over between us, you do know that? We'll see each other, in classes, but I won't date you any longer.' Even if she had found some measure of feeling towards him, Giselle was too proud to be romantically connected with a man who had treated her so in public. She would not be made a fool of.

Giselle stared at him, trying to find some sense of what had attracted her to him in the first place. Now, she felt not even the slightest jot of chemistry between them. Had she when they first met? She hadn't even known what chemistry was, or how things ought to feel between a man and a woman. Perhaps that was the problem. They were as inexperienced as each other.

'What now then?' he asked her. 'Do you want something to eat? Another drink? Or . . .' He stared at her hopefully.

Giselle sighed. It was up to her again to make the final move, to decide their future. She was tired of always having to lead things between them, as though he was a puppy dog and she his master.

'Let's go back to yours, then,' she said, shrugging into her cardigan.

She let him pay the bill. God knows, she scrimped enough to get by, and he had money to spare, and always insisted on paying anyway.

They huddled together on the pavement near the diner's doorway, trying to avoid the rain and waiting for another cab to come. He tentatively drew his arm around her, and she let him. She knew what was coming next, and that it would be the last time. It hardly mattered now.

Memorable firsts and lasts. Was that what their relationship boiled down to? A beginning and an end.

He held the door of the taxi open for her when it arrived, always the gentleman, and Giselle relaxed against the seat and thought back to their first time together.

In Paris, there had never been the opportunity or, to be fair, the right guy. There was something 'ordinary' about the boys she frequented, drawn from family circles or school, or once removed friends of friends. A lack of excitement. There was nothing sentimental about Giselle, but in her heart she still wanted the first boy she would go with to be different, memorable. She'd always known it would happen in London. The boys there were surely more exciting. They had a cosmopolitan edge. Experience. And tonight was going to be the night.

She'd arrived three months earlier and settled down at the ballet school. The students in her year came from all over, although curiously enough she was the only dancer hailing from France. There were firm-arsed Brazilians, a bunch of fiery Mediterraneans, Nordic girls who appeared to have come off a conveyor belt, with cheekbones to die for, skinny as hell and beautiful to quasi perfection if also distant and unemotional, a bevy of Eastern Europeans who stuck to each other and barely spoke a word to anyone else. The teachers were exacting and the lessons hard. She would invariably return home to her bedsit in the East End every evening, her body screaming in every joint and her mind floating in a fog of exhaustion. The first days had been like a slap in the face; she'd had to forget most of the things she had learned back at the dance studio in Paris that she had been attending since the age of seven, and quickly came to the realisation that the majority of her fellow students were actually so much more proficient, naturally talented and attuned to the art of dancing than she was. Their bodies were invariably the perfect shape, their lines instinctively clean and sharp, their movements effortless, where she was too tall and thick-limbed and strained in silence just to keep up with them and follow the unceasing instructions and corrections.

Giselle looked out of the window at the whitewashed façades of the buildings on the other side of Lansdowne Road. The trees were shedding their leaves with the approach of winter. The sky was beginning to darken as dusk neared. She shivered briefly in anticipation of the next few hours, but the house was warm.

Olen had gone to the kitchen to fetch some wine. His room was just enormous, so much larger than hers, high-ceilinged, tastefully furnished and tidy, prints of old maps and legendary ballet dancers, Fonteyn, Nijinsky, and others she knew she ought to know but failed to recognise pinned at even intervals across the far wall. A plain beige throw was spread across the top of the crisp white bedspread. She glanced nervously at it. Unlike the narrow bunk that took up almost half of her Dalston rental, the bed was spacious, large enough to accommodate even more than a couple, she thought.

'Here we are.' He'd tiptoed back on bare feet without Giselle hearing him, and handed her a glass. 'I could make coffee, you know, if you prefer . . .'

'No, this is fine.' He seemed to be eager to assure her that he wasn't trying to get her drunk.

She took a sip. The wine was rich, fruity and pleasantly warming. It tasted expensive. Not that she knew much about wine, despite her French heritage.

Over the past months, they'd slowly gravitated towards each other, thrown together in classes, rehearsals, breaks.

He was good-looking, in a slightly camp, ethereal sort of way, with his chocolate-coloured eyes and the dark curls that hung over his pale forehead. He could have played the part of an elf, or wood nymph; all long limbs and cat-like grace that made his astonishing strength a surprise, when he performed lifts as easily as if his partners weighed no more than a feather. He was laid back, amusingly flirtatious, and had the most delightful arse, like two peaches balancing perfectly on top of his long, muscled thighs. Sometimes when Giselle saw him stretching on the barre, she wanted to kneel behind him and bite into those firm cheeks. He'd made it clear early on that he liked her, asked her out to dinner on the pretence of practising the French he had learned in high school, and they had kissed a couple of times as the evenings dragged on in smokey pubs around the Cromwell Road and Earls Court where the students from all years often ended their days. One night she had even allowed him to slip his hand under her blouse and touch her breasts. It had felt electric, and daring, with so many of their friends present and egging them on. There had been a sense of inevitability about it all.

And now here she was in his bedroom, planning to go from first all the way to final base in one go, having accepted his invitation to join him on this Saturday evening. They had agreed to go to a club deep in a cellar in Soho to hear some American folk singer perform, and others from their class would be joining them there, but he had suggested they first stop over at his place so he could change following an aimless, quiet, wander together up and down the Portobello Road in the afternoon. They both knew this was a pretext and that they would not be going out again tonight, neither of them being particular fans of folk music anyway.

Giselle could feel the warmth of his body, close to her. There was a faint background smell of lime from the shower gel or deodorant she guessed he used, but also a spicy, darker layer of fragrance, muted but powerful, which she imagined might be the smell of his lust. What did she smell of, she wondered?

His lips grazed her ear lobe and she shuddered.

No one had ever touched her there in such a way.

It felt shocking, but deeply exhilarating. Far less ordinary than a simple kiss on the lips.

She closed her eyes.

She knew this was the calm that preceded the storm, that these caresses would soon become heavier, and that eventually, tonight, she would give her virginity to Olen. That realisation was like a door opening, a vibration birthing in the pit of her stomach and racing across her whole nervous system, the busy canals of her bloodstream, a dam bursting.

His breath hovered inches away from her hot cheeks.

She turned her head. Their lips made contact.

Olen's tongue met hers, the indescribable taste of him penetrating her mouth. The moist warmth. The welcome softness. As Giselle began to process the feelings, the emotions this new private embrace provoked inside her, trying to record every moment so that she could pore over it later, dissect every detail, she felt his hand unbuttoning her cashmere cardigan, and then another hand tugging on the zip of her jeans. How many hands did men have that they could multitask with such octopus-like efficiency? She was rooted to the spot, rigid but compliant, her own hands redundant, not knowing where they should initially travel in response. His face? His hair? Below his belt?

He pressed himself against her and she felt the hard bump tenting his jeans. She knew what it was, although it was the first time she'd ever felt a man's erection.

Still in the throes of the lingering kiss, their lips communing, Olen's tentative hands exploring the bare flesh under the garments he had somehow loosened, Giselle retreated a step backwards, then another, towards the bed. Olen followed her movement, an unsubtle pas-de-deux across the small gap. Her calf made contact with the covers and she began to lower herself down, pulling Olen along with her.

The soft mattress gave and welcomed them into its deep pit of comfort.

Her heart was beating faster.

How often had she dreamed of this moment? Wondered what it would truly be like?

Her lungs felt like bursting and she realised she had stopped breathing, so busy in her thoughts she had forgotten the needs of her body. She pulled her lips away and inhaled. Olen was above her, heavy, his own breath irregular. His eyes peered deep into hers. Impossibly dark pits, decorated by nutmeg-coloured flecks. Warm. Questioning her silently.

'Yes,' Giselle said, assenting to the question that he had not yet asked.

'Are you sure?'

'I am.'

'It's not the reason I asked you back here, you know ...' he lied, struggling for words, as if what was happening was occurring too fast and he was no longer in control of the situation.

'I realise that,' she said. She'd known exactly why she'd agreed to come here tonight, and why he had asked her. She kicked her boots off, recalling with a smile how her parents always chided her for dragging her shoes on her bedspread back home in Paris.

Olen watched her, with a look of adoration.

'Do you have any ... protection?' she asked.

'Of course,' he said hurriedly. 'In the drawer, over there.'

'Good.'

Giselle pulled off her socks and then her tight jeans. She knew her legs were among her best assets. They truly did go on for miles. Olen stared and she began to feel self-conscious.

She took hold of his hands and moved them to her breasts, and he shook out of his torpor.

He briefly struggled with the clasp of her bra. Now he was the one with less self-assurance, although Giselle knew he was a year or so older than her at least and had all along assumed he was more experienced in matters sexual than she was. Apart from his pleasant disposition and looks, it was also one of the reasons Giselle had deliberately settled on Olen as her first lover. Too many girlfriends back in Paris had complained repeatedly of disappointments with younger boys, unseemly fumblings and mini fiascos and a nagging feeling of 'is that all there is?' and she was determined her entry into the world of sex should be more satisfactory.

Once they were both fully undressed and were embracing with a semblance of tenderness, battling their respective impatience, Giselle relishing the feel of his warm, hard penis pressed against her thigh, she had a terrible urge for them to part briefly so she could take it in her hand and inspect it properly. Of course, she had seen boys' cocks before, though never hard. In summer on holiday, the previous year, she and a group of friends had innocently stripped on a nude beach in the south – but this was a new sensation altogether. She didn't want to appear wanton or immodest, and feared that if she were too forward, Olen might think the worst of her and she would acquire a bad reputation. It wasn't easy to ignore a whole lifetime of bourgeois education and conventions.

His hands explored her, shyly journeying across her bare skin and venturing hesitantly into private places. She could feel the beat of his heart, the rhythm of his breath, the incursive velvet of his tongue inside her mouth, again the limey tang rising from his body. Her fingers raked his back, her nails delicately grazing the flesh of his firm arse.

23

Her nipples were hard, and she could feel a familiar heat rise inside her, a slow wave taking shape, radiating outwards from a world within her that had hitherto been wilfully neglected.

It was nice, but she desired more.

Between half-closed eyes, she observed him hurriedly fitting a condom on his cock and they slipped between the sheets, where Olen pulled himself above her. Giselle obediently parted her legs. He adjusted his stance, his eyes focused on hers, his hands diving beneath the covers and aiming his sheathed cock at her epicentre.

His first attempts at sliding inside her were unsuccessful. She was too dry, and they paused for a few awkward moments as he wetted the ends of his fingers and wiped the makeshift lubricant over her entrance.

'You okay?' he asked.

Giselle sighed. 'Yes. Do it. Now.' She held her breath and braced herself for some pain as his cock head finally breached her and encountered some resistance but ploughed on. It was no more than a sharp spasm which faded quickly, immediately soothed by the torrents of endorphins released and a ton of new emotions coursing through her.

They were finally doing 'it'. She, Giselle, was having sex, making love with her boyfriend.

Hands gripping Olen's shoulders, she squeezed them tight, holding him against her and he began his slow thrusts inside her. Giselle abandoned herself to the moment, filled, opened, and she hoped complete.

Less than ten minutes later, no longer joined, awkwardly coexisting between the bedcovers, neither of them could find the right words to say, struggling to understand the etiquette of post-coital conversation. Not that Giselle had come, she knew. Her feelings had been teased, caressed, tempted, but never quite allowed to explode, emerge into a new, shattering light. With an inaudible sigh of regret, she recalled the revelations of her girlfriends' own disappointments. So, as it turned out, neither was she special. It had happened to her too. Maybe it was because Olen was too nice, she reflected, a lovely guy but somehow she couldn't summon enough affection for him. Oh dear, I'm awful, Giselle thought, I've used him. A means to an end. And promised herself that she would learn to love him. Become a girlfriend, a companion, work on it.

'You can stay the night,' he whispered. It was dark outside although the curtains were not drawn.

'I'd like to,' she said.

In the morning, Giselle was determined, they would make love again. And it would prove better. Transport her somehow.

'That was great,' Olen said and put his arm around her and pressed his body against hers.

'Yes, it was,' Giselle lied. Maybe the sex with Olen wasn't

bad. Maybe this was all there was to sex? But somehow, she didn't think so. She can't have been so wrong in all of her dreams, fantasies.

Soon, she was fitfully dozing, her mind a buzzing crowd of questions and doubts.

Giselle wondered idly where this next chapter of her life would lead her. She glanced at the young man sleeping close, his head a mass of darkly angelic curls, his thick, plump lips trembling, a wry smile illuminating his dreaming features. Her first man. And already she knew deep inside there would be others. Many others. She wanted to taste more men, try them, ride them, love them, devour them. But for now, as she gave in to tiredness and the accumulative weight of conflicting emotions that had occupied her all day and still moved deep below the surface of her skin and mind, she was determined to make things with Olen work. She would be his girlfriend. Learn to love him. Be good.

At dawn, each of them woken early by the presence of another in the bed, they fucked again, and Giselle deliberately held Olen's cock in her hands and found it a thing of wonder, and they took it in turns to explore the other's body further. And it was better. Maybe in time it would become perfect, Giselle hoped.

And so it continued. Girlfriend and boyfriend. Lovers together. Until tonight's gig at Dingwalls where she had caught him kissing Simone.

As the black cab drew up to his building in Notting Hill and Olen dug into his pockets to find some banknotes, Giselle's thoughts returned to the present. The rain had stopped.

They walked up to his room.

The bed where she had first slept with him.

'It just happened,' Olen blurted out, covering old ground again. They'd been over this already at the diner. 'I ...'

'Shut up ...' Giselle cried out. And from what she'd seen, it probably hadn't been the first time either.

'But ...'

She didn't wish to learn anything more about him and Simone, whether it had been a random kiss or, more likely, the revelation of deeper betrayal. It no longer mattered. Her anger still simmered but was now beginning to ebb.

'Shut up,' she said again and moved towards him and slapped his face hard. He stood there open-mouthed, in shock. Giselle lowered herself to her knees and unzipped his jeans and pulled his cock out and took him into her mouth. It had taken her a few weeks following their initial tryst to gather her courage and finally suck him, but from the reactions in his body and across his face, she knew how strongly he enjoyed it.

'What are you doing?' he asked, even as he grew hard.

She pulled his cock out of her mouth so that she could reply to him.

'What do you think?'

'But . . .'

'But, but, but, Olen, it's your pity fuck. Our last time,' Giselle said and mouthed him again.

She was not even tempted to bite him.

And in the morning, a final wall of silence drawn between them as she'd occupied his bed and he had been instructed to sleep on the sofa, she returned to Dalston to change her clothes and pick up her dance kit and then headed on her bike to the ballet school for the day's lessons, something she had overnight lost all appetite for.

There had been a time when Giselle had loved every moment of her lessons. Right from the time that she had taken her first steps as a child, she had enjoyed the rigour and the structure of ballet. It had felt like a form of self-control, something that she could channel her energy into, work at, perfect.

A lonely child, without many friends after uprooting from Orléans to Paris, she had relished the chance to assuage her boredom with daily dance practice, and then revelled in the praise from relatives and teachers that her dedication garnered. She improved quickly at first, and she liked the way that her body responded to the various exercises. With concentration and focus she was able to easily master first through to fifth position, but it was not until she began to dance en pointe that she felt her soul fly. Giselle knew that of all the girls in her class she was the one who practised most. Her body was the strongest. And she was determined. Where others would cry after just a few minutes on their toes, Giselle danced on, and became stronger and stronger, ignoring the numbness in her feet, the pain, the blood that sometimes seeped into her tights and shoes.

At home she treated her stinging blisters with water as hot as she could bear, a dab of disinfectant and then a trick that her ballet teacher, who hailed originally from Kiev, had taught her. After cleaning the wound, she cracked an egg, and carefully pulled out a layer of the thin membrane from the underside of the shell and placed it over the blister like a second skin, held in place with a tightly wound piece of pointe shoe ribbon, tied shiny side down.

The next day, and the day after that, Giselle danced on.

But as she grew older, Giselle learned that hard work was not a replacement for natural talent, and while she was no stranger to the former, she did not possess the latter. Her mother and her grandmother were not actresses, models or dancers; they were ordinary housewives accustomed to physical labour, in possession of sturdy legs and strong torsos but lacking the fine-boned, delicate grace of Giselle's doll-like classmates. When they began the swift and tumultuous journey from adolescence to adulthood the other girls flowered slowly like small buds beginning to bloom. Giselle, though, shot up like a weed, several heads taller all at once, and her breasts seemed to quadruple in size overnight. She was not fat, by any means, thanks to her regular strength training, but she was long and lean and by the time she was barely fourteen she had a bosom large enough to create cleavage so that she had to strap her breasts down when she performed on the boards in her leotard to avoid standing out any more than she already did from the other girls.

Still, even when her parents tried to gently suggest that perhaps a different course of study might suit her better, Giselle insisted that she would not give up ballet. If she worked hard enough, she thought, she would improve. Deep down, she knew she'd been lucky to win a place at the academy in London. The audition had been a good day. She'd performed well. Her old Russian ballet tutor, who approved of Giselle's work ethic, had given her a good reference. And her father had paid her fees up front despite his reservations. Now, here she was.

Giselle often stayed later than the other students, and tonight was no exception. She had agreed to meet a bunch of girls at a bar in Notting Hill that served cheap cocktails in plastic jugs for students every Thursday night, and had about an hour to kill. The others had gone home to their respective shared rooms and apartments to change, do their hair and cake themselves in make-up. Giselle instead had chosen to stay at the barre and work through an additional stretching routine. She was strong, but as a result her muscles were short and tight and she struggled to maintain the necessary degree of flexibility.

She also wanted a chance to be alone and think. The ballet studio, when empty and quiet, had a wonderful sense of solitude about it. All that space, and just Giselle's long body reflected in the vast mirrors that lined the walls. With only the gentle in and out of her own breath and the occasional, muffled sound of a passing car on the road outside, she felt apart from the rest of the world, truly alone.

It had been three weeks since she had ended things with Olen. She hadn't missed him at all. Though she did, admittedly, miss the touch of a man's hands on her body. Even if sex between them had always been a little brief and awkward, and failed to drive her to the heights of arousal and release that she longed for, she had enjoyed being filled by Olen's cock and the firm press of his body against hers.

There was a good chance that she might see him tonight. The club in Notting Hill with its usually over-priced cocktails, sleek chrome and violet-coloured leather stools and elaborate glass chandelier-style light fittings was one of Olen's regular haunts.

Beth, one of the few girls in her classes that she had confided in about the break-up, had invited her over to her shared flat off the Portobello Road to get dressed before they went out.

31

'You can try on one of my dresses,' she'd said, looking at her own reflection and flipping her long blonde hair over her shoulder as she spoke. 'I have loads. And I can do your make-up,' she'd suggested, moving across to Giselle and staring at her bare face with a calculating eye as if mathematically decoding what line and shade of eye shadow and blush would best improve her features. 'Show him what he's missing.'

Giselle just shook her head. 'No, you go on, I'll meet you there. Exams are next week and I need the extra practice . . .'

Beth hadn't argued. She knew, as Giselle did, that something was missing from Giselle's movements. She was too methodical, her lines not quite clean or sharp enough. No matter how many hours she put in at the barre, she couldn't replicate the easy grace that came naturally to Beth and others, so that an outsider watching would think that she was barely putting in any effort at all.

Giselle grimaced as she stretched one long leg out in front of her and bent forward to reach past her toes. Her hamstrings never seemed to get any looser, no matter how often she worked on releasing them.

She stood and glanced at the clock; already two hours had gone by since Beth had left. Giselle had been at the studio most of the day. Her stomach rumbled, her muscles ached, and she now had less than an hour to change and make her way to Notting Hill to meet the others. Giselle was never late.

She collected her bag and made her way to the small unisex shower room down the hall to freshen up before changing into a pair of soft black leggings and a deep red cashmere cardigan with a V-neck that she knew clung to her breasts and made her cleavage visible when she leaned forward. She combed her hair and spritzed on a little perfume, but refused to add lipstick or high heels. She would not let Olen think that she wanted him to want her. She would not lead him to believe that he had crossed her mind even for a moment.

'Giselle,' Beth shouted when Giselle arrived, as though it had been weeks since she had seen her friend, rather than hours. 'You've got some catching up to do,' she insisted, taking her by the hand and pulling her through the already crowded bar to the corner that the ballet students had nabbed. Heads turned as the girls made their way through. They were a good-looking pair; one blonde, one brunette, with lean, athletic bodies from years of dance practice, and about the same height as Beth wore high heels with the silver-sequinned mini-dress that just skimmed the top of her thighs, more like a tunic than a frock.

'Olen's here,' Beth whispered, 'at the back. I wanted to warn you.'

Giselle tossed her hair back and raised her chin.

'I don't care,' she replied.

She caught a glimpse of his face turning towards them, but pretended she hadn't, and studiously avoided making eye contact.

Beth handed her an icy-cold pink concoction served in a frosted Martini glass decorated with a glacé cherry on the end of a swizzle stick.

'Thanks,' Giselle said, and winced at the shock of cold against her teeth as she threw her head back and took a large sip.

She hadn't planned on imbibing tonight. Her exams were scheduled for tomorrow, and goodness knows, she needed to be on form if she was going to obtain a decent grade, and retain her place at the school next year. But it was still early, and one drink wouldn't hurt. Maybe letting her hair down might loosen her up a bit, put more flow into her limbs.

Olen was looking over at her again. He was standing next to Simone, whose full lips were red with rouge and slightly open as though she was ready for another kiss. They were both probably sipping mineral water, Giselle thought, and planning to head home before midnight. Home to Olen's bed. A sudden surge of anger made her blood run warm and quick in her veins and brought a flush to her cheeks. She slugged back the rest of the sickly sweet drink in one and picked another up off the table which was littered with left-over drinks since the bartender was serving two drinks with every single order until 9 p.m. and most of the students were staying sober in expectation of their performances tomorrow.

'You okay, sweetheart?' Beth asked. 'That's your fifth drink, and that bartender isn't mixing them weak ... I think he might have the hots for you.'

The music was now so loud that normal conversation was impossible and Beth had to lift a hank of Giselle's hair and speak directly into her ear to get her point across. Giselle had never given much thought to her sexuality and took her straightness for granted − women didn't turn her on − but with her veins full of alcohol and strawberry syrup and the incessant wild beating of Motown rhythms that filled the bar, the closeness of her friend's body and the sensation of Beth's mouth so close to her skin a familiar heat began to radiate between her legs. She was tipsy, and horny.

Giselle turned in the direction of Beth's gaze. She was right, the bartender was staring at her, or the pair of them together more likely. He met her gaze and responded with an obvious wink. Had Giselle been sober, it was the kind of clumsy gesture that she would find immature and lacking in style, but in her current mood the bartender's leering filled her with excitement and a heady sense of her own power over men.

'Hold this,' she said to Beth, placing her empty glass into Beth's waiting hand before turning on her heel and approaching the bar. Even in flat shoes, she was unsteady on her feet, but Giselle felt as though she was dancing across the floor.

'Hiiii,' she drawled.

'Ready for another?' he replied. He took a step back from the bar and flung the spirit bottle that he was holding into the air where it flipped twice before landing neatly back into his other hand.

Giselle giggled. She was fascinated, not by his display of acrobatic mixology but by his bicep muscles which strained through his tight black T-shirt.

He put the bottle down onto the bar and leaned forward, close enough to her that their lips could meet if Giselle so desired.

'I think I've had enough,' she said. 'My exams are tomorrow.' She felt the words pop out of her mouth as though she was speaking into a bubble.

'You're not a schoolgirl, are you?' he teased. 'We have laws against schoolgirls drinking in bars, you know.'

'No, no! University. Kind of. The Ballet Academy.'

'A ballerina . . . that explains your great arse.'

'Thank you,' Giselle responded, without any false modesty. She was proud of her arse.

'I know a few moves, you know. From football, not ballet, but we have to be light on our feet.'

'Why don't you show me?' Giselle purred.

He wasted no time in swinging open the latch on the partition that separated the bar staff from the customers and then swinging Giselle into his arms.

'Hey, that's not what I meant!' she complained, but her voice was teasing rather than angry.

'Well, I only have a minute because I'm on duty,' he insisted, 'and I'm not going to waste it.'

He tipped her head back and kissed her. And Giselle kissed him back.

The fire that stormed through her wasn't just arousal. It was a satisfying mixture of revenge gratified – she hoped that Olen was watching, and that seeing her kiss the bartender cut him – and a rebellious sense of freedom, knowing that after all these years of working for little in the way of results she could say to hell with it, and have a good time for once.

His hands kneaded her arse in a firm, possessive manner so different to Olen's light touch and Giselle responded to this new and delicious force immediately, relaxing against him, opening her lips to allow his tongue to explore her mouth, running her hands up inside his T-shirt and caressing his bare back.

'I want your number, babe,' he whispered as he pulled away. His colleagues at the bar were shouting at him to stop flirting and serve some drinks.

'Sure,' Giselle whispered. She was dizzy and breathless.

But before she could even tell him her name, Beth was dragging her away off the dance floor and out of the door into a taxi.

'Gizzy! Come on! It's nearly midnight.'

Giselle hated being called that, and Beth was the only one she let get away with it.

'Let's get the night bus ...' she muttered. 'I can't afford a taxi.'

'I'm taking you back to my place, and I'll pay for the ride. It's the only way to make sure you'll even make it to school tomorrow.'

Giselle relented, and within minutes was leaning against her friend's shoulder, snoring softly as the city streets flashed by.

In the morning, it was only the strength of several cups of coffee, Beth's insistent nagging and a handful of painkillers that roused Giselle from her bed, into her ballet shoes and plain black dance costume and down to the studio.

She had practised the routines so frequently that she didn't need to think as she danced, which was fortunate, as her brain felt as though it was locked in an ever-tightening vice. But she knew that her movements were formulaic. Her lines were far from clean. There was no joy and certainly no spring in her lifts.

It was all she could do just to make it through to the end without being sick in front of the grim-faced assessors who were judging her so intently that she felt the weight of their disapproval like a lead blanket hanging over her shoulders as she danced.

When it was finally over she collected her things and went straight home, ignoring her classmates' invitation to celebrate with another trip to the pub. Even the thought of another drink made her stomach turn.

She collapsed onto her bed and fell straight to sleep, dreamless, but overwhelmed by a strong sense of dread.

They kept her waiting a full fifteen minutes before she was finally called in. Giselle, sitting motionless in the dean's antechamber, felt both exhausted and resigned to her fate. She knew she had not been summoned for a round of congratulations or small chat about how she had settled down in London or to discuss how tuition was different in France. The small office was brightly lit and the neon strips crisscrossing the ceiling glared mercilessly at her. She expected a stern reprimand and, possibly, the threat of having to repeat a semester. Which would present her with financial uncertainty and the possibility of having to go back to her family and beg for more money.

The door to the main chamber opened and the desiccated lines of Mrs Olga's head peered round.

'Giselle, dear ...'

Giselle rose from the narrow chair, straightened her

anthracite-blue pencil skirt, checking that the red leather belt cinching her waist was at its tightest, and stepped forward, her posture as rigid and professional as she could manage.

She remembered the first and only time she had been in the dean's office previously. It had been during her induction week and she had been part of a group of newcomers to the school. Though welcoming, even then his tone of voice had a deliberate severity that could be chilling.

'Mademoiselle Denoux, thank you for attending,' the deep bass tones of Principal Pinborough's voice greeted her. He sat behind his immense oak desk, while Mrs Olga sat to the side of the desk on a wooden antique chair, her legs elegantly crossed, the exquisite curve of her thin ankles delineated by a pair of black sheer tights, or maybe she wore stockings? Yes, she would, thought Giselle as she took her place on the low-slung sofa that faced the dean's desk.

Giselle nodded.

Pinborough cleared his throat and looked down at her. Mrs Olga's smile was fixed in a rictus of understanding, but it felt too unnatural and forced.

'I assume you know why we wanted to see you, Mademoiselle Denoux?'

'I think so.'

'Are you happy here?' Mrs Olga asked, taking Giselle by surprise.

'Yes . . . I suppose so . . .' What else could she say?

The dean sat back in his tall black leather padded executive chair. Exchanged glances with his colleague. Mrs Olga, whose Lithuanian name few of the students had ever managed to pronounce properly, was in charge of the first-year intake and college lore had it she had been at the ballet school longer than anyone else.

'But it's not working out, is it?'

Giselle's mind went blank for an instant. Then it switched on again, a blur of words and thoughts.

'Well . . .'

'We realise you've been working hard and your attendance record is admirable, but at the end of the day you're just not reaching the standards we expect of you, and all of our other students . . .'

It hurt.

But it was the truth.

For some time now, Giselle had tried to suppress the inner knowledge that she wasn't actually good enough, but to hear it from the mouth of others was like a stab to the heart. She'd had leisure enough to observe her fellow students and knew most had skills far superior to hers. The ability they had to merge their movements with the rhythms of music, the way their bodies reacted to the dance like second nature, it was still beyond her. It wasn't just a question of work or talent: somehow they carried a flame she was unable to conjure in spite of her deepest desire to dance with grace and technical precision. For months, she had been lying to herself. Hoping confusedly that she could coast along and make it to the second year and everything would miraculously click into place and she would flourish, become the butterfly she'd always wanted to be.

'I know,' she blurted out. Panicked. 'I'll put in more practice hours. Apply myself. I know I can improve,' she continued.

The reassuring accent of Mrs Olga interrupted her.

'It's not a question of work, my dear Giselle. You are a lovely girl. But experience tells me that despite all your efforts you have come as far as you can. You're intelligent, attentive, move elegantly, but we just don't believe we can take you to the next level. I know it's painful to hear, but maybe a less exacting environment, another school, might suit you better.'

Giselle tried to repress the tears and the sorrow welling up inside her. Ever since she had been a small child in Orléans, she had wanted to be a ballerina and had danced around the house and the garden and the streets of the town in a joyful daze, imagining herself on a vast stage surrounded by other girls of her age in white tutus and flying swans leaping through the air in a semblance of battle. It had been more than a dream. It had felt like reality. She remembered the hours of negotiations with her hard-faced father trying to convince him that the London school would bring out the best in her, as her mother sighed silently at his side and refused to get involved in the conversation.

And even when she had grown into a woman, and the confused mirage of sex and love had clouded her horizon, it had always somehow been the dance that had felt like a priority. A destination.

How could she now return to Paris, with egg on her face? How would she explain it?

But part of her also knew Dean Pinborough and Mrs Olga were right. She had to accept reality.

She would be allowed to complete the academic quarter, and the news of her departure from the school would not be announced until the end of the recess so that other students would remain unaware of her status until then — this to avoid embarrassment. Giselle gladly accepted.

She skipped the next day's classes and spent the whole time walking around London, looking at places and people with a new perspective. Fixing images in her mind as a form of farewell.

The daytime emptiness of Camden Lock where she had decided to break up with Olen.

The shelter of a tall, green tree by the Albert Memorial where she had allowed him to kiss her and determined he would become her lover.

The tall Kensington building in which she had lost her

virginity and guided a penis into her mouth for the first time, been filled, escorted towards the threshold of pleasure but never quite completed the journey.

She felt sad, but she also knew now there would be others and that Paris would offer as many opportunities to live, move closer to the inviting shores of pleasure and maybe even attain it.

It was something Giselle looked forward to.

Next week, she would pack her bags.

2

Nude in Paris

It would take many years for Giselle to finally complete that long journey from Orléans all the way to New Orleans.

Back then, her mother had given birth to her a week or so earlier than her parents had expected, while the family were in summer residence at their country villa near Orléans, in the French provinces by a curve in the Loire river.

Throughout her childhood she would hear people, relatives and friends, talking of New Orleans in America and she always imagined it as a newer, sleeker version of the sleepy regional city where she was born. It was only in her teens that it became evident to her that New Orleans was in fact rather different, a city of darkness, secrets and legends, as evoked by books and movies. It made an uncommon impression on the young child she was.

A city of future promise, summoning her in confused ways from far across the ocean whenever her mind wandered as, later, adolescent minds often do. The other Orléans, the distant one, the mysterious one.

When she was only five, her parents disposed of their country house and acquired an apartment in a luxurious new development by the sea in Cap d'Agde in the Languedoc, and she would spend her summers by the pool or sea there and the fragmented memory of Orléans faded for a while. It just happened to exist in the clouds of her memory, a name in black ink on her birth certificate, and it was only when she reached her early teens that her town of birth began to take on an extra dimension in her often fevered imagination. Joan of Arc, her history classes taught Giselle, had also hailed from Orléans.

And at night, when the family household was quiet and just the occasional creak of a floorboard or the patchy flow of water in the central heating system, flowing hiccup-style from radiator to radiator, broke the silence, Giselle lay in bed and, her cheeks on fire, would compulsively imagine how Joan, the legendary Maid of Orléans, had been tortured after her capture by the enemy. A prolonged period of intense suffering before she had finally been burned at the stake. Recurring and sharply visual thoughts of the torture and violation both fascinated and repelled the young Giselle, and her guilty thoughts couldn't help but focus on every intimate, single detail of Joan's degradation while pruriently imagining it was somehow happening to her. At the same time, an alien warmth rushed through her body and she would begin to feel an unstoppable wetness rise between her legs as well as sweat trickling through her pores as the madness took hold of her. Discovering this curious form of pleasure and excitement – so terribly arousing – was deeply shameful and she took great care never to share these feelings with schoolmates, brothers or sisters, let alone grown-ups, instinctively guessing it was quite wrong, if not twisted in the extreme.

But time and again, she would picture herself stripped of nightgown, mercilessly spread across a cold slab with shadowy priests and uniformed soldiers gathered around her, defiling her in every way possible, cruelly toying with her and laughing along to her screams.

Until the day she tentatively touched herself in search of relief for the first time, and the guilt and confusion unaccountably faded and she began to find the experience pleasurable.

It had felt like emerging into a brand new world.

But one she held private, wary of making this important discovery in any way public. And then she had begun growing up and things in her mind had become both clearer and more confused, and the complicated feelings had slipped into the background, while she negotiated the thin line between studies and dance school and later moved to London and met Olen. And then ultimately broke up with him.

It wasn't until, a few months into her work for William, when he had casually asked her to pose as Joan of Arc, the Maid of Orléans, as a result of a new commission he had obtained from one of his mysterious clients, that those troubling memories had returned with full hurricane force. By then, she had become William's lover, maybe also his muse.

Giselle had arrived back in Paris and initially camped out on a friend's sofa for a week before she'd summoned up the courage to contact her parents and announce her return to France.

Her mother took her into her arms and asked no questions, her support unwavering. But it was not until the evening when her father arrived home from his surgery that things became sticky.

'Back for good?' he asked, with already a hint of disapproval.

Giselle sat at her usual place at the dining room table, nibbling with a lack of conviction at the salted caramel shortbread which had once been her favourite dessert. Only her younger sister was present in addition to her parents. Her two elder brothers had both, as planned, left the family home while she had been in London, one to work in Brussels as a translator for an NGO and the other to live with his Italian girlfriend in Rome where he worked as a sous chef in a Michelin-starred restaurant.

'I think so,' Giselle admitted, lowering her eyes to avoid his austere scrutiny. His thick black-framed reading glasses were perched on the end of his nose and the lenses magnified his pupils so that Giselle felt like a small rabbit caught in the gaze of a barn owl.

'What happened? Did something go wrong? The school throw you out?'

'Not really. I'm just not good enough.' Giselle bit the bullet and blurted out the inconvenient truth. 'A dancer . . .'

'I see,' was all he said in response.

She expected him to begin berating her for the waste of money the London adventure must have cost but he didn't, and his continuous silence wounded her even more. As if by remaining mute he was confirming her lack of sufficient talent had been known to him all along. Deep down, Giselle knew that it had. Her father had never praised her dancing.

'It's not the end of the world,' her mother interjected. 'You're still a wonderful dancer. Maybe a less classical environment might suit you better?'

She had always encouraged Giselle to pursue artistic aims.

Her mother rose from her chair and walked over to the kitchen to get the coffee pot. She looked older than she had the last time Giselle had visited home, but was still a handsome woman. Her hair was fully grey now and hung loose around her shoulders, thick and lustrous. The strings of her apron tied taut around her waist indicated that she had so far escaped the advance of middle-aged spread and her posture remained straight as an arrow. She stood erect and proud even when undertaking simple chores, and she moved across the kitchen floor with firm, deliberate steps. It was clear where Giselle's figure and bearing had come from; unfortunately, though impressive in its own way, her physical inheritance, which might have been perfect for the rigid solemnity of a marching band, was not best suited to the fluid grace of ballet.

When she returned, Giselle's father asked, 'So what are your plans now?'

'I'm not sure I'd want to go back to my old school. Maybe I should forget about a dancing career. I think I'm just too tall for ballet.'

'Probably. So, what else?'

'I was thinking I could take some new courses, see what I'm best at. Enrol at the Sorbonne maybe?' Before the move to London, it was something he had proposed and encouraged and that she had vehemently rejected, and it felt humiliating having to fall back on this, and prove her father right.

'And you'd want us to underwrite it all?'

Resenting his tone, she recklessly rebelled and announced, 'No need. I'll find some part-time work. If it's okay with the two of you, I'll live here until I can afford to find my own place, save up a bit first.'

Her mother argued this wouldn't be necessary, but her father just nodded.

'It's your life, young lady.'

No more words were said on that initial evening. Though she tried to pretend otherwise, Giselle's pride was a little wounded. She had hoped her father would at least try to talk her out of giving up ballet, or soothe her feelings by suggesting her teachers must have underestimated her skill. But he was too honest and too blunt for that.

That night, back in the room that had witnessed her transitioning from little girl to young woman and that she had since outgrown, Giselle slept fitfully, thoughts rushing in all directions, frantically trying to grasp a firm point of reference, her mind a maelstrom of emotions. Every second of her London sojourn was now indelibly imprinted on her memory, the good times and the bad. The wonderful few occasions that she had reached a zone of silence and grace while dancing. The soft touch of Olen's lips. The unsettling and then welcome feeling of having him inside her. The rhythm of his timid thrusts. That constant balance between navigating the slope to pleasure and the nagging knowledge she had always been just a few inches, just a few seconds away from reaching her goal and coming, but never managing the feat. The highs. The lows. The shame of the confirmation other dancers were better and that, despite her best efforts and hard work, she couldn't reach their standards and make it all look so wonderfully effortless as most of them did.

Where now?

Sleep eluded her.

The following morning the post brought two letters from Olen posted in London a day apart. She swore not to open the envelopes and read them, and when temptation crept across her mind, abruptly tore them up and disposed of the pieces in a bin on the Boulevard Saint Germain. Giselle knew she had to close that chapter. She didn't love him, and that was the end of it; there was no point in maintaining any lingering communication between them even if in her current low state kind words from Olen would have brought her some measure of comfort.

A clean sheet, that's what she needed, and the inflexible inner discipline to, from now on, follow her own agenda and not allow herself to be distracted by the superficiality of others, or the contradictory feelings about her body and sexuality flowing inside her veins. The tingling in her limbs had become a constant accompaniment to her waking hours, accompanied by the knowledge of her incompleteness and the impatience that gnawed at her heart to find a solution to it, a man, but Giselle now realised he must be able not just to satisfy her bodily needs but also to soothe that cauldron of simmering desires that kept her alive.

She ended up finding a part-time job at Aquarelle, a large flower shop on the Rue de Buci in the Latin Quarter, just metres away from a flourishing food market. Five daily shifts between five in the afternoon and eight when the shop closed, and also Sunday mornings. An old school friend of hers knew the owners and had put in a good word for her.

But the money she would earn there was, for now, wildly insufficient for her to find a room or a small flat of her own, even in the furthest reaches of the capital, so she had to continue living in the family apartment in Neuilly. Because of her hours, however, she managed to avoid the tense meals together on most days.

She also signed up for a course at the British Council on Rue de Constantine to improve her English skills. Back in London, she had mostly socialised with other foreign students and had been unable to get involved with enough Brits. There was Beth, of course, but part of the reason that she and Beth had become friends was because they both valued silence, and when they did talk it was mostly in the colloquial way that friends do, so the conversation between them had never been enough to achieve the real improvement she knew her grammar and her accent needed. The English course allowed her to obtain a student card, and although she wasn't actually registered she was able to gain access to the university's Censier-Daubenton campus where she began to follow lectures on American literature in the vast, booming amphitheatres, lost among the crowd of official students, taking notes and discovering a whole world of words that had eluded her until now, fixated as she'd been by music, dance and performing to the detriment of words.

Unlike the others attending the classes, Giselle wasn't planning to take any exams or undergo individual tutoring. She was just a hanger-on, thirsty for knowledge, keen to open a window on new worlds, and the complicated universe of American letters was so much more vibrant than the staid progress of French culture, with its bad school-day memories of straight-jacketed plays by Molière and Racine and the mechanical rhymes of too many poets who had always sounded more constipated than inspired to her.

The only drawback was that too much of her modest income now went on books, even though she managed to acquire the majority of them cheaper second-hand at Gibert on the Boulevard Saint Michel, a continual expense which delayed her hopeful independence even further. Most of the friends she had renewed contact with since her return from London and the sparse, new acquaintances she had made around the university halls and cafeterias were as broke as she was, surviving on shrinking bursaries and parental hand-outs, and few of them had any worthwhile suggestions as to where or how more money could be earned, and even menial jobs in stores or waitressing were impractical as the regular required hours would inevitably interfere with the schedule of lectures she wished to attend.

But Giselle was content. She was evolving a quiet routine and the days passed in peace, even if she always felt as if she stood unsteadily perched on a diving board, poised to leap into unknown waters.

It was ten o'clock on a grey and windy Tuesday morning, the first time she saw him. Freya, a buxom Norwegian girl who worked day shifts at the shop, had called and asked her to come in and help, as one of the other student workers had phoned in sick and they were expecting a large delivery that would keep Freya busy sorting buckets in the large cool room out back. Giselle had agreed to forego one of the classes she usually attended in order to cover the till. She needed the money, and after all wasn't officially enrolled, so didn't have an attendance record or exams to be concerned about.

When the bell rang to signal that a customer had entered the shop, Giselle felt a rush in her veins that made her glance up. It wasn't a premonition — even if she had believed in such things — there were no accompanying visions of the future, chills up her spine, nor goose pimples rising on her arms. Neither was it a gust of cool air. It was blustery enough outside that she'd brought the sign in to save it from being blown down the street or into passing traffic, but the angle of the shop door was mostly sheltered by the awning out front.

No, it was something else that had caused her to turn her attention to the man who walked into the store. Later, when she turned the memory over in her mind as if she was examining a precious gem for further fine details, she decided that she had sensed his presence before she had seen him or heard the doorbell ringing.

Male customers at Aquarelle were not an unusual sight. Quite the reverse. Many of their customers were male. Some were regulars – they either came in person or they had regular diary orders set up to request a bouquet delivery to their mothers and wives and mistresses for birthdays and other special occasions that demanded flowers. Others came in evidently flushed and visibly sweating with nerves, having realised at the last moment that they had forgotten Valentine's Day or a dinner engagement or had committed some other relationship faux pas and were desperately seeking some token to stave off a woman's anger. None of these men really cared for the flowers. Giselle was equally attentive over every order regardless, but she knew that in most cases she could have sent the guy out the door clutching a bunch of cabbages with a ribbon around them and he'd never have known the difference.

This man was unlike the others.

Giselle found her eyes drawn to him like homing beacons as he stepped softly around the room, carefully checking each bloom for health, colour and whatever other criteria he evidently had in mind while making his selection. He touched some of the petals ever so softly in the way that a seamstress might run her hand admiringly over a fine piece of silk. He was almost waltzing from one plastic pot to another, and apparently as utterly absorbed in his task as she was in him. He did not look up at her once until he had finished filling his basket, so Giselle had ample opportunity to study him.

What struck her most was his sheer bulk, such an odd juxtaposition in contrast with the tiny buds on the stems he collected. He wasn't fat, but he was tall and broad with thick biceps and forearms that swelled through his rolled-up shirtsleeves. His skin was deeply tanned, the colour of nutmeg, and his hair was jet black, thick and a touch too long. He wore the hairstyle of a man who has neglected to go to the barber's for a few too many weeks, but his beard and moustache were close cropped and trimmed neatly, with geometric precision.

Giselle longed to know if his chest hair was equally thick.

'Can I help you, Monsieur?' she asked boldly, although

he didn't seem to require any help. Her voice caught in her throat and came out with a distinct croakiness. The sound made her blush.

He lifted his chin, startled, and shifted his shoulders back, but did not turn around.

'No, no, thank you,' he called over his shoulder and carried on making up his bouquet, stem by stem.

Finally he finished and took his purchases to the cash register, laying the whole bunch down on the counter with the same care and tenderness that a mother might employ when putting an infant to bed.

How would he be with a woman, Giselle wondered? The thought just popped into her head, and once it had reached her brain she was unable to forget it. When she noticed the slight hook in his nose she thought of it brushing against her clitoris. Not that cunnilingus was an act she had ever actually experienced. Olen had never gone down on her, although she did on him. She had learned all about the wonders of tongue on vagina from Beth, and to Giselle, who was all too familiar with the pleasures she could bring to herself by applying the right pressure to certain parts of her mound, it sounded wonderful.

When she drank in his mouth, those full, deep-red lips, she thought of how they would feel pressed against her own. The slightly upturned edges almost formed a smile and softened the severity of his thick brows and high cheekbones. His jaw was the shape of a comic superhero's, sharp and angular with a square chin. His eyes were a warm brown, like melted milk chocolate, and his lashes were thick and full, the sort that would have belonged to a woman if God or evolution or whatever was responsible for the creation of the human species had been fair.

'Would you like those arranged into a bouquet, Monsieur?' she asked him.

He reached into the pocket of his jeans, extracted a bunch of crinkled-up notes and began counting them out, smoothing each one as he did so. Evidently he did not carry a wallet and his neat precision in other matters did not extend to his finances.

'Just some paper would be fine,' he replied, indicating the loose grey sheets that covered the countertop and were used just to protect the bench from the inevitable stray leaves and dampness that seeped from the stalks of flowers as Giselle was arranging them.

'Are you sure? I could wrap them in plastic with a water pocket at the base to keep them fresh.'

'No, no,' he insisted, furrowing his brow in an effort to cover his impatience. 'I don't have far to go.'

Giselle obliged, expertly wrapping the bunch in a couple of sheets to protect his hands from any thorns and protect the petals from the wind.

'A special occasion?' she enquired as she rang up his

purchase on the till and the register sprang open, her curiosity driving her to push the man further although she could tell that he was now eager to leave.

'No. For me. I happen to like flowers. That is all.'

She felt embarrassed that such an admission should seem strange to her. There was nothing wrong with a man liking flowers, after all.

Giselle handed him his change and he stuffed the coins into his jeans. They were dark blue and tight, she noticed, as she leaned forward and briefly glanced down at his crotch. Warmth radiated in her own groin as she imagined how thick and long his cock must be. It would be a cruel trick of fate if his package were not in keeping with the rest of his stature.

He nodded his thanks, picked up the wrapped bunch, and turned and left. Giselle's eyes followed his arse all the way out the door.

'Ah, I see you've met William Tremblay,' said a voice behind her.

Giselle jumped. She hadn't noticed Freya emerge from the cool room and wasn't sure how much of their exchange the older blonde woman had observed.

'Is he a regular, then?' Giselle asked.

Freya was rubbing her pale hands briskly against her apron to warm up. Giselle knew from experience how cold it was working in the chiller. The temperature sneaked up on you. At first the coolness was refreshing, especially if you had been tasked with lifting some of the heavy plastic containers full of water and flowers from the delivery van parked on the side street to the shop and into the fridge. But if you spent too long in the cool room sorting the vats so that the oldest blooms that needed to be used up first were closest to the front then gradually the cold seeped into your bones, like the persistent icy touch of a malevolent spectre that only a long soak in a hot bath could assuage.

Work at the florist was far more labour intensive and vigorous than Giselle had expected from a profession that she first considered rather feminine and delicate. But that was one of the reasons that she enjoyed it. At least her body was still getting a workout in the absence of dance practice.

'He comes in every Tuesday,' Freya replied, 'to get the best of the new shipment.' She blew on her fingers as she spoke and had begun jumping up and down. The motion made her large breasts bounce and for the second time that morning Giselle found herself mesmerised by the body of another. Since so many of the flower-shop duties involved bending over, and Freya often worked double shifts, Giselle had often been unwittingly exposed to Freya's expansive cleavage and had wiled away many a quiet moment imagining whether the Norwegian's nipples were large or small, dark or pale pink, insensitive or easily inclined to hardness as Giselle's were.

'For his wife, girlfriend?'

Freya snorted.

'No, he's single, as far as I know. Probably has lots of lovers, though. The man's seen half of Paris naked, or so it's rumoured.'

'Really?'

He seemed so brusque and disinterested to Giselle. She couldn't picture him as a ladies' man. In truth, she'd been a little surprised, and somewhat miffed, that he hadn't looked at her admiringly or bothered to flirt at the counter. Giselle wasn't a vain woman but an honest one, and the truth of it was that most of the male customers did normally give her a second look.

'He's an artist. Paints, draws, so on. Nudes, I'm told, and some of them pretty racey.'

'Have you posed for him?' Giselle asked.

'Gosh no!' She paused and ran her tongue over her lips. 'I would like to. But I don't have the courage. He's awfully handsome but has such a hard look in his eyes, I think I'd crumble before I got my pants down. You should apply, though. With that figure of yours, I'm sure he'd welcome the idea, and I think he pays.'

'Pays?'

'Oh, probably not much, but he's posted fliers in here once before, seeking models for art work. I might even still have a copy in the desk drawer out back. Or we certainly have his phone number in the diary. He may still be looking. Why don't you call and ask him?'

Giselle's heart beat like a drum. She pictured herself spread naked under that severe stare and the thought was enough to make her dizzy. Besides which, she could do with the extra money, and it didn't seem like a difficult thing to do, just sit there with her clothes off.

'I think I might,' Giselle replied, lifting her chin to strengthen her resolve.

'You do know he's much older than you, dear. Be careful, won't you?'

Giselle hadn't really noticed his age. She supposed he was older than her. Probably more than ten years older. He had looked to be in his mid-thirties, she guessed. But she knew that with some men appearances could be deceptive. He could even have been older.

But then, she remained convinced that one of the reasons things hadn't worked out with Olen was his youth. He might have been a year or so older than her, but it was always said that girls matured so much more quickly than men. And besides, she was only going to pose for William, wasn't she?

Freya found his phone number, and with shaking fingers and an even shakier voice Giselle dialled and asked him one day later if he was currently in need of any life models. She didn't mention that they had already met, in case the call went horribly wrong.

Yes, he would see her. They set a date for the following Thursday.

That night Giselle lay in her single bed, blanking out the sound of her parents snoring softly in the room next door, and she imagined William's fingers tracing a path from her mouth to her cunt, as gently as deftly as he had touched the petals of flowers in bloom.

She looked down at the scribbled address on the crumpled piece of notepaper she held in her hand. Yes, this was it. The door to his studio was painted dark green, the colour of a Christmas wreath, and stood at the top of several concrete steps. A rusty iron railing ran down one side, badly in need of repair. Even though she was tall, from her position on the footpath the knocker hung well over Giselle's head, as if the door itself was looming over her, just as he had.

William Tremblay. Could she call him William? Or should she continue to call him Monsieur? She smoothed down her skirt – cream with a floral pattern, it reached nearly to her knees – and lifted the knocker. It made a dull sound, the metallic thud of brass on brass, and Giselle frowned. No one would hear that, surely. Then she realised that of course this was the door to the main entryway, and the knocker was totally unnecessary. A panel of buzzer buttons was situated at her right and she pressed the one labelled 'WT'. He was on the third and top floor. There was a click sound, as if someone had picked up the entry phone, but no words were spoken over the intercom. Giselle continued to wait. A chilly gust of wind rattled along the street and she crossed her hands over her chest and briskly rubbed her arms, wishing that she had worn something warmer than her high-necked silk blouse.

The door swung open.

'Giselle,' he said to her, by way of greeting. He was dressed in a pair of slim-fitting navy-blue corduroy trousers and a black collared shirt that looked as though it had seen better days. He was barefoot. His hair was unkempt, as if he had spent all morning running his hands through it. He was as tall and as muscular as she had remembered.

She nodded.

'Come,' he replied, and turned his back, indicating that she should follow. She stepped over the threshold, and followed him down the length of the gloomy hall to the lift.

'I usually take the stairs,' he murmured, indicating to the flight of steps alongside them, 'but I don't want you red-faced, for the portrait. Even if it is a drawing and not a photograph.'

Giselle was about to protest that she was perfectly fit enough to climb a few steps without huffing and puffing when the elevator dinged to indicate its arrival and William folded the screen across and pulled the metal slatted cage door open. It was a claustrophobic space designed for one person, and certainly a smaller person than William. Giselle followed him inside, holding her breath and hoping that he would not notice how dizzy his presence made her feel. How the light-as-air touch of his skin briefly brushing against hers as he moved his arm to his side and bumped against her made her sway on her feet. She inhaled, analysing the peculiar scent that clung to him. Cigar smoke – her father smoked cigars, so she knew that smell – and the sharp note of lemon. No, not lemon, lemon verbena, Giselle inwardly corrected herself, a herb she recognised as it was one that her mother grew in small pots on the kitchen windowsill. She looked down at his hands, the thick, strong finger ends blackened with charcoal so they resembled used match sticks, but much larger. She was grateful that he could not read her thoughts. The dreams that she had evoked about those fingers. How much she wanted him to unbutton her blouse and take her breasts in his hands. And yet, she wanted him to know how she felt, for surely she would not have the courage to tell him, ever, and then how would they move beyond artist and subject?

'Would you like some mint tea?' he asked her, when they arrived inside. 'It's all that I have, I'm afraid.'

'Oh yes,' she said. 'Please,' although she had never drunk mint tea before. She usually drank coffee.

She looked around for somewhere to put her bag down,

and in the end just dropped it on the floor by the door. There wasn't much furniture in William's studio. Just a large bed at one end, a chair in the middle of the room, under a skylight, and another chair by an easel across from that. The small kitchen that William now stood in was separated from the main part of the room by a wooden bench, and on the bench stood a vase with the flowers that he had purchased from the shop. The buds had now opened, but they were not past their bloom. Giselle walked across and smelled the flowers, cupping a yellow rose in her hand so that she could deeply inhale the scent. Its petals tickled the end of her nose.

'I recognised your voice on the phone,' he said. He had plucked a handful of mint leaves from a small pot of the herb that stood alongside the kitchen tap, placed them into large white mugs, and was pouring boiling water over them. He added several spoonfuls of sugar to his cup and she stopped him adding any to her own.

'I don't have much of a sweet tooth,' she remarked, by way of explanation. He raised an eyebrow.

'You work at Aquarelle,' he continued. 'But I hadn't seen you there before.'

'I usually work the late shift. One of the other girls called in sick.'

'And you saw one of my fliers? I did leave some,' he mused, 'but that was a long time ago. I was working on a commission with something of a botanical theme. Thought that subjects with an appreciation of matters floral might suit, but it didn't work out that way.' He shrugged. 'You're here now, though; perhaps I gave up too soon.'

He sipped his tea, and looked her over. His gaze was both appreciative and calculating. Giselle felt as though he was taking her apart with his stare, inch by inch, weighing up the respective value of each of her parts with mathematical precision and then putting her back together again. A model, both literal and figurative, like a doll that had been crafted limb by limb for the purpose of posing for him.

She could think of no particular reply, so instead took a gulp of the hot drink he had made for her. It was pleasant and warming; the mint had its own sweetness. She was waiting for him to take the initiative and hoped he would do so quickly before she lost her nerve.

'Ready?' he asked. 'We should get started, while the light is still good.' He reached his arm out towards her and took the mug from her hand although she hadn't finished. 'Go', he said. 'Stand there. Where the chair is.' He walked over and removed the chair. 'Take off your clothes.'

Giselle stepped out of her skirt and tugged down the elastic of the pristine white cotton Prisunic knickers she had after much deliberation decided to wear today.

Her clothes pooled around her feet on the dark wooden floorboards of the artist's studio.

She was naked.

She didn't look up, conscious of the older man's gaze.

In her mind, she had rehearsed this moment several times during the course of recent days, but her feelings still came as a surprise. She felt no shame or embarrassment at being so crudely exposed in the sharp cone of light illuminating her from above, as the bright glare of the midday sun surged through the large square skylight. On the one hand, there was a latent fear he might not actually take a liking to her body, would not appreciate her lean frame and the subtle bend of her hips, both in stark opposition to her full breasts which did not belong on a dancer, even an ex-ballet student. On the other hand, a defiant part of her silently screamed out to be noticed, excavated a kernel of sexual madness at the thought, the sheer need to flaunt herself in front of a man in this manner. It was a fight between decorum and arousal.

Instinctively, as the clothes had fallen aside, she had curved her shoulders and brought her hands forward to protect the dark cupped mound of her tight pubic curls, even though she knew how useless the gesture was in the circumstance.

'Straighten up, please.'

His tone was so brusque it was obvious that he had tacked the 'please' on for politeness' sake. He was articulating an instruction, not a suggestion.

She looked up and her eyes locked with his as he examined her with an appearance of indifference. How many naked women had he seen already in his career? A hundred? A thousand? Maybe for him she was just another piece of meat, something impersonal. She didn't know how the mind of artists, painters worked.

Giselle moved her hands away. Swallowed hard. Still, he looked dissatisfied.

'Your posture is terrible. All that slouching,' he added.

Her cheeks went red. He was right. She hadn't realised how hunched she had been. The involuntary consequence of her frayed nerves and insecurity, her body's automatic attempt at modesty. She imagined that she was back in ballet school. Remembered the instructors' constant reminders, orders. She pulled her shoulders back, held in her stomach, and her breasts jutted forward, her strong dancer's legs moving just an extra inch apart to retain the solidity of her balance. Almost as if she were flaunting herself. But never had she had to do this in the nude before. Or for the benefit of an audience of just one. A man.

William walked towards her, his gaze unflinching. Giselle shivered briefly. He began to circle her clockwise, then again but anti-clockwise this time, observing, measuring, weighing, she guessed. Smelling her too? He was a head or so taller than her. Before coming here she had washed her hair, using her favourite shampoo with just a hint of magnolia fragrance, brushed it endlessly to capture just the right sheen. Since arriving back from London, Giselle had begun to grow her hair longer. He'd just asked her to come as she was, do nothing special, insisting she wear no make-up even, but she had felt more was required. Had she subconsciously planned to seduce him or was she hoping to force him into seducing her?

'I like your perfume,' he said.

Yes. A minor triumph.

His voice behind her. His eyes no doubt examining the cleft of her arse, the line of her legs, the olive-tinged pallor of her skin. A familiar tremor birthed in the pit of her stomach. Taking a grip of her heart, precariously shimmering in the orbit of her clit, projecting pins and needles into her extremities.

'Get dressed again,' William said and she felt a sudden sense of disappointment. 'There is a rack over there.' He pointed to the far wall of the studio where a rail, laden with an assortment of outfits, stood. 'I want to begin by doing some charcoal sketches of you.'

As Giselle walked over, she was acutely aware that his eyes were fixed on the way her backside inevitably swayed gently from side to side as she moved and repressed any attempt at exaggerating the natural, wanton rhythms of her flesh for his delectation. She had his full attention already.

She was confronted by the tall rack of garments.

'What would you like me to wear?' she asked.

William had turned his back to her and stepped over to his work bench, where paints, brushes, pencils and uneven piles of material and sheets of art paper were scattered.

'Anything,' he called back. 'It's not important.'

'Really?' she queried.

'Yes. I'd like to spend our first hour together drawing just your face. To get the measure of you. So your clothing will be of little matter.'

She could have kept on the skirt and blouse she had been wearing to visit him, Giselle realised, for all he cared. But he had requested to see her body first. She felt confused.

She pulled a V-necked top at random from one of the hangers, a deep red shapeless confection in chenille material, which she slipped on, its smooth but distinctive pitted skin grazing against her hardening nipples, and walked back to the chair where she had left her skirt and pulled it on, neglecting the white cotton panties she had earlier been ordered to jettison.

William was still ignoring her.

'Where do you want me to stand? Or sit?' Giselle asked the artist.

'In the centre,' he said. 'Where you stood before when I inspected you.'

Giselle moved back into the cone of light. It felt like

being on a stage, the crude illumination of a spotlight shining on her, highlighting her silhouette, awaiting a hypothetical performance.

For a moment, she was lost in thought and was taken by surprise when, suddenly, William arrived by her side, his progress across the wooden floor of the studio quite silent. He handed her a backless stool. 'Here. Sit.'

Giselle installed herself on the narrow seat.

'As a model, you must learn not to move,' William said. 'Try to find a position that will not prove awkward. Best is, I'm told, to attempt to just blank your mind. It works for some. Daydream.'

Giselle nodded and shuffled her backside into a semblance of comfort. She looked around at William, expecting him to erect some sort of easel, but he was just drawing rapid lines on the sheet of paper he'd spread across his lap for now.

'Don't move,' he reminded her.

'Oh, sorry . . .'

He kept on drawing, broad strokes racing across his sketch, assured, fast, precise.

'Would music help, maybe?' William asked.

Giselle thought. 'No. I'll be okay.' She feared any music might make her want to sway even more, suggesting rhythms and movement to her body, her senses.

An hour went by in almost total silence as William worked away. Giselle was curious to see the results as sheet after sheet of paper joined an untidy pile and he ceaselessly moved on to yet another sketch.

Finally, with a deep sigh, William stopped.

'I'm done,' he proclaimed. 'You can move those long limbs of yours now,' he suggested. 'I'm sure it will come as some relief. I know how difficult it always is the first time.'

Giselle slipped off the high stool, her bare feet slightly numb as they made contact with the unyielding wood of the floor. She stretched her legs. She badly wanted to see the work William had produced, to find out what she might look like through his eyes, but guessed it would be bad form. She knew artists had their habits and it would do her no good to rush him. Would her features be broken up into geometrical patterns like a Picasso odalisque? Would he have added kilos to her cheeks and chin, like a Rubens matron? A Mona Lisa smile, a frown, a sadness?

He offered her a coffee and a bowl of fruit and distract-edly bit into a shiny red apple himself as he did so, enquiring whether she was willing to pose for a further hour following this break.

Giselle agreed.

'Clothes off.'

She undressed, shedding the two pieces of clothing she had been wearing, and stepped back towards the stool, already fearful as to how she would raise herself onto it without being even more immodest.

'No, not there.' William stopped her.

He waved his arm in the opposite direction and pulled back a heavy curtain that served as a divider between the actual studio and what Giselle guessed might have been his living quarters. A vast four-poster bed carved out of burnished metal sat there, its sheets a grey shade of white away from the now fading beam of the skylight.

'There.'

Giselle sat herself on the edge of the bed, while William took hold of a long hooked pole standing against the nearby wall, raised it towards the ceiling, connected with a latch on another skylight and pulled it open, and a shadowy, dusky light poured in, warm and fuzzy and so unlike the sharp, crude and possibly unflattering glare she'd had to withstand when sitting earlier on the stool. A bedroom light. Having set the tone of the scene, William moved back towards her and the bed, looked down at her, contemplating the spectacle of her naked body, pensive but keen.

'Let me,' he said.

She felt his large, surprisingly warm hand alight on her bare shoulder, and then the palm of his other hand cup her left buttock, as he gently hinted she should lie down on the bed and no longer sit stiffly on its edges. Giselle's mind was in a tizzy but she forced herself to relax and follow William's firm pressure. She lay down.

'No, not like that.'

She looked up at him. His crown of curls was haloed by the muted light avalanching down from the studio roof, his features an indistinct blur. He loomed above her, his stocky shape briefly blanking out the day.

Giselle loosened. Allowed his soft, expert hands to sculpt her into the right position, until she was spread across the sheets, her arms at an odd angle, her thighs delicately parted, on her side, the deathly white sheen of her skin offered to the fading light, her breasts in shadow, her eyes facing the metal rods of the bedstead. Disposed like a puppet of flesh and bone.

William tut-tutted his approval, took a step back to admire his handiwork.

'Hmmm ...Yes ...'

Giselle held her breath. God only knew what he was seeing right now. All of her, exposed, truly naked.

'Will that position be comfortable enough?' he asked her.

Her throat was dry. She merely nodded.

'Good.'

He took a few steps back and, this time, set up an easel. She could only glance at him sideways because of the angle at which he had placed her head, with her long flowing black hair draped across her left shoulder before cascading halfway down her back.

To compound the unease brewing inside her, she could sense a faint welling of wetness between her legs and bit her lip, hoping to all heaven that in the muted light he had created he would fail to notice this revealing seed of her involuntary arousal. Could he even see inside her? She swallowed hard.

He drew swift, nervy lines across his canvas. The skeleton over which his painting would be anchored. Giselle frantically tried to blank her mind but too many thoughts danced inside her skull and her heart was beating, she felt, much too fast. Seconds passed that felt like minutes, minutes floated by that felt like hours. She counted sheep, swans, and a ceaseless procession of identical blank-faced dancers in matching tutus and pink ballet shoes.

The dampness in her cunt was now like a dam, waiting for the signal to shatter, pour out, flood the bed-sheets and shame her. Her cheeks were on fire. But, just a few steps away, William was busy, merely shooting glances at her, to fix her image or checking up on her immobility, his brush travelling across the canvas, lost in a world of his own of which she had now become the centre.

In a blinding flash, it came to Giselle that she was actually now the one in charge. Not the artist. It was her body that had become the focus, the crux around which all else orbited. She was the sun, the stage and without her, presently, William was less than nothing, guided as he was by her attraction, hypnotised. Sensing this affirmation, her breath slowed and she began to regain her composure. Peace of mind washed over her, the awkward wetness between her thighs no longer a source of embarrassment but a source of intense pride. And curiosity.

When the session finally came to an end, and not too soon as her whole side was frozen in cramp, William brought over a silk dressing gown for her to slip on. It was now dark outside and he had grown unhappy with the quality of the light, and Giselle was beginning to feel cold. He'd covered the canvas with a sheet and again refused to let her see what he had achieved so far.

'That's not how it works, my dear. You must learn to control your impatience. When the time is right, when the work is ready, then you will be allowed to view it.'

He turned his back on her as she shed the dressing gown and slipped into her street clothes. She felt like saying to him, 'Why do you look away now? You've seen all of me. I want you to continue to see all of me ...'

That was it. She had shown all of herself and been dismissed.

It was not enough for Giselle. She was consumed by a feeling that she couldn't name. A mixture of rage and desire burned through her with savage intensity and made it impossible for her to settle back into her ordinary life.

Food lost its flavour. Arranging bouquets at Aquarelle, a task that she usually took pleasure in, now bored her. The stems of flowers pricked her or made her skin itch. The regular stretching and toning routine that she continued to perform each night to keep her body supple seemed pointless. She was not a dancer, she would never be a dancer, why did she still dance? She could not concentrate on her lectures, nor read. Words swam on the page like random patterns made by spiders running through ink.

It was pouring with rain the night that she returned to William's studio. In search of what? Giselle didn't know. Her emotions were irrational and yet she felt bound to follow them. Her spirit would be unable to rest until she saw the artist again, of that much she was sure.

Water streamed over the cobbled streets and soaked through her thin shoes. Her clothes were stuck to her skin. Her coat had been hanging on a hook by the front door and her walking boots and umbrella were tidily stacked on the shoe rack below. To avoid disturbing her parents she had clambered out of the window so by necessity she had not been able to don either and so was unprepared for journeying through the streets of Paris in a rainstorm.

She hurried through the dark, almost running to ward off the cold and escape the fleeting glances of strangers who noticed the tall girl striding through the storm wearing just a thin chiffon top and a pair of jeans.

The muted sound of the buzzer made her wince. She pressed it three times in quick succession and huddled against the door, seeking protection from the elements as she waited and hoped that he would appear. In the empty minutes that passed she began to wonder how she would explain her bedraggled appearance on his doorstep in the night and what she would do if William was out, or worse still, busy with another model or a lover. She was about to turn and rush home as hurriedly as she had rushed here when the door swung open.

'Giselle?' he said.

She stood mute as he processed her arrival, mouth half open in shock.

'You're frozen,' he muttered, and wrapped one of his large hands around her upper right arm and pulled her inside. Even through the wet, stiff fabric of her long-sleeved top his touch was hot in comparison. She let him drag her along the hall to the exiguous elevator, relieved to be in his presence again. Somehow just being near this burly, rough man made her feel safe and relaxed.

He banged the elevator screen door closed and pressed the button for the floor to his studio then turned back to her and placed his other hand on her left arm and rubbed briskly to warm her.

'What are you doing here, Giselle? You're lucky to find me. By now I'm usually back at my apartment. Had just stayed behind to clean up the mess a bit.' His tone and his words were soft, as if he knew the answer to his question already. She knew that the expression of her desire must be painted across her face, and why else would she have come here, in the dark, in the night, through the rain that she could still hear hammering on the rooftops and the gusts of wind that had made windows rattle as she passed them? How had she not even realised he didn't actually live here, that it was just his place of work? But luck was on her side tonight.

She reached forward and slipped her hands under his T-shirt to warm them against his waist. His torso was broad and as solid as a tree trunk, she longed to feel the crushing weight of his body against her own. He flinched in response to the ice cold touch of her palms and removed his grasp on her arms, taking her hands in his own instead.

'I needed . . . I needed . . . I needed you to . . .'

Giselle tried to vocalise the fragments of thoughts and emotions that ran ragged through her mind but it was like trying to sculpt a solid form with liquid, she could not make words hold together.

'You needed me to what?' he whispered.

'To do that,' she replied softly, as his hands travelled up to her wrists and he gripped her tightly.

'This?' he asked, and he reached forward to touch her chest, brushing his knuckles over her nipples, so hard in response to the stiff, cold fabric of her top that rubbed against them that they ached.

Giselle arched her back and pushed her breasts forward towards him. A low moan escaped her lips.

'Yes,' she said.

The elevator shuddered to a halt and he ripped the door open so energetically she feared the ancient contraption might rattle apart.

William pulled her down into his studio as if she were a rag doll. Her shoes squelched and rain dripped down her legs leaving a trail of water along his wooden floors. She began to visibly shiver, shaking with cold.

He led her to the spot under the skylight where she had posed nude in vain for him just a few days earlier and began to remove her clothes. His fingers made quick work of the small buttons on her blue blouse, although the storm had soaked the fabric. He peeled the chiffon over one arm and then the other and carefully hung the garment over the wooden stool that stood alongside them.

Underneath, she was wearing a navy lace bra with a red trim. Her expansive breasts were firm enough that Giselle did not need the support; she wore a brassiere out of habit and for modesty's sake, to prevent her nipples from showing through her clothes. The cold had turned them to fierce, pink nubs that pressed against the lace, clearly visible. William lowered his head and took one into his mouth, warming her with his lips. She buried her hands in his mop of shaggy hair, marvelling at the bulk of his head, the solidity of his jaw.

'I'll get you a towel,' he said, 'before you freeze,' and he left her standing there, shirtless, wet and aroused.

Giselle didn't move. She felt bizarrely as though she was posing for him again.

He wrapped the towel around her shoulders and began to dry her so briskly that her skin hurt. He unceremoniously unclipped her bra at the back in one swift motion so that her breasts fell free and then he rubbed them in the same rough manner. He was quick and thorough, even wiping behind her ears and beneath the crease line of her bust. As the subject of his attentions, Giselle felt like a small child or a dog. They had not yet kissed, but she knew that his cock was hard. She could see the bulge straining through his trousers.

He finished drying her top half and then unclasped the button on the waist of her jeans. The denim was water-logged and clung to her like a second skin that gentle tugging would not shift. William dragged the stiff fabric halfway down her thighs with such force that Giselle was nearly off balanced and she wrapped her arms around his shoulders and clung to him to avoid falling over.

She inhaled his scent, a strange mixture of the paints that he used, cigarette smoke and soap – he was not a cologne sort of a man – an odour that Giselle instinctively associated with masculinity. He dropped to his knees, peeled her sheer panties down and buried his head between her legs, raising his face to her mound and lapping at her entrance as though he were dipping his tongue in the purest natural spring.

'Oh,' Giselle whispered, a moan of pleasure, surprise, and recognition. So this was what it felt like to have a man's lips caress her there.

She tried to shift her stance, to spread her legs apart wider so that he could delve further inside her but with her jeans on it was impossible, she might as well have her ankles tied together.

Giselle pulled at his hair, tried to encourage him to stand upright so that they could tumble back on the sofa behind them together, in much the same way as she had fallen into bed with Olen on their first night together. But William wouldn't have it. The more Giselle struggled, the more insistent William's tongue became hunting her pleasure.

He gripped her ankles with his hands to hold her still and ran his tongue between her folds, sucking the dampness from her lips, a mixture of her juices and the rainwater that had soaked through her clothes. She looked down, trying to catch a glimpse of his face, the expression that he wore while he tasted her. Olen had always liked to watch as Giselle took his cock into her mouth, and she had known it, so turned the experience into something of a performance, being sure to always wear a smile as she sucked him, to flutter her eyelids suggestively.

This was different. There was nothing theatrical about William's caresses. The way that he touched her was earthy, primal. He licked her pussy as if he was feeding on fine wine. He had a vitality about him that bypassed all of Giselle's pretences and fears and tapped straight into her soul.

The rhythm of his strokes soon made her forget her discomfort, her cold legs and her wet feet, and her vulnerability, standing in front of this man she barely knew as he worshipped the most intimate part of her.

Giselle began to feel something that Olen had never made her feel, a sensation so strong that it overshadowed everything, drowning her thoughts and her petty insecurities, even quieting the voice in her mind that said she was a fool to have come here. None of that mattered, nothing did but the pressure of William's tongue sliding over and around her clitoris, his hands holding her tight, the warmth of his head as she clung to him, half collapsed and barely able to hold herself upright any longer, so strong was the thrum of her blood burning through her veins.

She screamed aloud, 'Oh!' as she orgasmed, and crushed his face against her, pushing her mound as hard as she could against his nose, his jaw, his mouth. It no longer even occurred to her to worry that he might suffocate between her thighs.

'Oh.'

She couldn't speak. She was shaking and flushed. Her mind floating blissful on a cloud, aware of her surroundings and yet so infused with peaceful afterglow that the floor beneath her, the walls around her, everything besides the man who still knelt in front of her might have been a dream. The snatched, muffled orgasms that she gave herself as she fantasised in her narrow bed at night were not a patch on this.

He continued to lap her gently until her tremors subsided, but even after she had come, she could not find the strength to straighten her body up and instead she rested half of her body weight against him. Her knees began to buckle. William shifted into a crouch and pushed himself up, then lifted her in his arms as easily as he moved his stool and easel, and carried her to the bed. He laid her flat on the sheet, belly up, and dragged her wet jeans from her body. Giselle wiggled her hips and pushed down the waistband with her thumbs to aid him. He pushed her hands away.

'Shh . . . ,' he said. 'Lie still.'

Finally, she was naked, and he pulled away, returning a moment later with the towel and dried off one of her thighs, and then the other. He left her pussy damp, her juices still running, her bush wet with rainwater and his saliva. Wild.

'You're beautiful,' he stated simply, and then lay down alongside her and pulled her into his arms.

They fell asleep cradled together, bathed in the pale rays of the moon that fell through the skylight.

3

Gardens of Earthly Delight

Within a month, Giselle had moved in with William.

He did not reside at the studio, but had an apartment on the Rue Monsieur le Prince, not far off from l'Odéon. It was a fourth-floor walk-up and there was no lift in the imposing turn-of-the-century building. The rooms in his flat were spacious and airy, the walls a cacophony of art-work, not just his own but including work by other artists too, some of whom even she had heard of or recognised. The ceilings were crisscrossed with sturdy beams of dark wood in parallel formation and from the narrow flower-box-strewn small balcony outside his bedroom you could see Notre-Dame, the Ile de la Cité and on a clear day glimpses of the river.

Giselle had lied to her parents and informed them she was

sharing with a girlfriend who attended some of the same lectures at university. She couldn't see them approving of her co-habiting with a man almost a decade and a half her senior, and a wild-haired brute of a painter at that. Either they preferred to believe her or they didn't outwardly care, but she chose an afternoon when her mother was out busy with her charity work in the suburbs to move her clothes and other belongings to William's flat to avoid fielding further compromising questions or offers of help in transporting the stuff.

Neither had she mentioned the existence of her new lover to any of the rare friends or acquaintances from the university corridors, or from her pre-London life. William was her secret, and it was none of the others' business.

He was an easy person to live with, not that she had much previous co-habitation experience with anyone. A man of few words, of great physical appetites and an attentive lover, who was devoted to his art. Whenever Giselle asked William about his life before her, he was careful to deflect the question and she soon learned not to enquire more insistently. The one thing that troubled her was the women he had known, loved prior to her. She was curious about them. Had he touched them in the same way, painted them all too, whispered the same words to them in bed under cover of darkness? She wanted to feel unique.

William was not French but Canadian, and it appeared

that he had lived in Paris since his teens. He never mentioned his parents, any close family or details about his background. He was under contract to an art gallery in the Rue Mazarine and planning a new exhibition there in the near future, following a successful debut two years back. In addition, he also undertook private commissions for a series of individual collectors, an aspect of his activities he would sometimes refer to although he would pointedly never provide much in the way of details. Giselle had, when left alone in the studio or his apartment, carefully looked through the scattering of remaining paintings or prints he had not sold or had held back and, to her great satisfaction, had noted that he had used a wide assortment of female models prior to her arrival on the scene, but barely a handful had ever been the object of more than a couple of pieces of art, as if William had cast his net wide and hadn't yet settled on a permanent muse.

She was determined to become that elusive figure. Not just his mistress but his inspiration.

By now, she had grown more comfortable in her skin and posing for hours on end came more naturally, as did wandering in a total state of nudity around him, not only in the high-ceilinged studio but also in what was now her home. It felt right, and a constant prelude to sex, making herself available to him fully, gently teasing him with her assets and her desire to be seen and taken.

William loved to cook, and after a few culinary fiascos when Giselle had attempted to recreate from memory dishes she had seen her mother prepare, only to make a real mess of the balance of flavours, it was agreed that William would prepare their evening meals whenever they stayed in. He insisted that she keep out of the kitchen on these occasions and spend the time studying, determined that their relationship should not affect her academic progress. She had finally got round to enrolling formally, at his insistence, after she had revealed her dilettante status.

'One day, you'll see, you will find that degree useful. I won't always be around, you know.'

He was particularly conscious of their difference in age, and much too often complained that he was too old for her and they could have no long-term future. 'You'll soon tire of me,' he said. 'Find someone your own age.'

Initially, Giselle would dismiss this thought with a petulant shrug, but with time, she learned to ignore his protests and, under the sway of her youthful enthusiasm, threw herself into the affair with the divine blindness that insists on believing first loves last forever.

She was reading an essay on the symbolism of Gatsby's green light while William was preparing a lobster risotto in the kitchen. The smells of simmering food and a delicate equilibrium of spices wafted in her direction, interrupting her concentration. She wondered briefly about the way that food and sex seemed so intimately connected in William's mind and actions, and in what position he would fuck her tonight and what new levels he would transport her to in his hedonistic quest for some kind of perfection, refining his gestures, spreading her, forensically orchestrating the underground stream of her own sensations, the awakening of her taste buds right now at a distance a mere overture for the grand opera he would conduct later. She smiled at herself in the empty study, relishing the thought, setting her dog-eared copy of the Scott Fitzgerald novel aside while diving deep into her anticipatory daydreams.

Triggered by the appetising smells of food, the call of pleasure already beckoned.

There was a strong touch of hyperrealism about William's art. His sketches were so anatomically precise and the foregrounds of his canvases so like photographs that an initial and superficial sighting could sometimes confuse even experts as to the nature of their origin. Unlike others working in the same style, though, like Jack Vettriano or Robin Harris, the often phantasmagorical and at times frankly surrealist tapestries of grotesques against which the characters inhabiting his work floated quickly set him apart, panoramas in the style of Hieronymus Bosch or refined, sophisticated versions of other-worldly vistas familiar from old pulp covers or cheap paperbacks. The contrast proved startling and at times unsettling. The first painting he'd completed of Giselle had her standing nude against the multi-dimensional landscape of a stage on fire, a white-skinned captive of a roaring inferno, vulnerable, unprotected, about to be consumed by the flames coming from all directions. But when it came to Giselle, he had captured the sheen of her hair to utter perfection, the living shades of her skin, all the way to the small birthmark below her left nipple and other rare blemishes, and even the thin scratches on her arm from the roses she had pruned at the flower shop that same morning. It was like a photograph of her, faithful to life but also just an inch or so disconnected from reality and bordering on the uncanny, and conveying emotions she didn't know she harboured within her.

It was this realistic approach he brought to sketching bodies and faces with such meticulous attention to detail that also attracted his private collectors of a rather particular kind.

Some years previously, at a time when he had been short of money and his work was not selling often enough, William had connected with a small group of wealthy individuals who enjoyed commissioning specific paintings or drawings of an openly pornographic nature from talented artists who had not yet broken through into the limelight. They were not unlike the collectors who, decades before, had ordered erotic stories from the likes of Anaïs Nin and Henry Miller. Although he was now no longer as pressed for cash as he had been, he still enjoyed accepting the occasional commission, seeing them as a challenge. Naturally, none of these pieces was ever signed and they seldom saw the light of day, being secreted away in the collectors' vaults for their own private enjoyment.

'Giselle, darling, can I ask you something?'

They were side by side in bed, still catching their breath, a thin sheen of sweat illuminating their exhausted bodies. William's hair was mussed and he looked even wilder than usual. Giselle was still vibrating inside from the joyful ferocity of his earlier thrusts which she had loudly invited in terms that had surprised even her. Loving this man as she did and relishing the sheer physicality of their embraces made her swear like a fishwife.

'What is it?'

'I have another special commission, and wanted to know if you're willing to pose for it?'

'There's no need to ask, William. You know I'm always available. I can't say no to you.'

'It's just that this is somewhat different. A private commission of a different nature. Not like the work we've done before.'

Giselle wiped her hair back from her forehead, opened her eyes wider, intrigued by her lover's hesitation. He'd always been a force of nature, sweeping everything along with him in his wake. It surprised her to see him so tentative.

'Absolutely. Anything.'

He explained the background and who Emile Saffy was.

'Do you have any of the preparatory sketches you made for the pieces you previously did for him maybe?'

'Yes, I suppose. Somewhere.'

'I'd like to see them,' Giselle suggested. Saffy's taste was for the re-creation of well-known historical scenes, with a penchant for the erotic elements brought alive and skirting the edge of pornography.

'*The Rape of the Sabine Women, Salammbô at the Fall of Carthage*, the violation of Marie-Antoinette prior to her execution at the guillotine, an explicit version of *The Raft of the Medusa* . . . Those sorts of twists . . .' William said.

'And he pays you a lot?'

'A lot.'

'And what has he ordered this time?' Giselle asked.

'Joan of Arc. A multi-imaged fresco about the successive stages of her capture and death. Her interrogation and torture, her incarceration, when she was burned at the stake.'

Giselle felt her heart stop.

Images from her past came pouring back, irradiating her mind with electric-like impulses, throwing up memories of her fantasies in sharp relief.

'And you want me to be Joan?'

'Well, pose as her . . . And no one but us and Saffy would ever see the end result.'

She felt as though an extra dimension of sweat was seeping through the pores of her skin, something both wonderful and perilous being released.

William rose from the bed, as Giselle's eyes gazed at the sheer male magnificence of his heavy body. She so loved the square mass and solidity of his arse.

He stepped towards the bedroom door then stopped and turned. 'Some of my early Salammbô sketches should still be around at the studio, I've just remembered. If you're interested. Should give you a fair idea of the material he likes to see done. Not the sort of stuff I'd want to keep around the apartment.' He smiled.

He was facing her as he spoke, his thick cock half hard and unavoidably catching her attention. Giselle could not help but stare. Damn, she loved this man. Every single part of him, but some even more than others.

'I will,' she said. 'Pose. Be Joan.'

Her lips opened and she crawled off the bed towards him and lowered herself to her knees.

Joan in a torn rough burlap nightshirt, sleek metal chains crisscrossing her body, from the neck downwards like the embrace of a snake, tight around the chest, restricting her breath, a swipe of blood across her damp forehead, her arms stretched, hanging from hooks.

'I'll sketch in the background later,' William said. 'A

dungeon with humid stone walls and just a thin line of light piercing the ambient darkness.'

Giselle looked down at the quickly executed drawing William had just completed. All it lacked was an actual face. Her face.

The image made her shiver.

'Later, I'll set up the right light and you can sit and I can do your face,' William suggested. 'Not that I couldn't do it from memory,' he added. 'I'm getting used to every line and curve of your features.' He smiled.

'Just that?' Giselle questioned.

'Sure,' he answered. 'There should be no need for a prolonged session. This is just prurient material we're doing to order for a rather perverse collector, not something I'd want to include in an exhibition. But it pays the bills.'

'William?'

'Yes?'

'Why don't we do it properly? I'd like to.'

'What do you mean?'

'I'm happy to find, create, an outfit like that, to be ...' she hesitated, '... chained.' She looked him in the eyes. 'Surely, it'll make it more real, more authentic?'

'Would you?'

'Yes.' She tried to hold her voice steady.

They found an old white shirt of his he hadn't worn in ages in the back of a drawer and studiously slashed it with a knife, then in a closet a set of chains that had once been used to hold luggage or heavy loads on a car's roof rack and filleted it, revealing the metal under the plastic. Giselle stripped. William sprayed water across her to simulate the sweat, although she already felt as if she was on fire inside. He dabbed some paint across her features and her wrists to represent the blood. Once it dried it was evident it was the wrong shade of red, but this was of no matter, as he would correct the tone in the actual painting. He erected a stepladder to reach the ceiling beams and slipped a rope through a narrow gap between the wood and the ceiling and allowed the rope to fall loose to the level of her raised arms where he could tie it to her wrists.

'Is that okay? Not too tight?'

'It's fine.'

A war between desire and rational thought was battling inside her stomach as she assumed the position in which Joan had been in William's preliminary sketch, itself inspired by a 1930s illustration he had found accompanying a magazine article about the final days of the Maid of Orléans.

Every time she moved, which she tried not to do too often, although it was awkward to remain immobile standing as she was on tiptoe with her arms pulled towards the ceiling, Giselle could feel the now torn, uneven edges of the white shirt brush against one of her nipples, daring it not to turn hard and peep out impudently, wondering whether William would keep this pesky detail in the painting or not.

As always when he painted, William was in a world of his own, his hands in constant movement, racing across the canvas, his brow furrowed. Immobilised, Giselle could feel the wetness between her thighs seep madly down her legs, totally out of her control. She had never before felt both as excited and as scared by the tide of emotions rising inside her.

Two hours later, William released her hands and her whole body ached with a pleasurable form of pain. She had persistently refused earlier to have a break every time he had asked.

'You look so flushed,' he said.

The words died in her throat. She badly needed some water.

He brought a glass to her lips and she sipped avidly.

He loosened the improvised network of chains circling her. Then detached her from the rope.

'Was the chain too heavy maybe?'

Giselle sighed.

'You looked wonderful,' William said.

'I need to take a shower,' Giselle said.

'Of course.'

Normally they would have returned home to their apartment. It was only a ten-minute stroll from the studio and they would have walked in silence, he still in the euphoric state he often reached after good work, she in another world full of dangerous thoughts. But Giselle knew that if they left the studio, her mood might evaporate. She insisted on using the exiguous shower William had installed in a corner of the loft, and which could be reached up a spiral staircase an architect friend of his had built, to ensure that his habitual models could clean up following sessions. She showered but still the irksome fire kept on simmering inside her, like a subterranean stream in full flight from an even hotter lava torrent.

Coming down the stairs, she emerged into the vast open space of the studio. William was sitting reading, waiting for her to be ready to go home. Normally she would have automatically asked him what the book was. From where she stood, all she could see was an anonymous white cover, similar to a thousand others in French editions. Normally, he read a lot of biographies, of artists, writers, seldom fiction, unlike Giselle.

'I want to go to bed,' she declared.

'Isn't it a bit early? I was thinking we could go to Chez Fernand and have a bite before.' It was one of their favourite restaurants, a small haven of terroir cooking on the Rue Guisarde. 'Sleepy? Tired?'

'No. I want you to make love to me ...' Giselle felt the strong need. To be filled. Used. Torn. Thrilled. Also a touch tentative; normally it was mostly William who led on these occasions, took the first step. But this late afternoon, a pale sun barely breaking through the latticed shutters shielding the studio window, she knew she had to be bold, take the initiative.

William gazed at her with a look of intense curiosity. Surely he could see how aroused she already was? How this uncommon warmth had taken a grip over her.

He opened his mouth, but before he could say a single word Giselle had thrown herself against him and wrapped her arms around him. Now he could feel the warmth radiating from her naked body. It was unmistakable.

'Fuck me,' she ordered.

Holding on to her slender frame with one hand, he pulled his shirt off with the other, tearing at the buttons in his haste, clumsily negotiating his arms out of the narrow sleeves.

Her sharp nails raked his shoulders. Her breath slowed as he hugged her tight and gently pushed her down until her body was laid out on the couch that he sometimes used as a prop.

He was about to undo his baggy trousers and free himself when she took him by surprise.

'Bring the chains,' Giselle asked.

Deep in her eyes, a harrowing well of despair. William knew not to object and raised himself slowly then stepped back into the work area, bent down and gingerly picked up the chain which had been dropped to the floor following the session.

He walked back to the couch where Giselle lay and was offering him her hands, in what could have been construed as a gesture of prayer.

He wrapped one end of the improvised chain around her wrists, noting as he did so that she had not cleaned the paint there away under the shower, and still bore the marks of seemingly torn skin and bondage.

'Tighter,' Giselle said.

He bound her hands together, knotting the end of the chain around the links.

'Are you sure about this?' William wasn't new to sexual games, but never this early in a relationship or with someone so young.

'I am,' Giselle confirmed. 'Now use the belt from your trousers.' She witnessed the moment of hesitation in his rigid posture as he processed her verbal demand. 'Please,' she continued.

He unthreaded the belt from his trousers. Stepped out of them. Held the brown, cracked leather at arm's length and made to circle her ankles with it.

'No,' she interjected. 'Around my neck.'

He swallowed hard. She was so full of surprises.

But his excitement was rising. Fast. And his anxiety about where all this might lead.

The belt fitted her neck like a dark collar once the burnished metal buckle clicked into the final notch available.

Giselle briefly blinked several times in succession.

William looked down at her with new eyes. Both touched and immensely aroused by her vulnerability.

Her bound hands reached out for him, her fingertips brushing against his abundant chest hair.

It would be like fucking Joan of Arc, he reflected.

Eyes still closed, disorientated by the flow of emotions, feeling the binds, experiencing such a total lack of control for the first time, Giselle was likewise imagining she was the incarnation of Joan of Arc, like in her twisted childhood dreams, transported by the knowledge that she was going to be violated.

William's hand made contact with her arse, and she jumped.

'Fuck me now,' she asked.

He vigorously seized her by her waist and turned her body round so that she was on all fours, her rump and parts offered to him. Yet again, he marvelled at the darker shades of her outer labia, like a stain against the pink warmth of her cunt opening, and his gaze was caught by the even darker corolla of her other hole.

He had never penetrated her there.

Would the soldiers, inquisitors and fanatical priests have

buggered Joan during the course of her torture, he wondered? Probably. It was said she had died still a virgin.

'It's going to hurt, Joan,' he said in a whisper, or was it a growl as his passion grew out of control.

'Yes,' she said. Then again, 'Yes. Yes.'

When daylight broke the next morning, they were both sore and exhausted. The chain and the leather belt still adorned her, although in different configurations, no longer binds but an integral part of her body, jewels of passion, branches of transgression that she had earned by her wanton abandon. His cock ached but refused to deflate, the transformation that Giselle had endured a constant provocation, keeping him in a semi-permanent state of hardness. It felt as if they had broken through an invisible barrier and landed fully formed and naked in another world altogether. He felt like a new man. Eager to test further limits, discover how far Giselle would be willing to travel along this royal road to pleasure.

Most of all, he wanted to draw and paint again. Her. His wonderful priestess of sex, his beautiful sorceress.

Giselle was daydreaming, suspended between sleep and another state altogether.

He looked down at her, curled up nude on the stained sofa, fed, almost purring.

'I'll rush down and get some coffee and croissants from the café on the corner of the Rue de l'Ecole des Beaux-Arts,'

William said. 'And I'll be right back. I want to start another painting. Right now. Are you game? While you inspire me madly.'

'Sure.' She opened her eyes. The dark brown of her irises appeared even darker than before.

When he returned a quarter of an hour later, Giselle had moved an old trestle table he normally used to keep his brushes and materials on, and placed it at the very centre of the studio floor, just below the skylight so it was caught in a cone of sunlight. She had draped a sheet over it and lay across it, her limbs spread at their widest, indecently exposed, open, like a sacrificial lamb on an altar awaiting the whip of her master.

He recognised the image. It was also in the old magazine full of engravings about the life of Joan of Arc. But in the illustrations, the virgin had been clothed, not fully disrobed and humiliated in the process. Giselle was visibly now improvising.

'Tie me down,' she begged him.

He needed no reminder and diligently obeyed.

As he lowered his body down against hers a few minutes later and placed his throbbing cock at her entrance, his lips kissing the side of her neck, Giselle whispered, 'If you hurt me, I will tell you all my secrets.'

His initial thrust burst through, savage, rock hard, unforgiving.

She confessed to him about her childhood fantasies of Joan of Arc and how, in the heat of the moment, the shame of her sexual excitement had merged with this new, uncertain but welcoming form of rapture. The terribly mixed feelings about her craving for degradation.

He held her down by the wrists, his weight almost suffocating her.

She unveiled every single sin she had imagined and was freed at last by her admissions.

He rode her wildly, smacking her arse as he did so, pulling her hair until breath failed her briefly.

She became an open book.

Under him, she bucked, resisted his taming, relished the girth of his cock invading her, growing inside her until she felt that her walls could take no more pummelling, her sex lips no more stretching.

Giselle screamed. In pain. In joy.

William growled, sighed.

They rode the waves.

By the time they finally left the sex-soaked atmosphere of the studio several days later, William had completed a trio of paintings and a series of studies, each more obscene than the one that preceded it, resplendent pornography from which Giselle's radiant features shone out like a sun. Not once since that first evening had she been any longer clothed, having grown accustomed to a state of total nudity, both physical and mental, and walking down Boulevard Saint Germain finally dressed again felt curiously alien to her.

'I think I'm finally done with Joan,' Giselle confessed as they showered the days of excess away together under warm jets of cleansing water.

'Me too,' William admitted. 'Maybe we should try something new, dredge up different buried memories? Goodbye Joan, hello Giselle.'

Giselle stretched languorously as she exited the cubicle and reached out for a towel.

'Would you like to travel?'

Gravel crunched beneath the wheels of the car as they pulled into the long driveway that led to the enormous, layered house ahead of them, like a stalk leading to the head of a flower. The sound was thick and rich in Giselle's ears and reminded her bizarrely of the sensation of biting into a cream cake. Or perhaps it was just that she was tired from a surfeit of travelling, and arriving on a day as bright as a newly minted coin was the final bizarre element in this whole adventure, and her imagination had begun to run away.

They'd flown out in the evening, but unforeseen delays and a mislaid suitcase had meant that instead of arriving late on Friday night they had spent an extra couple of hours propped up against each other in the airport terminal waiting for the case which had followed them on a later flight and they had pulled into their accommodation just in time for breakfast, rather than bed.

It was Giselle's first time across the Atlantic and everything from the sound of the engine, sending them skywards on great metal wings, to the flow of the luggage carousels seemed both strange and exciting to her eyes. She knew that looking at the two of them together people might wonder if William was her father rather than her man and so she had worn a demure linen trouser suit for the journey, now horribly creased, and tried to project an air of knowing sophistication, as if New York were just another stamp in an already full passport. In reality she had spent most of the time staring about her wide eyed or snoozing against his shoulder.

No one seemed to know who owned the sprawling maze of a house that was to be home for the next few days. Giselle hadn't wanted to skip her lectures, or take advantage of Freya's kindness by requesting more than a few shifts off work at the flower shop, so they had agreed just to make it a long weekend. William had intimated that he might stay on longer, if work required it, as many of the private collectors who commissioned his more exclusive pieces would be present and it was a good opportunity to network with them.

And to show off his latest model, Giselle wondered?

The stones that covered the sweeping parking area, already peppered with expensive vehicles, were sharp and pricked Giselle's feet as she picked her way across them. Her shoes were flat and thin soled. She preferred them that way, perhaps a habit that ballet had ingrained in her. She liked to feel the ground beneath her feet. It made her feel more balanced, more at ease in her core.

She looked up at the house. It was three storeyed, with white walls and a pale mint-green roof and surrounded by a wide expanse of lawn that seemed to stretch on endlessly, as though the building itself were floating atop a great grass ocean, a ship in the centre of a perfectly flat lime bay. And with its tall gate that had closed behind them, swallowing them up as they passed through, and the line of trees that separated the property neatly from any prying neighbours, they might as well have been on an island.

A large marble fountain stood in the centre of the parking bay. Giselle stopped to admire the lifelike arrangement of limbs that adorned the statue. A couple, locked into an embrace so fiercely that they seemed to be one person, like a mythical creature with one head and an additional set of arms and legs. Each figure's grip on the other appeared to be so strong that the embrace could have been mistaken for a battle, were it not for the way they leaned into each other.

'Beautiful, aren't they?' William had approached so softly that Giselle hadn't noticed, presuming he was busy getting their cases out of the car. Not knowing what to wear, or any real details of what they would be doing for the next few days or the style of their hosts, Giselle had packed light, bringing just the linen trouser suit that she was wearing, a slinky cream short-sleeved T-shirt with a V neck, several changes of underwear, and a small zip purse with her tooth brush and the few cosmetics she occasionally wore. She hadn't thought to bring a swimsuit, and now regretted it. A place this size was bound to have a pool. She could happily have climbed over the low marble bench that encircled the embracing couple, removed her shoes and paddled in the ring of cool water at the base of the fountain right then, to both wake her up and wash the journey from her feet.

'Have you sculpted,' she asked him, 'or thought of it?' She could see the similarities between William's style of painting – the hyperrealism he favoured – and the piece of work in front of her. And she could picture him working with something in his hands. Creating life with those strong, large palms of his, the way that he sometimes ran his fingers over her body as though he was peeling away an invisible outer layer to expose the parts of herself she normally kept hidden.

He shook his head, causing his mass of dark curls to bounce wildly in the breeze, and rubbed his hand over his beard, the gesture he made when he was feeling impatient or frustrated.

'No,' he said, 'no. I like to paint. Bringing a person alive with colour ... it's different. With something like this ...' he leaned forward and touched the marble statue in front of them, 'the expression is in the musculature, the angles of the body. What I do, it's in the skin, the light. Do you see?'

Giselle frowned, and was about to respond that yes, she did see, but she was thinking that experimentation with different mediums could never be a bad thing for an artist, when the double doors swung open and a man strode towards them.

'William!' he cried, throwing his arms wide in a gesture of exuberance ready to embrace a long-lost friend, although he was still metres away.

'Hello, Sebastian.' William's tone was warm and easy, and his face had transformed into a wide grin. More relaxed than Giselle had seen him in ages.

Sebastian was not quite as tall as William, but only half his bulk, which made him seem taller than he actually was. His white hair was cropped close to his head, and his skin shone through it a little, a shade of pinkish-white that along with his long body made him look a bit like a white rat. He wore a floor-length red velvet cloak as though it were a gown, and when it flapped open as he flung his arms out, he revealed a three-piece pinstripe suit underneath, complete with pocket watch and a feathered cream bow tie. His shoes were black-and-white patent two-tone leather that gleamed in the early morning light like sunbeams bouncing off clear water.

He could only be an artist, Giselle thought, which would explain how they knew each other, despite Sebastian being probably twice William's age.

'And this must be your latest muse,' the older man said as he reached them, and before bear-hugging William bowed low and kissed the top of Giselle's hand. She bristled at the word 'latest', and only politeness prevented her from pulling her hand away. Sebastian's fingers were covered in rings. One was particularly large, an orb of onyx set into gold. It was blacker than black, as if a sorceress had carved out a lump of shadow and turned it into a jewel.

'Giselle, Sebastian, Sebastian, Giselle.' William introduced them. 'Sebastian is also a painter. As you might have guessed,' he explained to Giselle, cocking his head towards Sebastian's flamboyant outfit and raising an eyebrow in explanation.

'You have a beautiful house,' Giselle said.

Sebastian burst into peals of laughter.

'Oh no,' he said. 'I'm just a guest. Thank you, though. I'm flattered to know that I might appear to be rolling in the sort of dough that whoever owns this place has.'

'Does nobody know who our host is, then?' Giselle enquired, curious.

'An ageing society queen, it's rumoured,' Sebastian

answered. 'But sometimes it's best not to know certain things, don't you think? A bit of mystery is romantic.'

He insisted on helping William with the bags, and picked up Giselle's case as they walked into the house.

They entered a long hallway with so many doors leading from it that Giselle felt as if she was surrounded by a row of dominoes on each side. Her head snapped from one to the other as she caught a flash of the occupants of some of the rooms.

They paused at the bottom of a flight of stairs while the men changed their grip on the luggage, and Giselle looked around her. She gazed at a group of women playing ping-pong in pairs who were wearing dresses covered in tiny sequins that shimmered like schools of fishes as they dashed back and forth around a large table to catch the ball before it tumbled to the floor. In the room directly opposite, the floor was covered in grass instead of carpet, and on top of it a game of croquet was taking place between a group of young men, all of them dressed in striped trousers and red braces, with no shirts underneath. Their chest muscles rippled when they laughed.

Giselle sniffed. She had thought the 'grass' must be a type of carpet, and yet she could smell the sharp tang of a freshly mown lawn.

'That can't be real?' she asked Sebastian, pointing to the sheet of green on which the boys were teeing off.

'Oh yes, darling,' he said. 'Everything you see here is real. Some of it is so unreal, it seems more real than real. Hyper real, like your friend's paintings, and mine. Fantasy is so much more lifelike than reality, don't you think? And fantasy come to life is life trebled.'

Giselle wasn't entirely sure that she understood. His words were like the lyrics of a tune half-remembered. She grasped a part of what he was saying but couldn't quite make out the whole. She thought of her Joan of Arc fantasies, and how the colours and sounds and emotions those dreams conjured had been brighter and louder and more acute than the humdrum detail of the small bedroom that surrounded her as she experienced them, but that was the nature of dreams, wasn't it?

Laughter reached her ears from either side, a fluid mix of the young women and the young men, high- and low-pitched sounds bubbling over one another like a brook flowing over rocks.

They continued their journey upwards. The stairwell was round and spiralled, and as she looked down from part-way up Giselle saw another bunch of people reclining on cushioned beds hidden behind the base of the steps. They were not sound asleep, but rather appeared to be in a dazed state, drugged out and blissful.

It occurred to her then that they had walked into the remnants of a party and the inhabitants of the house were probably now winding down from the excesses of the previous night rather than getting up for breakfast.

They turned off into another hallway on the first floor. It was wide and light and airy, and the walls and ceiling were covered in a startling array of vivid paintings. Giselle simply stopped dead for a few moments, and stared. The work covered a varied mix of subjects but every piece she cast her eye upon captured both sensuality and unease. There were lovers coupling alongside animals tearing one another apart, swarms of bees like dark clouds invading pure white landscapes, fruits red and purple and dripping juice the precise shade of blood, Dali-esque clocks melting and Wonderland rabbits, men dressed in suits with the heads of fishes or beaks of birds and other men with human faces behaving like beasts. Women were bare breasted and open thighed with expressions that spoke of horror and desire in equal measure, assorted folk with the beauty of youth displaying the fanged smiles of monsters or with blank faces that suggested a maturity beyond their years.

'Wait until you see the painted woman,' Sebastian said. 'This is just a prelude.' He beckoned for them to follow.

Giselle was too polite to say so out loud, but inwardly she hoped that their own quarters were not similarly decorated as she was certain she would never be able to sleep. Did any of the people here sleep, she wondered, as they were passed by another troupe of party guests, these ones dressed in full

Victorian riding gear and leading a pantomime horse. One of the women, dark-haired, tall and buxom, with a hooked nose and a black hat twice as high as any Giselle had ever seen before, decorated with an even taller plume of playing cards, winked at her as she passed by. When Giselle turned to watch her walk away she saw that the woman was only half clothed – her corset and long skirt appeared full from the front but did not cover her back half at all, apart from a harness device that held the garment on, looped over her shoulders, her buttocks, thighs and calves. The woman, perhaps sensing Giselle's gaze, turned back and winked at her again. Her wink was slow-lidded and reptilian, the deliberate gesture of a woman who is either devoid of all morality or simply the unnaturally slow movement of a person who has been awake far too long.

Finally they reached their rooms. They had been assigned two, despite insisting that they would sleep together and didn't need the extra space. To Giselle's immense relief, the rooms were painted white, bare of any disturbing furniture and, with the door shut, quiet. The two rooms were adjoined with a door in between and shared a large en suite bathroom.

Giselle's eyes drifted to the bed. It was white-covered, pure, yet large enough for six, a strange juxtaposition of images. She was deathly tired and yet indefatigably curious. She felt she was awake in a dream yet she didn't want to fall asleep in case she missed the best parts.

'Let's join them for breakfast,' William said, as if reading her mind. 'Eat, and meet a few people. Then come back and rest.'

Giselle nodded her assent, and began to strip off her clothes. She hung her suit jacket and trousers over the high-backed chair tucked against the writing desk that spanned the length of a whole wall alongside the bathroom. William came up behind her as she slid the shower room door open and placed a hand on either side of her hips. He nestled his face into the slope of her neck and pushed the white lace panties that she was wearing down to her thighs. She could feel the hard point of his erection jutting against her buttocks, and instinctively began to turn her body around so that she could kiss him, then unbutton his trousers and fuck him on the bed before they washed.

'No,' he said, 'stay there. I want you like this.'

He lifted her arms above her head and placed her palms against the sheet of glass that lined the wet room area.

There was the faint click of his belt buckle unlatching and then the schtick, schtick soft sound of the brown leather rasping against the waistband of his trousers before thudding gently to the floor. Giselle could not help but conjure a visual image of William when they fucked like this; him with his broad arse and legs bare, his trousers pooled around the floor and his socks and shoes and shirt still on, his calves spread apart to keep his balance, perhaps the loose, soft flesh

117

of his ball bags visible between his spread legs. It was a position that struck her as innately perverse. There was something about the thought of being naked while he was mostly clothed, and of facing away from him, of being spread-eagled and unaware of when he might choose to slide his cock inside her, that made her feel powerless. And by not even removing his trousers – fucking her with his shoes and socks on – she was an afterthought, a vehicle for a lust that was short-lived before it even got started, not even worth getting undressed for.

Giselle was torn by these thoughts in the same way that she had been over her Joan fantasies. She felt that she ought to be revolted by her own desires and yet the more she focused on the subject of her revulsion, the more turned on she became. She knew, in her heart of hearts, that she was not an afterthought for William, nor simply a place for him to put his dick, and yet the idea of that very thing caused a spring of sexual appetite to well up inside her. These were thoughts that sparked her mind and wetted her cunt. As if it was the transgression that turned her on far more than the physicality of the thing. Not his cock sliding inside her, as it was now – and she clung to the glass with her palms as best as she could as he thrust and moaned behind her – but why he did it so. Sex, sometimes, was not about sex at all, Giselle decided, as they both fell forward together slumped against the shower screen.

It had only lasted minutes, and she hadn't come. Yet she took satisfaction from his orgasm and from the hurried nature of it. The overwhelming strength of his desire for her evidenced by the sort of need that had him fucking her against a bathroom door half-clothed before breakfast made her feel wanted, loved. She was aware of her conflicting feelings and yet satisfied. There was no need, in Giselle's mind, to tease apart all of the whys and wherefores of pleasure. It was enough for her that it felt good.

William moved her to one side in a loose embrace as he fiddled with the tap, and one after the other they washed away the dust of the previous days.

Giselle wrapped herself in one of the large, lemon-yellow bath sheets that she found folded and tucked away on the wooden shelves beneath the sink and watched William rinse himself off. He liked to stay beneath the water longer than she did, and often followed a hot shower with a strong jet of cold water. He said that it awakened his mind and made him feel alive.

'I brought along some extra clothes for you,' William said, still rubbing himself vigorously with the towel. Giselle could hear the pause in his voice that signalled he was about to ask her something that he was unsure of, or that she might not like what he was going to say next.

'Oh,' she replied. 'I would have packed properly if I'd known what to pack for.'

'I doubt that you would have clothes for such an occasion,' he pointed out.

'What exactly am I dressing for?' She thought of the attire that she had so far witnessed on the other guests they had passed.

'It's difficult to explain,' he responded. 'Better just to experience it, without too much thought. There's a dress hanging in the closet.' He pointed to a tall cupboard in the corner of the room. It reached nearly to the ceiling and was narrow, plain, and made from a very dark wood, well polished. The sort of wardrobe that would no doubt give a child nightmares. It looked like a coffin, Giselle thought, as she hesitantly pulled the door open. Inside, just one garment hung on the rail. She examined the fabric between her fingers, and then pulled the gown from the rail and held it up to the light. It was voluminous, white, almost shapeless and totally sheer, with long bell-shaped sleeves that trailed past the wrist, Maid Marian-style, and a low-cut V neck.

'There's a belt, too,' William said. He was watching her attentively, waiting for her reaction.

She reached back into the wardrobe and pulled a long, thin rope cord from the rail. It fastened with a knot threaded through a gold loop.

Giselle didn't ask if he had also purchased a matching chemise to go under the dress. She knew that the answer would be no. Her heart beat a little faster at the thought of appearing in front of William's friends and acquaintances covered only in this film of mesh. She laid the gown over the bedspread in front of her and then slipped it over her head, and turned to the wide, long, gilt-framed mirror that hung across the wall directly opposite the bed, the only piece of ornate furniture in the room.

'Shoes?' she asked.

'We won't be eating outside, I think. Your slippers will be fine, if you need them.'

His eyes shone as he stared at her, drinking in the vision of her firm body visible through the sheen of thin fabric that draped loosely over the curve of her buttocks.

'You look like a sculpture,' he said, 'made of marble. But not so cold.' His mouth lifted into half a smile.

Giselle smoothed her fingers through her hair – slightly damp still, from her shower, although she had taken care not to stand directly under the water – and decided simply to leave it as it was, flowing around her shoulders, with a slight curl caused by the humidity of the bathroom. She considered applying a touch of rouge to her cheeks, or lip gloss. Even though it was morning time, she felt as though they were attending a party.

William had changed into a fresh pair of navy-coloured trousers and a clean shirt, plain white, and added a pair of heavy silver cufflinks that hung at his wrists. The trousers that he had travelled in were still lying in a heap near the shower door.

'Ready?' she asked him.

He nodded, and took her hand as they stepped together into the passageway. The images that covered the walls seemed to loom out at Giselle as they passed, mocking, leering, laughing at them. If she had believed in dreams, or in nightmares perhaps, she would have suspected the eyes in the painted faces that surrounded them of following her as she walked.

Breakfast was unlike any meal that Giselle had eaten before.

The table was set out upstairs, rather than downstairs as Giselle had expected. They followed the winding staircase up one more level, and arrived in an enormous room, the length of the entire floor. A trestle table, set with chairs and elaborate silver cutlery, spanned the space – half the size of a football pitch. Conversation at the table was strangely muted considering the number of people, at least a hundred, Giselle guessed. The sequinned ladies that she had seen playing ping-pong earlier were seated directly in the middle, opposite the croquet players in their red braces, none of whom had put on shirts before sitting down to the meal.

Sebastian was at the far end, and stood and waved to catch their attention.

'William, darling!' he cried. His voice cut easily through

the crowd, who all turned to stare at the newcomers. 'I saved you two a place next to me. Come, come,' he beckoned.

He was clothed in the same long red robe, and as they approached Giselle noticed that his sleeves were narrowly close to dragging through a pot of cream that was positioned next to his plate, alongside a large scone and a hefty mountain of jam. On top of his head was now perched a black top hat with a silver ribbon tied into a large bow at the front, dangling just a few inches above his left eye.

'I do like your costume, my dear. You have beautiful breasts. I would like to paint them, sometime.'

Giselle was taken aback by the bluntness of his compliment, which rang out across the quiet room.

'Thank you,' she replied, slipping into one of the seats that he had pulled out. She was sitting opposite William, in between Sebastian and a corpulent man with an almost perfectly round and totally bald head. He might have resembled a large flesh-coloured baseball if it weren't for his long, black moustache that had been so carefully curled with wax that it managed to defy gravity and stick out from either side of his lips like a set of thick whiskers. He wore a bright violet-coloured waistcoat and black pinstripe shorts that turned up at the knee.

Two waiters appeared, one by Giselle's side and the other by William's as noiselessly as if they had somehow materialised out of the air instead of walking across the room to reach them. Both were young men and entirely naked apart from a crisp white neckerchief tied into a cravat around their throats and a length of white linen folded over one forearm, positioned rigidly in front of them with military precision.

Giselle's gaze was automatically drawn to the body of the nude attendant who positioned himself alongside William and was asking him if he would like to drink tea or coffee. He carried a silver serving tray and balanced atop it was a shining jug filled with steaming liquid. He was tanned – the deep golden-bronze colour of a brand new penny – and every muscle was as clearly delineated as those of a Michelangelo statue. His penis was long and straight and jutted out slightly from his body as though he was verging on a semi-erection, and matching the rest of his 'uniform' was a thin silk ribbon knotted around the base of his shaft.

His balls were heavy and apparently warm, since they dangled so low and, Giselle thought, invitingly. She was so mesmerised by the sight that she didn't notice that the waiter next to her was asking what she would like to drink until he had repeated the question twice over and Sebastian interrupted in his booming, high-pitched theatre of a voice 'He'll stir your sugar in with his cock if you ask him nicely my darling, won't you?' and then reached across and slapped the waiter's bare rump, causing the contents of the serving tray to rattle but not bringing so much as a flinch to his poker-faced composure.

A deep blush spread over Giselle's cheeks when she realised that she had been caught out ogling while sitting opposite the man she loved. But William only looked amused.

'There's no harm in looking, my dear,' Sebastian continued, patting her wrist with the same hand that he had used to slap the waiter's rump.

'Or even more,' William added in a low voice, quiet enough for the sound to almost be drowned out by the noise of cutlery scraping and tea pouring into the china tea cups, but the words flooded into Giselle's ear in one hot rush.

Sebastian nodded his agreement without raising an eyebrow at William's meaning and added, 'There will be plenty of time for that later, once you've rested. Some of these folk have been at it for days, now,' he said, staring down the table.

Giselle turned to follow his gaze.

At first, she had only noticed the costumes of her fellow guests. The glitz and glam, feathers and silks, satin and leather and lace, all of it beautifully cut and even the most eccentric outfits carried off with the aplomb of the most dazzling European court. Now she noted their faces. All of them were laughing, smiling or peacefully content and quiet, piqued with the bright-eyed flush that Giselle had only ever witnessed on the faces of dancers who she knew had thrown caution to the wind and come up trumps with the riskiest and best performances of their careers. It was the open-hearted look of the truly free, those who had tossed their hearts like dice and won the jackpot in the throwing.

They were openly affectionate with their neighbours to the point of obscenity. The sequinned girls were squeezing each other's breasts and comparing their firmness to the various types of fruit decorating a platter that served as the table's centrepiece. The croquet players were feeding one another teaspoons of jam and cream and kissing this makeshift dessert from each other's mouths. Further down the table, guests who were becoming uncomfortable in tightly boned corsets were untying their laces and revealing bare breasts and torsos, marked with red striations deep as valleys in the smooth mould of their skin.

A young woman in a sky-blue dress with an enormous flounced underskirt that swept around her like a sundial was down on her knees, sucking the cock of one of the waiting staff as he held a bottle of champagne aloft and poured the bubbling liquid from such a height that it created a fizzing stream that tumbled like a waterfall into the waiting guests' champagne flutes. Instead of drinking it from their flutes, they poured the cool liquid over each other's bodies and then lapped at the champagne brooks that ran over aligned nipples.

Giselle's attention was again distracted, this time by the rumbling of her belly. She hadn't eaten a proper meal in what felt like ages, and while she had been absorbing the antics occurring around her, breakfast had appeared on her plate, deposited by one of the naked waiters. There was a boiled duck egg, cooked just as she liked it with the yolk still runny, balanced in the smooth hollow of a golden egg cup, and a basket full of toasted brioche cut into dainty fingers. Alongside that, tropical fruit carved into tiny flowers, cool jelly served in balls like scoops of ice cream and a large cupcake, frosted with cream cheese icing. When she bit into it, lemon curd oozed out from the centre onto her tongue.

She ate, and drank, and once she was finished she felt revitalised, as though she had fed her tiredness, at least in part, as well as her thirst and hunger.

She and William returned to his room and fell into a sleep as deep as a drugged coma, waking abruptly when Giselle heard a tap on the door. She slipped out of bed and opened it, realising as she did so that she was entirely nude, not that it mattered.

Outside, the hall was empty. Giselle looked one way, and then the other, wondering if she had dreamed the knock before staring down and noticing a package wrapped in tissue paper on the floor in front of her feet, and on top of it a large cream envelope sealed with a lump of red wax. She picked it up, turned it over, and tore it open, since the sweeping calligraphy spelled out both her and William's names. The sealing wax was still warm. She flipped open the card and a cloud of fine silver dust floated to the floor. Inside were the words 'Top floor', written in tall, navy-blue letters.

Giselle shut the door behind her and crawled back onto the bed where William still lay. She planted a kiss on his forehead, handed him the card and began to unwrap the tissue paper.

Inside was a black satin robe. Giselle held it up. It was taller than she was, and far too large for her. She handed it to William. The only other item in the parcel was a glass bottle, about the size of the bottles of cream that her mother ordered from their local dairy at home. It was cool to the touch and contained a white liquid with a shimmer running through it that sparkled through the glass when Giselle held it up to the light.

'If you drink it, will it turn you into a frog?'

'You flatter me too much,' William replied. 'From a frog, into a prince, more like.'

He removed the lid from the bottle and dabbed a smear onto his wrist.

'Body paint,' he announced. 'I think this is intended to be your costume.'

'Well,' Giselle replied, 'I don't suppose that it will be any less revealing than this morning's chiffon, and that doesn't seem to matter here.'

'It has a wonderful shine to it,' William said, studying the line of paint on his wrist. 'You will look like a moon goddess, covered in this.'

He glanced at the watch lying on his nightstand.

'Midnight,' he said, 'we slept the entire day, and half of the night away.'

They bathed again, hurriedly this time, and Giselle dried herself carefully and moisturised her skin as William instructed, to ensure that the paint would go on smoothly and sit well.

He poured a stream of it down each of her shoulders and expertly spread it over her body, not lingering as he usually did when he caressed her breasts and buttocks with paint-covered hands. Giselle stood perfectly still, and held her arms out in a posture of crucifixion as he blasted her with the hairdryer to speed up the drying process.

When he proclaimed her finished, Giselle glanced in the mirror. She was covered in a thin layer of the glittering white paint, part goddess, part ghost. He had left her face and her throat bare, along with a line of nude that travelled between her breasts and formed a spiral pattern over her belly. Her normally pink nipples seemed redder contrasted against the pallor of her bust. Her thick triangle of pubic hair was a forest of black covering her groin.

William appeared behind her. He had washed the paint from his hands and had donned the black robe. Giselle turned round, her eyes fixed on the naked length of his midsection. The robe did not come with a belt or the loops to attach one, and even if it had, there wasn't quite enough fabric to cover all of his body. It hung from his broad shoulders and hovered just a few millimetres from his feet as if made for his length and breadth by a tailor who had sewn the garment to suit his precise measurements but purposefully left his penis, now almost fully erect, on display.

He kissed her cheek, then pressed his mouth to her ear lobe and reached between her legs to test her wetness.

'You're soaking,' he whispered. His gentle caresses became firmer, and then he found her clitoris, and began to play a rhythm in slow, concentric circles against her nub.

'Ohhh,' Giselle moaned. She could feel her blood beginning to pump faster in her veins as he played with her, his fingers now forming a makeshift cock and filling her entrance, one, two, three thrusts and then sliding back to continue exploring her labia, and toying with her clit.

He withdrew suddenly and she groaned with the shock of his withdrawal.

'I want the others to watch,' he said. He lifted his fingers to his lips and licked her juices from them, then kissed her, transferring the sweet salt of her arousal from his mouth to hers.

He took her hand in his and they walked through the

wide hall and up one flight of stairs, past the door to the breakfast room and then up another. The gradient felt somehow steeper to Giselle the further they climbed, and although she knew it was only three floors, when they reached the door that led to their destination she felt she was about to step into another world altogether.

She laid her hand upon the door and pushed, but it didn't budge. William reached past her and turned the handle.

The sound reached her first. The combined choir of so many people making love that they formed a chorus, a melody of sighs and moans punctuated with the occasional joyful scream against the percussion of rhythmic thuds, body parts banging against furniture and against each other, the wet slap of skin on skin.

The night air was cool against Giselle's flesh and as a gossamer breeze brushed over her breasts she felt her already hard nipples stiffen even more. She longed for William to bend his head to her chest and suck them, to soothe the aching need that burned inside her. Her cunt was slick, a cauldron of lust between her thighs.

There was no roof overhead. They were outside on a terrace. Fire burned on flaming torches that lined the balcony on each side. Every so often a gust of wind would send an abnormally large flame skywards, lighting up the bodies that writhed ahead of them, some on beds, blankets and cushions, others just against the hard concrete floor.

Dead centre, a woman stood, tied onto a plinth with tight black coils – whether rope, leather, silk or chain, Giselle could not make out. Her eyes were closed but she was not asleep. Her body twitched and jolted as though she were undergoing an exorcism. No, not that. An orgasm, Giselle realised. Her mouth was transfixed in a smile, her face a picture of radiant joy. Rivulets of sweat, or tears – blood, even? – trailed over her skin.

But none of that was the strangest part. What caused Giselle to blink, to question whether she had again woken up mid-dream, was the canvas that covered the woman's flesh. A bacchanalia of images, etched into her skin, leaping, dancing, lighting up the darkness that surrounded her. Like pornographic tattoos come to life, or a mirror image of the bodies fucking in front of her.

'Come,' said William. 'Let's join them.'

He took her hand again, and together they walked ahead.

4

Of Bodies and Light

Giselle spent the weeks that followed her return from the Ball in a daze, still processing the images and sensations she had witnessed with a sense of both shock and delight. The trip to the opulent property beyond Long Island still felt like a dream to her sometimes. If it had not been for certain mundanities, such as the difficulty of removing the ghost-like paint from her skin, or the plain white card that Sebastian had slipped into the pocket of her linen jacket on the morning she left, she might have thought she had dreamed it all. The fantastical nature of the intoxicating party and the strange array of guests that she had met there made the rest of her life pale into ordinariness by comparison, so that she now felt as though she was perched on a precipice, hanging between two different worlds. Between the world of daily domesticity, the lectures she wished to attend and the work at the flower shop on the Rue de Buci, which she insisted on still doing if only to retain some form of financial independence despite William's selfless offer to support her, her mind never had the leisure to settle. She became a traveller in her own life. Even when her body was settled, her mind drifted.

They had just made love – a tender, untroubled affair – and William had showered and was walking back from the bathroom, his hair wet, curls askew, drying himself with a thick brown towel. She would be taking her shower next, had unusually declined to share the cubicle with him, intent on allowing the inner heat of her orgasm to die down slowly, lazy in the fuzzy clutches of the receding pleasure plateau, in her own time, her body still tingling and now blissfully bone tired. An unwelcome thought occurred to her.

'William?'

'Yes?' His head emerged from the loose folds of the towel, his dark eyes and aquiline nose peering out from its soft surroundings, his ordinarily stubbly beard a lion's mane since he had now left off shaving for a few weeks rather than days as he usually did.

'When you look at me here, in bed, in real life, when we're together, do I look the same as when I pose or do you see someone different?'

'What a strange question.'

'I was just wondering.'

Noting how earnest she was, William paused, reflecting.

He allowed the now wet towel to drop to the floor, gazed intently at Giselle. Fell silent.

'I meant ... when you gaze at me, and draw, paint me, is it the same everyday Giselle, or is it some form of abstract object, rather than me as a person?'

'I'm not sure I properly understand you.'

Giselle sighed, realising that the confusion reigning in her mind was twisting her words, rendering her in part inarticulate.

Unable to communicate as she wished, she turned round and buried her face in the pillow.

'What is it?' William asked.

Remembering the faces and bodies at the Ball, Giselle could not help recalling the radiance that shone through them, the way the pool of the moonlight tripped over their features, their sublime curves, how deep inside their eyes an eternal flame appeared to burn.

Was that the way William saw her when she posed? Transfigured. Could she ever be that way? In a contradictory manner, it made her doubt his feelings for her.

When she later peered nervously at William's paintings in which she appeared at the centre of things, all she could see was herself, a pale imitation of life despite the acute hyperrealism of William's pictorial style. Despite his talent and the love he professed for her, she didn't shine like others had. Would she ever?

By now, William had become accustomed to her fleeting moods and knew better than to encourage them, and remained silent, moving to the kitchen under the pretext of getting them some coffee. By the time he was back in their bedroom, Giselle was asleep. As he had hoped. He lit up a cigarette.

The next morning, Giselle enquired if he would mind her posing for others. Since she had begun working for him, she had received a handful of offers from artist friends of his whom they had met socially at dinners or gallery openings. And, in America, there had been Sebastian. Until now, she had ignored them all.

'Not at all. I actually think it would be good for you. I can't hold you back, can I?' William remarked. 'It will provide you with invaluable experience.'

'You wouldn't be jealous?'

'Of course not.'

She contacted Sebastian first. Following the weekend at the mansion in the States, the three of them had met up a few times to talk and drink and smoke cigarettes and she had many times now listened to William and Sebastian debate the various merits of their artistic preferences and styles of working. Sebastian was a much older and solidly established artist who was under contract to the same gallery that William was. His work was, according to William, more traditional, vast canvases full of broad sweeps, natures mortes, classical nudes and delicately etched portraits. Giselle had never actually seen any of his paintings, just heard them described, and she intuited that he was also part of the same close circle of artists who agreed on occasion to produce more daring and sexually provocative pieces for Emile Saffy and other collectors who were even more protective of their anonymity when it came to matters pornographic. On the occasions when they had met as a threesome, neither Sebastian nor William had directly raised the topic of the party beyond Long Island – the Ball, as she had overheard other guests refer to it – and without a prompt, she was too shy to ask for further details. In normal circumstances, Sebastian was flamboyant and eccentric as he had been that weekend, but not quite to the same degree. In public, he was like a butterfly in a fog, hiding his brightness under cover. Giselle hoped that in his own home he would be less guarded, and she could learn more, perhaps ask some of the questions that William had brushed away without properly responding to. Since William had an eye for the surreal, Giselle was of the opinion that something like the Ball didn't seem out of the ordinary to him. That was the way that his mind worked, after all. Maybe the Ball, to William, was reality, and everything else somewhat dim and grey by comparison.

'That's grand,' Sebastian said. 'Could you do next Wednesday? I happen to have a session scheduled and I was in need of a second model. Would it bother you to pose alongside another woman?'

'Not at all.' It would be something new, Giselle reckoned, and provide her with some exposure to expressing herself, holding her limbs in a different style of pose than she was accustomed to.

The fee he suggested was more than generous, although this wasn't Giselle's primary concern. She just wanted to know how it would feel modelling for others, how she would be perceived. It felt important. To find out how she fitted into his world.

It wasn't until Giselle began in earnest to pose for others that she came to realise how characteristic the smell of paint was in William's studio. Unlike the new artists she visited, as she discovered later, he preferred to mix his own paints, a devil's brew of pigments, sachets of strange powders, water, oil, alcohol, solvents, egg yolk, binding potions and a pinch of mysterious ingredients unique to him, a secret cocktail that had him poring meticulously like an alchemist over his jars and cups for ages to prepare, random specks of ash from the cigarette dangling on his lip floating down at times into the mixture. Was that why the surface sheen of his canvases proved so unique, as if the texture of the drying paint harboured a beating pulse of light within its strokes and superimposed layers? At any rate, few other artists could equal the supernatural illusion of life that his paint contributed to his images. Often, when queried by strangers about his trademark pigments, he would hint mischievously that he added a precise amount of sperm collected at just the right moment of the strongest orgasm as an extra ingredient. And then would roar with laughter at the look on their face.

But the material thus prepared also generated a strong odour, an astringent fragrance that now permeated the wooden beams and floors of his Latin Quarter studio in permanence, like a smell of dead flowers and a distant echo of strong booze, rotting leaves and ash that clung to the air. It had taken Giselle several sessions to get used to it, until she reached the point that she no longer noticed it.

As she walked into Sebastian's airy atelier just by the banks of the river at Nogent sur Marne, the difference in scent was the first thing she noted. The immense rectangular space, with its paint-stained floors displaying an intricate, involuntary mosaic of cabbalistic maps, bathed in the heady fragrance of sweet flowers, its sliding patio doors open to a nearby garden where rose bushes grew untrimmed in a mass of untidy beauty. The contrast with William's studio and its lingering odours and studied darkness couldn't have been greater.

Unlike her lover, the thin–as–a–stick Sebastian never

bothered himself with preliminary sketches or studies and worked straight onto canvas, and the material he used came in carefully aligned squat tubes of paint laid out on a trestle table within reach of his hand, his brushes carefully disposed in a row where they sat aligned in decreasing sizes.

The other model hadn't yet arrived.

At the far end of the room, a table laden with plates full of succulent patisseries and a tall jug of orange juice had been set up, which Sebastian and his boyfriend cum assistant, Ellis, a dour but much younger and extremely good-looking, square-shouldered Breton in a striped top and baggy white slacks, invited her to sample while they waited for the late-coming model to make her appearance.

'It's Sunday, and the Metro is always slower,' Sebastian remarked.

Munching on a petit pain au chocolat, Giselle asked him if he'd worked with the missing girl before.

'No. It's the first time. I booked her through an agency. My client wants something ballet-themed and she has a background in dance, I was assured.'

'Me too,' Giselle pointed out.

'I know.'

'How come?'

'Giselle, it's the way you move. It's unmistakable . . .'

Giselle blushed slightly. Was she so transparent? The thought occurred to her, and this was not the first time,

whether people, men, strangers looking at her in the street
or wherever, knew when she had recently been fucked by
William. Did it show, in the way she walked, by the colours
of her skin, her cheeks? The reminder troubled her.

The chimes rang and Ellis left the studio space and headed
for the villa's front door.

The young woman who returned with him was tall and
blonde, her cheeks flushed, babbling away apologetically.
She had run from the nearby station. In an attempt to compose herself, she brushed her hair back and Giselle recognised
her. It was Beth. They both laughed out loud as they
acknowledged each other.

'What are you doing here?'

'I could ask the very same question!'

'I'm French. I live here.'

'And I'm just a tourist of sorts. Making ends meet with a
spot of modelling!'

'You know each other?' Sebastian chuckled, amused by
the coincidence.

'We studied at the same ballet academy in London
together.'

'Just over a year ago.'

'How quaint . . .'

Sebastian gave them a half hour to catch up and change
and apply their make-up.

'My client has ordered a slightly askew ballet scene,' he

informed them. 'You'll find the outfits on the rail over there. Your sizes, I'm assured.' He had a day or so earlier enquired about their measurements, which were remarkably alike it turned out. 'He's one of those rather perverse private collectors. Wishes one of you to be topless and the other . . . bottomless. I assume that's alright with the both of you? You decide between yourselves who does what . . .'

Neither of the models was taken back.

'You have the better breasts,' Giselle said to Beth. 'I'm okay with it.' Since the Ball, nothing could surprise or shock her.

Beth had failed the next exam at ballet school and had drifted to Paris shortly after, mostly waitressing until a now long-past-his-sell-by-date boyfriend had suggested she could improve her finances by modelling and had introduced her to an agency. The boyfriend had since been ditched, as had the waitressing, but her striking Nordic-like looks paid the bills. She'd even been briefly employed at the Folies Bergère as a naked statue, she informed Giselle with a giggle, in constant fear of family and friends perhaps visiting Paris and the famous risqué theatre and actually recognising her in the chorus.

There were two outfits, one white and another in a pale shade of pink.

'You take the white one,' Beth suggested. 'It will go better with your skin tone.'

So everyone seemed to think, Giselle mused. She had so often lately been put into white. And she was hardly the Virgin Mary, nor a blushing bride.

Ellis had spread a length of thick carpet in a corner of the studio and arranged the lighting. The two young women self-consciously stepped towards it, even though they both knew the two men were gay and therefore did not have the slightest interest in assessing their bodies in any sexual manner. Sebastian dictated their positions while his sidekick fussed around them, mussing their hair, adjusting a spotlight or smoothing out a fold in the bottom half of Beth's leotard, which looked forlorn and bizarre without the obligatory body stocking a ballet dancer would often wear with it.

'Giselle, if one of your feet was shoeless, it would look better, more suggestive, I think.'

She unlaced the pointe, taking great care to hold her legs together out of modesty as she stretched out to do so in her position on the dark carpet. Beth's majestic breasts, pink-tipped and firm, stared at her at eye-level. The assistant arranged the unlaced ballet shoe upside down just a few inches from her foot, an abandoned extension of her shapely leg, on the border of the carpet, like the aftermath of an unseen struggle or event.

Sebastian dismissed his assistant, who moved back into the house, softly closing the studio door behind him, leaving them alone.

'Just us,' the painter declared.

Giselle and Beth were sitting side to side, shoulder against shoulder, their bare skin lit by a concentrated beam from above where Ellis had attached a row of theatrical-like spotlights.

'Beth, move your hand, just like that, there, set it down on Giselle's thigh ...' Sebastian was giving orders now, though in the same soft voice that he used to offer tea, despite his growing frustration.

He adjusted their positions yet again, still dissatisfied by the overall composition he was attempting to shape. Gazed at them at length, tut-tutting to himself all along.

Still, he wasn't ready to begin painting them.

He moved forwards, circled them, paused, stepped back, returned, swept Giselle's long black hair back so that it was now partly draped across Beth's nape. Observed the end result of his composition and shook his head.

'Nothing wrong with you two lovely ladies,' he said, with a sense of disappointment, 'but I had this image in my head and it's just not coming to life. Doesn't work.'

Both Giselle and Beth knew not to comment. They had both worked with artists or photographers before and were aware how fickle and indecisive they could prove.

Sebastian walked away, adjusted the angle of one of the spotlights and assessed the scene again from afar. He asked Giselle to stand, extend her arm and loom over Beth's sprawled, long-limbed body. Then yet another infinitesimal twist of the incandescent bulb to correct the shape of the pool of light in the heart of which they were situated.

'You're both beautiful,' he finally said. 'But my gut tells me we need something more. I know this collector; he's very picky, won't be fobbed off with just anything.' He pondered a moment. 'Some form of contrast. Something quirky. Get up, Beth ...'

The two young women stood next to each other, almost at military attention, each in a different state of undress, blonde and brunette, the soft pink of Beth's areolae an isolated zone of warmth against the even porcelain landscape of her skin, the dark luxuriant curls of Giselle's pubic area a dense forest of black against the warmer tones of her nudity.

Sebastian hesitated a further moment, then asked Beth to pull her leotard, which was bunched at the waist, down and then her thin flesh-coloured knickers. He gazed at what she revealed. Her pubic hair was sparse, pale to the extreme, seemingly even more sun-bleached than the hair on her head now held tight in a ballet-apposite chignon. His eyes moved from Beth to Giselle whose dark as night intimate patch of vegetation was abundant but tidily trimmed, a habit that had been drummed into her back at the Ballet Academy.

The lanky artist considered the contrast, weighing ideas up in his mind.

'The other way around?' Giselle asked, suggesting that

maybe she should expose her breasts rather than the lower half of her body. Beth looked on silently.

'I have it!' Sebastian roared.

The two women awaited the result of his deliberation.

Under the table on which he kept his hoard of paint tubes, brushes and assorted work material sat a deep wooden chest which he dragged out.

'Here ...' Sebastian held out a handful of iridescent, opaque sequins and minuscule beads in his palm and presented them to Giselle. 'Would it bother you if you could somehow scatter these in your bush. I'm not being perverse, it's just a crazy idea. An extra touch of light, however incongruous that might sound,' he added. 'Sometimes, it's those small touches that make a piece look distinctive ...'

Giselle was not disturbed by the request, but stood there puzzled, thinking about its practicality.

Beth came to the rescue.

'Come with me,' she said and led Giselle to their changing area behind a set of drapes at the far end of the artist's studio, picking the sequins and miniature adornments from Giselle's hand, examining the trinkets closely, with a decidedly mischievous smile spreading across her lips.

Giselle sat on a chair, still attempting to get to grips with Sebastian's concept.

'Do you mind?' Beth asked. Her hand pointing at Giselle's genitals.

Two of her fingers delved into Giselle's thick curls.

'Good,' she said.

'What?'

'I first thought the only way would be to sew them on one at a time, or, worse, glue them ...' Giselle shivered as one of Beth's nails grazed her sex lips and her cunt registered the warmth of Beth's exploring fingers. 'But your curls are quite long and I think I could attach them naturally. Is that okay with you?'

Giselle nodded her assent.

'It's going to take some time,' Beth cried out to Sebastian who was waiting on the other side of the drapes. 'We'll need a half hour or so, I guess ...'

'That's fine,' he shouted. 'But make it look pretty ...'

'That I will,' Beth promised.

She settled on her hind, her surprisingly soft breasts cushioned against Giselle's knees. 'This is going to be tedious,' she warned. 'Spread a little, so I can get to work ...' There was a curious glint to her eye and Giselle felt hot all the way down to her soul. Never had she been in a situation like this with another woman peering at her sex from just a few inches away, as Beth carefully took hold of a single curl, gently pulling it straight and threaded one of the sequins down before twisting the curl's ends together to maintain it in place. Her movements were steady and precise. Never had the intimacy of Giselle's sex been contemplated at such length and close quarters by anyone, apart from William when he would go down on her, a practice she was still in two minds about despite the adventurous talent of his delving tongue and the restrained bite of his lips and teeth against her labia and clit.

Giselle's mind wandered.

'This is fun,' Beth said. 'And funny, you must admit . . .'

Giselle looked down, watched as the sequins were gradually spread evenly across the field of her pubic bush, catching the light with every microscopic movement she made, her legs wide open, her thighs welcoming Beth inside their harbour. The spectacle was fascinating. Beth worked with geometrical precision, interspersing the random beads into the sky of sequins now dominating her sexual landscape, a true craftswoman in her element.

The dangerous proximity of Beth's face to her opening had her mind wandering in confusing directions.

'I think that's it,' Beth said, and rose to her feet, glancing down with admiration at her work. Giselle's dark pubic hair was a bizarre field of stars. 'I can do no better.' She gleamed with satisfaction.

'Yes, yes, that's just right. It's fantastic,' Sebastian exclaimed as the two models walked out. 'Even better than what I had imagined.' He fiddled again with the spotlights as Giselle and Beth settled themselves into the new positions assigned to them, both facing his easel, supporting each other, each with an arm around the other's waist like two ballerinas exhausted following a performance and now pausing for breath, mouths half open, a touch unsteady and faltering. To an unknown observer, it would have appeared like a twisted and moderately obscene or provocative variation on a Degas composition, the pool of light cast on their bodies highlighting Beth's now incandescent nipples and the unnatural fire of Giselle's sexual parts, their respective faces neglected and partly left in shadow. Sebastian's movements across his canvas were fast and furious as he tried in haste to capture the image he had finally managed to compose and lay its foundations with paint and charcoal for posterity before it faded.

Sebastian worked rapidly, in a creative trance, now that the perfection in the disposition of the models in a *tableau vivant* had finally caught up with his imagination. By the time he had completed his rough draft of the painting and would no longer require the models, it remained light outside in the garden that overlooked the river and the dense woods on the far bank. As Giselle slipped into her day clothes, she noticed a couple swimming in the distance. The water was a grey shade of green. She had turned down Beth's offer to untangle the sequins and beads she had arranged in her pubic hair. Now, she just wanted to go home to William, buzzing with curiosity as to how he would react to the curious decorations adorning her below.

★   ★   ★

To Giselle's profound disappointment, William was not at the apartment when she got back to Paris an hour later. He had left her a note informing her he'd had to leave for three days at most, as he had been offered some work out of the blue by the Ball organisers, who needed some sketches for future events to be drawn and it was too good an opportunity to miss, he apologised. Her initial reaction was surprise, followed by resentment. Had he been flown to New York by the organisation or were they based elsewhere? She recalled the way other women had clustered around him at the Long Island mansion, and the wild glint in his roving eye that betrayed his evident interest and belonged as much to the man inside as to the detached artist he pretended to be in the presence of female beauty.

Forlorn in the empty Latin Quarter apartment, Giselle realised she had forgotten to ask Beth for her telephone number in her haste to return to William.

She nibbled a few slices of jambon from the fridge, made herself a baguette sandwich and picked up a book at random but was unable to concentrate and read properly. Her mind a total blank, she remembered she hadn't showered after the modelling session and rose, leaving the book opened at the same page she had been daydreaming over for much too long, and made her way to the bathroom. Once she had stripped, she looked at herself in the full-length mirror, appraising the long, straight lines of her body, the dryness of her plump lips to which small breadcrumbs were now stuck, the exiguous, shadowy valley separating her breasts, the eerie glossiness of her ebony hair which men always remarked upon, the rough texture of her nipples, inverted craters, the convex dip of her navel, and its mirror reflection, the concave hill of her mound now crazily highlighted by the multitude of sequins and beads Beth had so ingeniously attached, one at a time, her nimble fingers travelling like probes through Giselle's bush, decorating her intimacy like an incongruous Christmas tree. Giselle peered down at her reflection. The bathroom was a totally enclosed space, with no natural lighting, and the cheap costume jewellery no longer shone without the artifice of Sebastian's carefully directed studio spotlights, and looked tacky, if not ridiculous now. Maybe it was a good thing William was away. There was no way he would have found the spectacle arousing, more likely deserving of laughter, and the confrontation could have proved humiliating.

Giselle determined to untangle the sequins and beads later. First she badly needed that shower, to wash away the craziness of the afternoon and the disturbing emotions Beth's presence and the initial impact of seeing her cunt shine with such artificial brightness had raised.

It was only as the hot water washed down over her body, her face drowning under the cascading jet, that she realised her mistake, but by then it was too late.

She attempted in vain to correct the damage as soon as she had exited the stall and hurriedly dried herself but already the tangle of hair and jewellery now weighing down her bush had become impenetrable and each individual knot impossible to unthread or loosen, every effort to do so just making matters worse. She sat herself, despairingly, on the side of the bathtub and opened her legs impossibly wide to the gaze of the mirror but saw how tightly the cocktail of her curls and the now dull scattering of sequins were blending, almost glued together by the dampness. She should have attempted to untangle the mess before walking into the shower. How could she have been so stupid? William would laugh his head off when he returned and saw the state of her, she reckoned.

There was only one thing she could do, Giselle decided.

Precisely cutting each individual sequin and bead away from its allotted curl with a pair of nail scissors would leave her pubes looking like a decimated field following a bad harvest, she knew. It would regrow, luxuriant, in time but the sight of it would be dreadful in the interval.

She would have to shave it all off.

There was no other solution to the problem.

She guessed it would make her look like a plucked chicken, or maybe not. Back in the dance academy's locker room she had briefly caught a glimpse of the genitalia of a couple of foreign girls who kept their sex shaved for convenience sake. She had found the sight both odd and disturbing, and it had long lingered in her mind.

The second night with William, he had buried his head in her cunt with a deep sigh of pleasure and thrust his tongue into her folds, brushing her curls away and imbibing her like a wine connoisseur taking his first sip of a new nectar and said, 'I fucking love this dark forest of yours. I could live there.' Another memory that marked her to this day. The way words could carve a furrow across your heart.

Would he be angry finding her smooth and defoliated?

And, more importantly, how would this anger express itself?

How rough would he be with her?

How creative would his displeasure turn out to be?

Giselle extended her arms towards the medicine cabinet where the disposable razors were kept.

Took a deep breath.

How would she reveal the transformation to him? Deliberately expose herself as soon as he arrived back, or allow him to come across her new state of nudity accidentally in bed?

Her hand trembled.

Her cheeks felt hot.

She steadied herself, looked down at the delta between her thighs and began the meticulous task. It no longer felt like a chore, but sent a tremor of excitement racing through her mind and body.

The first tiny tangle of sequins and ebony curls slipped to the bathroom floor, floating down, knots of heavy dust dotting the grey tiles like random punctuation.

It was done. And she did not, as she had feared, resemble de-feathered poultry. Looking down at her bare slit, Giselle felt her heart leap in her chest. She ran a finger between her folds, marvelling at the smoothness of her skin. It was as if she had dropped an item of clothing. Without the cloak of her pubic hair, her mound was naked and inviting, permanently on display. She resisted the instinctive desire to cover herself with her hands. Even as she walked alone through the apartment, she noticed a change in bodily sensation. She had opened a window to clear the thick acrid smell of William's paint fumes, and a tongue of wind, soft as an exhalation of breath, danced over her nude skin like the lightest touch of an explorative finger.

She lay on the bed and closed her eyes, processing the new feelings that washed over her. Briefly, she was disappointed that Beth would not be called upon again to decorate her bush, or at least, not unless she chose to grow it back. She wondered what her friend would think of her new style. Would she be shocked? Doubtful. Not much shocked Beth. Aroused? Maybe. The thought of her friend glancing down at Giselle's smooth skin, testing how thoroughly she had depilated by running a fingertip over her lips and mound, caused a shiver to run through Giselle's body. Perhaps Beth would find a stray hair that Giselle had missed and slap her cunt gently with the palm of her hand to punish her for her laxness. Or she might fetch the razor, and run its cool blade over Giselle's flesh again. Or even bend her head down and nip away the errant strand with her teeth.

Giselle's pulse quickened at the thought and she rolled over onto her tummy and rocked her hips, pressing her bare cunt against the stiff fabric of the bed cover. It was a position that she had favoured when she still lived with her parents and figured that should someone interrupt her pleasuring herself, she could easily freeze still and pretend to be asleep. Now, she was still half angry with William for leaving her and she took some small satisfaction from rubbing her now wet, newly smooth cunt against his cream quilt with the raised embroidered pattern that felt so firm against her clit if she dragged herself against it at the right angle. Marking her place in his bed.

She came easily. It was always like that when she was alone.

When William returned at last his skin was flushed and he seemed feverish with excitement. He'd mentioned in his note this morning that he had been summoned by the Ball organisers to work on some plans for a future occasion. Giselle's curiosity battled with her other emotions – her loneliness and irritation that he had left her behind and the sharp teeth of jealousy that tore at her heart. Curiosity won.

'Tell me more about the Ball,' she asked. 'What have others you've attended before me been like?'

They were sitting cross-legged on the very same bedspread that Giselle had masturbated on top of two nights previously, eating a makeshift dinner of bread, cheese and fruit.

'I'm sorry, my darling,' he said, 'you know that I'm not allowed to talk about it. Everyone involved with the Ball signs an agreement. We're not even supposed to discuss it with each other.' He was silent for a few moments. Giselle recognised the break in conversation as a pause. Silence carries as much meaning between lovers as words do, and she knew by the pattern of his breath and the stiff way he sat, poised with a grape halfway to his mouth, that if she waited he would continue.

'Well, I suppose if I don't go into the specifics ...' He trailed off, popped the grape between his teeth and reached across to her and began to trail his fingertip over her collarbones as he spoke. 'The light they manage to conjure is the most incredible thing. One of their costume makers has managed to capture with fabric something I sometimes attempt to create with paint. I'm not sure how ... the dancers' dresses are often made of this stuff that looks like handfuls of the night sky. Like a Van Gogh painting. It's as though the light is dancing with them. You would look wonderful, in such a garment. I might paint a gown onto you.'

'Was it a rehearsal? Did you see them dance?' she asked him.

'I saw them perform, an impromptu act. They may have not even have agreed the final Ball routine yet, and all of the actual rehearsals take place in secret. It's like something organised by the secret service ...' He laughed. 'But I suppose that's how they keep everybody guessing and so eager to attend. They've been going on for centuries, you know, these parties. Even the costumes were only revealed to me because I might paint the backdrops. They wanted me to see the fabric, the way it made the dancers like stars ...' He had that faraway look in his eyes again, as though his mind was still travelling with the Ball although his body was back home in Paris.

Giselle set her hunk of bread and piece of cheese back down on the plate. She had lost her appetite. She saw the dancers in her imagination as clearly as if they were performing on the floor in front of them. A troupe of young women, each wearing the ecstatic expression that she had witnessed on the faces of the guests at the party at the mansion beyond Long Island. All of them beautiful, of that she had no doubt. Their bodies firm and lithe, skin luminous, eyes bright with the passion that comes naturally to performers when they are doing what they love, and know that they are doing it well. And an element of lust. Giselle suspected that everyone involved in the Ball possessed an appreciation of the erotic, a natural tendency towards the libidinous and a fearlessness that led them to dance down paths that others dared not tread.

The very same thoughts that had plagued her before William left on his assignment sprang up again and they erupted in her mind like a thunder cloud of bees shaken from their hive. She couldn't think straight. She felt as though she had been possessed. The image of the dancers moved like a large-screen movie in fast forward. Instead of watching them step in time, shimmering in their silver gowns, she saw them disrobe. One by one the women pirouetted, around and around like whirling dervishes until their skirts flew upwards from their calves to their hips and then higher, revealing naked bellies, breasts, bare throats as the garments drifted into the air, up, up and away, leaving them naked, still dancing, as William in his position as a voyeur in dreamland watched entranced.

'Are you alright, darling? You've turned pale. Would you like a glass of water?'

Giselle looked down at her hands; she was shaking.

Her throat was dry, and she couldn't find the words to speak. She nodded.

William rose from the bed and hurried to the kitchen. He filled a glass from the faucet and handed it to her.

As she sipped, Giselle tried to calm her nerves, but it was no good. She could think of nothing besides the dancers. How well they must dance, and how beautiful they must be. She despised herself for hating them. She'd always thought jealousy to be an emotion held by the weak, and here she was, sick with it.

William sat down next to her and patted her back as though she were a child. Suddenly she became aware of the fact that he had barely pecked her on the lips since returning home. Here they were sitting side by side on the bed, eating bread and cheese together like an old married couple. Shouldn't he have missed her so much that he wanted to fuck her the moment he walked in the door?

Or had he already had his fill of women, these past few days? And all of them no doubt sexier than Giselle. What kind of sexual tricks they might have learned as part of their employment with the Ball, she didn't know, but having seen the sorts of activities that took place at the American Ball, she could imagine.

'What were they like?' she asked him. 'These women.' There was an acidic tone to her voice that she wished she could erase, but it was too late, the words had already come out of her mouth.

He stared at her. 'They were exactly what you might

expect from dancers who work for the Ball, I suppose.'

'Beautiful?' she suggested. 'The best dancers in the world, I expect.'

'Well, yes,' he replied. 'Is that what this is about? You know what my work involves. And I don't see them that way . . . I know it's hard for you to understand but when a model is in front of me she's not a body, sexually. She's a vehicle for light, expression, art.'

'How do you see me, then? I must be one or the other. Am I art, or not art? Not beautiful enough to paint, or too beautiful to fuck?'

William ignored her question, which in Giselle's mind just confirmed that there was a flaw in his logic. He reached over to the bedside table and fumbled in the drawer for his cigarettes.

'Must you?' Giselle huffed, as he took a drag and smoke drifted into the air.

William's hand froze. He was flicking the end of his cigarette against the now empty plate that had sat between them. Giselle had never complained about his smoking before.

'I can go outside, if you like,' he replied, and glanced out of the window. 'It's a warm night. I wouldn't mind a walk, after sitting so long.'

He pushed himself up and reached for his jacket, the mustard-coloured tweed with the leather-patched elbows. She hated it.

'But you've only just arrived,' Giselle snapped.

'You've just asked me to leave.'

'I didn't ask you to leave, I asked you not to light a cigarette, when I've just been coughing.'

'Forget it,' William shouted. 'It's my own damn house. I'll smoke wherever the hell I please.'

He picked up the plate and glass and threw them into the kitchen sink. Then stalked back to the bed, picked up his box of cigarettes, shrugged into his jacket and dropped his lighter into his pocket.

'I'll be back later.'

There was a note of finality in his tone that brokered no argument.

Giselle stared at him with her mouth open.

William walked out of the room, slamming the door so hard behind him that the windows rattled.

She got up and pulled open the cupboards until she found one of his bottles of spirits. 'Remy Martin', the bottle said, and she knew that it was expensive as he drank it rarely and always accompanied by a distinct sense of ritual. Alongside the bottle was the glass that he used during his occasional drinking sessions, a squat, thick and heavy cut-crystal tumbler. Giselle pulled both out, sat down on the floor with her back resting against the cabinet door and poured herself a large measure. The sound of the liquid streaming into the glass soothed her, as did the thought that William might be annoyed with her when he tasted the booze on her breath. He knew she wasn't a big drinker and could have just as happily consumed a glass of the red wine that was already opened and her only motivation for imbibing the cognac was a petty form of revenge.

It was warming and tasted of honey. She poured another measure.

Her head slipped back to rest against the cupboard door, and she shuffled her feet forward so that she was slouched, crescent-shaped, relaxed. But just as she felt her anger and irritation were ebbing, another image of William would prick her. His hand on an unknown thigh. His tongue sliding over a nipple, pink and hard. His hands tangled in a hank of blonde hair.

Giselle's jealousy was like a bed of nails. No matter how she tried to direct her thoughts there was a pin prick ready to stab her.

Unable to find any rest, no matter how much of the amber liquid she swallowed, Giselle got up and began to search the apartment for more of William's paintings. She had always wondered why he had so few in their home and back at his studio. There must be more somewhere, she figured, he couldn't have sold or stored them all. Perhaps he had hidden them from her.

She got down on her hands and knees and crawled under the bed, lifted the mattress, pulled the bedding from the linen cupboard and searched between towels, pushed pots and pans to the side in the kitchen, looking for – for what? Some proof that he didn't love her as much as he said he did?

Having ransacked the whole house and found nothing, she at last turned to the set of drawers by his side of the bed, where he kept his cigarettes. Inside, beneath a couple of empty lighters, stray filters and papers, a couple of buttons that had popped off shirts and been put away for safe keeping, she found a sketchbook. She pulled it out, climbed onto the bed and flicked through the pages.

Nearly every picture was of Giselle. He had drawn her in a myriad different ways. In the first, she was nude, and holding a thorny rose to her breast, her mouth twisted in pain. In another she was the radiant centre of an orgy, her expression uplifted like a Madonna in prayer, as an unidentified man, sketched only in body and not in features, filled her from behind. There was a whole series of her as Joan, with her legs and arms wide open and inviting, despite the chains that bound her. Several depicted her as she'd been at the American Ball, naked through her filmy gauze dress. The most recent picture was not quite finished, and must have been drawn on the plane back when she had been sleeping. She was one of a group of dancers, the only one who had been sketched in full. He had pictured her nude in the night sky, her arms outstretched as if she were reaching for the stars, and might be able to scoop them up into her hands. Her lips were full and turned up at the corners and her eyes closed, as though she was remembering a kiss.

She looked up when she heard the key turning in the door. The sound brought her back to reality, like waking from a dream. She glanced at the tumbler, now lying on its side on the floor alongside the still open bottle of cognac. The apartment looked as though they had been burgled. Linen lay in piles where she had tossed it, cupboard doors were open on their hinges and the bench tops were covered with the debris of whatever items she had pulled from shelves in order to search behind them. It was too late now, by a mile, to slip the sketchbook back into his drawer and pretend she hadn't been prying.

William hung his jacket on the hook and sat down beside her on the bed. He looked around. Giselle waited for his response. She was clutching his book of drawings like a thief with loot, frozen on the spot.

'You've been busy, I see,' he said at last. He turned her chin towards him with his fingertips and kissed her gently, then slipped the book out of her hands. He tasted of cigarettes, but not of alcohol. Wherever he had been, the last few hours, it wasn't at a bar.

'I . . . I'm sorry,' she said.

'There's nothing to be sorry for,' he replied. 'I should have paid more attention to you. What were you looking for, in the pictures? Were you looking for you? Or for others?'

'I don't know.' Giselle paused, thought. 'I wanted to understand how you see me. And how you see the others,' she admitted. 'The women at the party. They were so beautiful.' She pulled away, embarrassed by her insecurity. 'I'm not like them. I don't mean their beauty, but their openness, the joy on their faces. I don't have that. I'm closed, in some way. It's why I could never dance better, as much as I tried. I always had the work in me, but never the letting go. Always one foot firmly on the ground, never in the stars. The other girls – they flew.' She frowned. If even she didn't fully understand her own thoughts and emotions, how could she possibly explain them to William?

'Oh, but you're wrong, my darling. Look at you.' He flicked through the pages, always pointing to the face that he had drawn on her body. But Giselle did not see the expression that William painted as her own, she had only seen it on the bodies of others. She did not reply.

'Would you feel differently if these were photographs? Rather than paintings?'

'Well . . . perhaps.'

In truth, she was aware, deep down, that the poison that ailed her – and her jealousy did feel like a poison, it pumped through her veins, white hot, sickening everything – ran far deeper than the superficial nature of her appearance. But she was afraid of losing William, and willing to agree to whatever he suggested to smooth things over.

'I have a photographer friend. He's very good. Would you pose for him? Maybe together with me? And then you will see how I see you. There's no arguing with a photograph.'

His eyes were glowing, begging her to agree.

'Yes,' she said. 'Yes, I will.'

He pulled her to him and they fell back on the bed together. The flow of Giselle's emotions changed in that moment of closeness. What had been a mix of anger and pain writhing through her, like a many-headed serpent that powered each of her limbs as well as her heart, became an explosive cocktail of arousal. She wanted him inside her now more than she had wanted him in as long as she could remember. Her longing went beyond want. She needed him.

Not until William began to unbutton her jeans and peel them down did she remember her hairlessness. She held her breath, waiting for his response as he unveiled her now bare mound.

For a moment that felt to Giselle long enough to fill a lifetime, William paused, and said nothing. Then he lowered his mouth and licked her, slowly, passing his tongue through her slit first and then lapping at her now smooth skin.

'You like it?' Giselle whispered. She couldn't see him, so

saying the words aloud felt odd, as though she were talking to herself.

William scooted up the bed to face her. He embraced Giselle's body, holding her close against him as he replied.

'I love you. All of you.' He kissed her again. 'I fucking loved your bush. But I love your cunt like this too.' He reached his hand down and ran his fingertips over her groin. 'It's so smooth . . . I can't wait to paint you like this. It will reflect the light in a totally different way.'

'Really? I was worried you would hate it.'

'I could never hate any part of you, Giselle, and this part of you least of all.'

He crawled down her body again and caressed her sex with his mouth, investigating every millimetre of her as though they were making love for the first time.

The photographer, Mandel, had a villa in Deauville, which he used for some of his commercial fashion shoots and as a country house to get away from the bustle of his day to day life in Paris.

Mandel spoke in half sentences and then filled in the other half, asking her a question and then answering it before Giselle had a chance to respond. The bar he stood behind ran the full length of the lounge, at a right angle to the wide expanse of glass that overlooked the meticulously clipped bright green lawn and the pool.

'Sugar? No, I didn't think so.'

Giselle sat mute and watched him as he pulled out bottles from a cabinet of spirits and tossed them into the air like an acrobat with juggling sticks, catching them again before removing the lids and pouring out a shot. Already, his arrogance annoyed her, and yet she found him undeniably attractive in a crisp white shirt, open at the neck, loosely tied navy blue cravat and slimline navy trousers, laundered and pressed to perfection. He wore dandy-esque, pointed tan shoes with a white trim and heavy silver cufflinks decorating his shirtsleeves that clanked against his cocktail shaker when he pumped it over his head.

She was perched on one corner of the white leather sofa that was too clean and shiny for her to fully relax against. William had disappeared to use the bathroom and had now been gone for over fifteen minutes.

'He's probably reviewing the work from my exhibition,' Mandel explained, as if he could read her mind. 'I've just had the pictures hung upstairs.'

He handed her a coffee in a Martini glass, complete with a large shot of rum and a splash of cream, artistically decorating one side of the glass. Two coffee beans floated on the top. A mint leaf punctuated the cream, draped over the rim's edge like a feather on a fascinator.

Giselle heard footsteps on the stairs behind them.

'Ah, excellent! You've met my glamorous assistant,' said

Mandel. 'And Flick, I see you haven't wasted any time getting ready for the shoot.' He glanced at Giselle, who was observing the woman walking down the stairs ahead of William. She was totally nude apart from a pair of sky-high vivid blue and green heels, and a peacock headdress that framed her face and stretched about two feet into the air from her skull in the style of a Las Vegas showgirl. Giselle's eyes were automatically drawn to Flick's sex, which was as bare as her own. It couldn't be a coincidence, she thought, William must have told Mandel that Giselle was totally depilated.

'Giselle, meet Flick, Flick, meet Giselle.' Flick strode across to the sofa and extended her hand. Her posture was overtly masculine, although she was evidently female, in anatomy if not self-identity. Giselle instinctively stood to greet her. She was at least a foot taller than Flick, who was tiny, both in height and in mass. She was stick figured, almost entirely curveless, but swung her hips as she walked with exaggerated femininity. Flick was a perfect mix of male and female, like a pixie who could inhabit either gender at will and bounced between them from one moment to the next. With her short hair, high cheekbones and full lips, Giselle could see why Mandel liked to photograph her.

She hadn't, however, been expecting company and was taken aback by the presence of another woman.

'Let's get this girl another drink,' Flick hollered, in a

strong American southern accent. 'She's as stiff as a board!' Her voice seemed far too loud for her petite body. She took Giselle by the hand and pulled her across to the bar. 'What do you like?' she asked, 'Rum, tequila? Something fruity? Something sour? Mandel, where's that berry mix stuff ya got?'

'Look in the fridge,' Mandel replied. Flick turned her back to him to open the fridge door and Mandel openly stared at her arse, which was, Giselle had to admit, pleasingly firm and pert.

Flick rustled around behind the bar, opening bottles and sniffing the contents before shoving them to the side and searching for yet another. Eventually she put another drink into Giselle's free hand, this one in a tall, slim glass filled with a thick, bright red and ice cold mixture.

She then reached toward Giselle and boldly opened the top button of her blouse. Flick, Giselle realised, was already half drunk, and Giselle could see why. The fruity drink she had mixed was as strong as rocket fuel.

'I'm getting my camera,' Mandel announced, and raced up the stairs, two at a time.

William stood awkwardly in front of the sofa, watching the two girls. 'Sorry,' he mouthed to Giselle. His lips twisted into an uncomfortable half smile.

She pulled away from Flick and walked over to him, noticing that she was already unsteady on her feet.

William pulled her into an embrace and kissed her cheek. 'Are you okay with this?' he whispered. 'I didn't realise that she would be here.'

'It's fine,' Giselle replied. She took another large gulp of the drink and winced. The icy-cold temperature permeated her nerve endings, as if her brain were being clawed by Jack Frost.

Flick sauntered across to them. She held a cocktail in each hand, and passed one to William. 'Catch up, Mister!' she said, then bent over, unstrapped her heels and kicked them both away. As she lowered down, her small breasts tipped forward, her nipples jutting out proudly.

Giselle drained her glass. She wanted to run her palms over Flick's nipples, to graze them with her fingertips and make them hard. There was something overwhelmingly sexual about the smaller girl's brashness, the confident way that she held herself.

Mandel returned with his camera. 'I was going to do this in the studio,' he said. 'Get some couple shots, as you asked for ... But if you don't mind, William, I'll start here. These two girls are so wonderful, and the light from these windows is gorgeous.'

Giselle registered a pang of irritation that his question had been directed to William, as though she was just one of his puppets and would meekly pose as directed, like any other model, even though this wasn't strictly speaking a modelling job. This wasn't why they had come. But the cocktails had started to work their magic on her brain, and Mandel had switched on a record – she didn't recognise the music but the beat was insistent and made her want to forget her worries and jive in time.

'Let's dance,' Flick said, right into her ear, her lips so close to Giselle's lobe that her whisper might as well have been a kiss.

Flick took hold of Giselle's hands and placed them onto her into waltz position with Giselle leading, and they took a turn around the room, both girls laughing at the absurdity of their contrasting heights. All the while, Mandel crouched and snapped around them at every angle, moving in close and then darting away like an irritating mosquito. If he wasn't handsome, Giselle thought, he would be intolerable. Then again, if he was less attractive, he might have developed a nicer personality.

They whirled and twirled, twice more around the wide expanse of the living room as the men watched, until finally Flick pulled her towards the couch where they collapsed together in a heap beside William.

'Gawd,' Flick said, breathing heavily. 'You're fitter than I am.' Giselle brushed the compliment away but was inwardly pleased. She did try to take care of her body.

Giselle turned to William but before she could open her mouth to say anything, Flick had straddled her and was again working on the remaining buttons of her half-open blouse. 'You've got too many clothes on, gal,' she said, pouting dramatically. 'I feel out of place.'

Well, it was warm, and she had come expecting a nude photo shoot. Giselle slid out of her skirt and panties, carefully lifting her hips and pushing the fabric down beneath Flick's legs, which were scissored open over her lap.

'No,' Mandel interrupted, 'leave her shirt on. And William ... get involved, man! Or move. You can't just sit alongside them like that, you're totally out of place.'

William began to get up and Flick hooked her fingers through his waistband and dragged him back down again.

'You don't mind, do you?' she said to Giselle, and then stretched across and pressed her mouth against William's, forcing him into a kiss. Flick was rocking her groin against Giselle's, as if she were riding a cock. Mandel edged around them, looking for a gap where he could get a decent shot.

'Can you shift, guys? Nearer the windows? I can't get anything decent like this,' he muttered. 'Flick, get them both over there, would you?' He pointed to a space on the floor where beams of sunlight filtered, leaving a dappled pattern on the wood. 'I'll fill up these drinks.'

Flick leapt up immediately and dragged a sheepskin rug that was draped over the back of the couch onto the floor. She unclipped her headdress, laid it on the glass coffee table, and shook her short hair back as vigorously as a dog that's just jumped out of the ocean.

'Come on you two,' she called. 'Let's get down to the real business of the day.'

5

A Halo of Light

Dawn broke.

Giselle half opened her eyes and experienced a strong sense of disorientation, still torn between the remains of sleep and the promise of the new day. Floating unsteadily. Floating?

The peaceful sound of water lapping randomly against a nearby swimming pool wall slowly reached her ears. A torrent of blue assaulted her senses as the light poured in. She was lying on her stomach across a shocking-pink inflatable lilo and drifting across water, a gossamer breeze caressing her exposed buttocks. She realised immediately that if she were to make any sudden movement she would unceremoniously capsize into the pool. She held her breath, maintaining her fragile equilibrium, composing herself.

How had she ended up in the swimming pool? Someone must have settled her on the flimsy embarkation and cut her adrift. In her sleep?

As memories of the night before rushed back, she'd somehow expected to find herself surrounded instead by a clutter of bodies and a sharp reminder of what had happened. But she was alone, sprawled indecently across the pumped-up plastic mattress, bobbing along in silence.

She carefully raised her head and looked around. Could barely see anything beyond the raised walls of the swimming pool but a cluster of dark bushes a hundred yards away and, when she twisted her neck, the glass and metal structure of the pergola where she now recalled having initially found herself having sex with the photographer, intoxicated by the sheer lustfulness of the moment and, to a certain extent, peer pressure.

Alongside Flick, who had been doing the same with William.

Giselle remembered where she was. The country house of the photographer, what was his name? Oh yes, Mandel . . . In Deauville.

Where the hell was William?

Had he unaccountably left her here behind on her own? Surely not? The striking image of his bear-like body embracing Flick's stick-thin frame, almost crushing her, the shorter girl's face a portrait of delight as she urged him on, flashed through Giselle's mind, like stitches inside her being severed again. And the fact that she, Giselle, had not objected and had watched the developing spectacle of her man with another in terrible fascination out of the corner of her eye while Mandel diligently swarmed all over her just a few breaths away, and she had, to her immense surprise, felt detached, madly curious, anything but indifferent.

For a brief moment, Giselle experienced a touch of panic at the prospect of getting back to Paris. She'd agreed to do a double shift in late afternoon at the flower shop on the Rue de Buci and had come along to the coast with almost no cash on her; at any rate, not enough to pay for the train fare. How could he have done this to her? Freya, at the store, would be furious.

She gingerly dipped her hands in the water and as best she could attempted to drift her way back to the pool's edge without upturning the flimsy lilo. Once there, it proved as awkward to actually get off it without descending into the water as the short journey itself had been. She pulled herself up and crawled onto terra firma on her knees.

She raised herself and cast her eyes around the pool area. She couldn't see her clothes anywhere. A cold sun was rising above the horizon and Giselle shivered. Goosebumps were sprouting across her skin. There was a lone towel draped over a white garden chair, and she tried to wrap it around herself as best she could but it only reached as far as her midriff. She tightened it around her chest. A gravel path snaked back to the house and she tiptoed along it. The back door was wide open and led to the studio space. It was still as she remembered it, a labyrinth of equipment, props, cameras and lenses, lightmeters and gizmos of all kinds, and crumpled expanses of unrolled sheets of thick cloth – or was it paper? – that Mandel had unspun as a background to his session.

He had bizarrely started casually with just his camera and the fading light coming through the wide expanse of living room windows, and as the three of them had gotten progressively drunker and more open, Mandel had become more professional until by the end of it she'd felt as though they were making pornography instead of erupting into a threesome that had happened to be caught on film.

The faint sound of music could be heard upstairs, and then a blur of voices and then music again. A radio.

Giselle took the wooden stairs one step at a time, fearful at the prospect of what she might encounter in the first-floor bedrooms. Would small Flick be lying in William's arms, her diminutive body sheltered by his welcoming bulk, or would they be spooning, or their limbs still be tangled together, the way she and William usually greeted the morning? Her throat felt dry. And what about Mandel? Would he be in the same room or bed as them?

Olen's face and the memory of his eyes avoiding hers flashed before her, a reminder of past betrayals.

Some scars never heal.

Giselle hesitated in front of the open door to the first bedroom. There were shapes on the bed, under the covers, knotted beneath the sheets. Adding steel to her resolve, she was about to enter the darkened room when a warm, wet kiss landed on the back of her neck, accompanied by the soft sound of steps.

Giselle swung round.

It was William.

His hair was all over the place. Wild and untamed. Like her, all he was wearing was a towel, but his was wrapped around his waist, leaving his chest bare, with its jungle of wild vegetation and dormant muscles.

'Good morning,' he said.

She was lost for words.

'Uh, you surprised me. Where did you come from?'

'The bathroom, over there.' He waved his arms at another door, all the way down the landing. Water dripped from his nose and chin. 'Just been to freshen up,' he said.

All Giselle could feel was relief. Realising that the couple snuggled under the covers was Mandel and Flick.

With her chin, she nodded at the sleeping shapes on the bed in the hazy half-light of the bedroom.

'Just the girl and the photographer,' William confirmed.

'I think the festivities went on until quite late, or it might well have been early this morning?'

Giselle was burning to ask him the question, but he beat her to it.

'I fell asleep by the pool. Watched over you all night.'

'How did I end up there?'

'Don't you recall?'

'Not really,' Giselle said. 'I remember us all making love on the rug and then in the studio, followed by the pergola, and drinking a lot.'

'It wasn't making love, it was just fucking ... But I must confess I've never seen you drink so much ...'

'Did I?'

'Oh yes. Then you expressed a petulant wish to go swimming.'

Only parts of it all were beginning to return, half-formed images, thoughts, like a lazy morning tide washing up against her consciousness.

'Did I?'

'I helped you onto the lilo and you fell asleep. It seemed safe enough, so I left you there, but sat by the poolside watching. I wished I could have painted you there. The whiteness of your skin, the black coal of your wet hair falling down across your back, your sumptuous arse, the blue-green shimmer of the water ...' William sighed. His words poured over her like a balm.

Giselle was about to say something when William put his hand against her mouth.

'Shhh ... they'll hear us. Let the others sleep. No need to wake them up.'

He took her hand and pulled her gently along the landing to another bedroom.

Once inside, he stood before her, gazing dreamily at her body, then abruptly undid the towel protecting her breasts and let it fall to the carpeted floor.

Giselle looked him in the eyes and instinctively pulled the towel around his waist off as if she had silently been ordered to.

His cock was hard and straight.

'One day you'll understand,' William said. 'Fucking another woman, as I did, makes me want you more than ever. As does seeing you with him. Reminds me what's so wonderful about you. And that, for now, you still are mine.'

He picked her up with all his gentle giant strength and dropped her onto the bed.

Giselle was more than ready.

Two weeks later, a large, stiff brown envelope, addressed to both William and Giselle, dropped through the narrow mail slot of the grey metal letter box beyond the main door that led to their apartment.

Giselle bent down and picked it up, then took the stairs, though not at a quick jog as she usually did.

'I'd forgotten how hard it is on the legs, coming up here,' she said to Beth, who was trailing behind her. The two of them had just returned from a long walk along the Canal Saint Martin, near which Beth had been casually attending ballet classes. Giselle refused to join her for the lesson, but had agreed to walk down and meet her there, to catch up. Both of them being broke, they had decided to return to Giselle's for a drink. William was away again, working with the Ball somewhere.

'Well, you might be out of practice, but you're not out of shape. Your arse looks great from this angle.'

Giselle stopped and turned to look at her. A mischievous smirk was spread across Beth's face.

'Thanks,' she replied. 'These stairs help.'

She unlocked the apartment door, pushed it open, walked in and switched on the kettle.

'Coffee?'

'Yes please,' Beth replied. She removed the baggy sweat-shirt that she had slipped on over the top of her dance clothes as they walked, and flung it over the sofa as though she was at home. 'I've got to say,' she added, looking around the apartment, 'it's not what I was expecting. What's that smell?' she asked, sniffing the air, nostrils twitching like a rabbit's. She reached behind her head and tugged at the hair band that had kept her long blonde locks restrained for the duration of the class. Loosened, her hair swept around her face, reaching all the way down past her shoulder blades at the back.

'William's paint,' Giselle replied. She walked across the room and pushed upon a window to let in some fresh air.

'Smells like kerosene,' Beth remarked.

'You get used to it.'

Beth shrugged. She perched on one arm of the sofa and stretched her legs in front of her, toes pointed out of habit. Giselle watched her from the kitchen. Ever since the afternoon they had posed for Sebastian, Giselle had been experiencing a new attraction for women that she had not previously been aware of. Now whenever she was with Beth she could not help but notice the fluid length and grace of her limbs, the pertness of her arse and breasts and the fullness of her red lips. There were other, smaller things too that captured Giselle's imagination, and caused her cunt muscles to twitch. The musky scent of Beth's shampoo. Her air of arrogance. The self-conscious manner that affected her every movement, as though on some level Beth was aware that everyone was looking at her.

The kettle boiled.

'Black?' Giselle asked.

'I'll have cream, if you've got it,' Beth replied.

Giselle hunted through the fridge and found a container,

hidden behind a round of cheese wrapped in paper and a jar of mixed olives. Satisfied, she tipped a generous portion of thick cream into each of their cups.

Beth took the mug from Giselle's hands and ran her tongue around the inside edge of the lip, licking up the splash of cream that lingered there. Giselle watched her, and could not help but imagine how that tongue would feel against her private parts. Again she envisioned how her blonde friend would react if Giselle was to inform her that following the photo session with Sebastian, she had shorn off her pubic hair.

'Well, are you going to open it?' Beth asked.

'Open it?' Giselle replied, confused.

'The envelope. The one that you picked up from the floor. It was addressed to both of you.'

Giselle glanced back at the kitchen bench and saw the thick brown letter lying there. 'Oh. No, I'll leave it for William.'

Beth crinkled her brow in a frown, her eyebrows like slim pale caterpillars hunching across her face. She stood up and stalked across the room, returning with the envelope clutched in her hand and tossed it at Giselle before sitting down again, legs tucked under her, Buddha style.

'You know I don't approve of you and William. Not as a long-term thing.'

Giselle's face turned blank, a sure sign that she had

switched off inside. She hadn't expected her parents to be happy about it, but she had hoped that her best friend would support her, or at least be ambivalent about her relationship.

'You didn't like Olen, either,' she replied.

'That's because you always choose the wrong men! At least Olen was your own age.'

'Age is just a number.'

'Don't spout that crap. He's nearly double your number. And there's something else . . . something weird about him.' Beth's eyes wandered around the apartment, as though she expected to notice evidence to support her remarks that had previously not been visible. Finding nothing, her eyes came back to Giselle. 'I don't like the way you always kowtow to him. He's not your father. Or God.'

'I didn't say that he was.'

'Open it, then.'

Giselle relented with a huff of resignation, and began to slide her thumbnail carefully under the seal.

Beth snatched it from her and ripped the paper open.

'There,' she said smugly, handing the contents back. 'Now you can't close it up again for him as though you haven't touched it.'

Inside was a bundle of large black and white photographs, protected by a folded sheet of white paper and wrapped with a black silk ribbon. There was no note.

'Bloody hell,' Beth said, as she caught a glimpse of the first one. Her eyes widened in shock. Beth rarely swore. 'What have you been up to?'

'Just a shoot,' Giselle replied, shuffling the photos back into the envelope. They were the pictures that Mandel had taken of her, Flick and William engaged in drunken fucking and looking at them would inevitably bring all of her emotions and jealousy back roaring to the surface again. She didn't want to risk bursting into tears with Beth looking on, especially since she knew her friend was not likely to take a positive view of her boyfriend making love to another woman.

'Not any ordinary shoot,' Beth insisted. 'And I've done some weird things for art, believe me.' She stretched out an arm, clamped her hand firmly around the photo stack, and tugged it out of Giselle's hands. 'Were you paid for these?' she asked, flicking through them.

'No,' Giselle confessed. She could feel a hot pink flush spreading over her cheeks.

Beth held up a photograph. 'I always thought you were a bit of a wild card, my dear, but I confess, I didn't realise that you were this wild.' The picture was of Giselle and Flick engaged in a deep, open-mouthed kiss. Giselle's hands were circled around the back of Flick's neck, her fingers knotted in the smaller girl's hair. Other shots showed bodies pressed together, pointed nipples, wet cunts, a cock sliding into an arsehole, Flick's arched back, William's fingers sliding through Giselle's slit. This one was less pornographic, and yet there was something raw about it. The muscles in Giselle's bare shoulders and fingers were tense as though she was pulling Flick against her with all of her strength. It was totally unposed, as if Mandel had caught two lovers una-wares in a passionate embrace. There was a sincerity to their posture that the other pictures, showing just anonymous parts, bodies recognisable only by their faces, lacked.

She picked up another that revealed a close-up of a man's hand, fingers clenched, squeezing a pert, petite woman's buttock.

'William?' Beth guessed. 'And the other girl?' She studied Giselle's face for her reaction, eagle-eyed. The hubbub of traffic whizzing by outside and pedestrians chattering was audible through the open window. It was a strange juxtapo-sition, Giselle thought, the ordinary minutiae of life bustling on while here, the two of them sat staring at nude photo-graphs. She wondered if children were walking along on the street below and experienced a sudden, and – she knew – irrational, feeling of shame and the desire to get up and pull the blinds across.

'Yes,' she replied at last. 'Her name was Flick.'

Beth seemed intent on pulling out every last detail of the experience. Not the detail of what happened, but how Giselle felt about it.

'And?' Beth pushed her. 'What was it like?'

'To be honest,' Giselle replied, 'I was so drunk, I don't really remember. We were all drunk. One minute she was coming on to me – coming on to both of us – the next minute I woke up on a lilo, floating in the swimming pool. But if you mean to ask how I feel about William with other women . . .'

'Yes,' Beth said impatiently, 'that's precisely what I mean to ask.'

'Well, I'm not sure. The thought of it makes me jealous. Wild. A bit crazy, sometimes.' She thought of the mess that she had made, looking through William's things to find the paintings that she was sure he must have, somewhere. 'And yet, on that night, I felt indifferent. Curious. Almost as if I was watching it all through a tunnel.' She shrugged. 'From what I can recall, anyway. We drank a lot of cocktails.'

'Will you see the girl again?'

'Flick?'

'Yes, her,' Beth said, pointing again to the picture of Giselle and Flick embracing. 'You seem pretty into her. Not like you're just putting it on for the camera.'

Was Beth jealous, Giselle wondered? She was aware that she felt an element of sexual attraction towards her friend, which had lately grown stronger and stronger, but it had never really occurred to her that Beth might feel the same way. She'd never really thought seriously about having a relationship with a woman, not even a fling, but if such a thing were to occur then she would have thought Beth was out of her league. She seemed untouchable, inhumanly beautiful. Giselle could not imagine Beth being attracted to her. It would be like making love to a movie star.

'I don't think so,' Giselle replied. 'I don't plan to, at least.'

Beth leaned forward, and at first Giselle thought that she was reaching behind her, towards the side table where they had balanced their drinks. But instead Beth placed a hand on each of Giselle's upper arms and pulled her in for a kiss. Their lips met. Beth's mouth was uncommonly soft, and her kiss gentle and slow. It was a damp kiss. Much more than a peck, and yet not a fully blown snog. There was a sour note to her taste, from the coffee and cream, but it was by no means unpleasant. Beth pulled away again before Giselle could be sure whether the gesture was meant sexually, or platonically. Later, she would wonder whether or not she had imagined the whole thing.

'I just want you to be happy,' Beth said softly.

She had to rush off, shortly afterwards, to a waitressing gig with an upmarket hospitality firm, serving canapés to rich businessmen and the occasional woman who would inevitably grope her arse when she couldn't do anything about it for fear of dropping a lobster-morsel-covered silver platter. 'I don't mind it,' she said, 'they tip well.'

After she'd gone, Giselle picked up the coffee cups and took them into the kitchen. They'd been so busy talking, they had barely touched their drinks, which were now cold. A layer of fat from the cream had formed over the coffee.

Was she happy?

It was a question to which she hadn't given much thought. Just presumed the answer to be yes.

She was happy, yes. But she was lonely, too.

When William was away working for the Ball, he would seldom keep in touch with Giselle, and she felt abandoned. Never a letter or a phone call, just the rare postcard with wish-you-were-here-words of reassurance or something harmless to that effect from places exotic or even unknown, some of which she had to check out on a map of the world to get an idea of where he was. All too often, the card would only reach her long after he had returned. Sometimes he would bring her back a souvenir, a snow globe, a trinket, once a gold ankle chain which she was reluctant to wear and kept more often than not inside her bedside drawer.

Surviving the days was fine; there was always something to do – lectures to attend, shifts at the flower store, some further modelling for Emile Saffy, most of which was now above board and academic, books to read, movies to see, daydreaming to do. Only once had Mandel, the photographer, been in contact with an offer of work, but she politely declined the opportunity on some pretext, too much of a coward to turn him down outright and advise him she never wished to pose for him again.

But the nights proved tough. Giselle was no longer used to sleeping alone, sundered from the reassuring mass of William's heavy frame and the familiar warmth of his slumbering presence. She felt like a well of emptiness, incomplete, and even the relief of touching herself and switching on her bodily senses when it all became too much was unsatisfying.

How quickly she had become addicted to this man.

Which made her angry, her soul bristle at the loss of independence.

One evening, as he was packing in haste following a telephone call from the Ball people and expecting the cab booked to take him to Roissy to arrive at any moment, he had glimpsed the quiet despair spreading across her face and said, 'You know … when I'm away …' he hesitated, 'I wouldn't mind if you saw others, men, women, it's no matter. I realise you have needs …'

It had drawn a tear to her eyes, but the thought had lingered on.

Another time, noting her underlying sadness, he had clumsily tried to explain himself.

'We owe it to ourselves to experience pleasure. It's all we have. Try everything, enjoy the life sensual. It doesn't mean that I don't love you or you don't love me. Far from it. Experiences become a part of us, renew us.'

Giselle had no doubt appeared dubious.

'You're still young, Giselle, one day you'll realise I am right . . .'

Paris at night was a bottomless pit of possibilities, each more attractive than the prospect of lying in bed in insomniac mode, unable to concentrate on the pages of books or the shadowy shapes that the moonlight cast against the ceiling.

Walking down to the river, past the closing bars and restaurants and the flickering lights of shop windows and art galleries, cruising by the graffitied walls of the Ecole des Beaux-Arts, emerging in darkness by the Pont des Arts, with the white sculpted silhouette of the Louvre on the opposite side of the Seine. Wandering by the banks, her hand drifting casually across the often splintered wood of the padlocked bouquiniste boxes hanging from the low walls of the quais, Giselle had no particular destination in mind.

It was just her and the night.

She crossed a bridge leading to the Right Bank and then crossed back again at the Samaritaine level. The river was a frontier, dividing Paris into two quite separate entities. As a child, she'd mostly known the northern areas, where her parents lived and she'd been brought up and gone to maternelle school, primary school and then the local Lycée, and had been familiar with the shrubs and greenery of the Jardin des Plantes and its tiny zoo and botanical gardens, the steep hills of Ménilmontant and the shady-by-night areas surrounding the train stations and further afield the teeming labyrinths of the Marché aux Puces which she was never allowed to visit alone. Somehow she'd never ventured much further south than Châtelet then, apart from incursions onto the Ile de la Cité and its heteroclite flower and bird market overlooked by the gothic bulk of Notre-Dame. The Left Bank had been shrouded in impossible glamour, a place of universities, fashion and, in her mind, the politics of the street. It was where the legendary May 68 riots had mostly taken place, a time she had missed by a generation. By now everyone said it had lost much of its cachet and was being swamped by fashion stores where once bookshops had dominated and, in its cheaper reaches, couscous joints, Greek kebab and fast food outlets were now spreading like an unwelcome epidemic.

Giselle wished she had been able to live here a decade or more earlier, but still the area was a maze of discoveries. Narrow streets with irregular lighting, airy boulevards kept alive by the neon of cinema façades, discreet brick buildings looming high away from the main roads, shielding inner courtyards, private mansions with imagined gardens just a stone's throw from civilisation, steeped in the past, harbouring passionate aristocrats and bourgeois dynasties whose secret life she could only take a guess at.

And, of course, all the late night bistros where she could shelter from the winter cold and sip a coffee for ages sitting in a corner without being bothered, or visit during the day for a glass of wine without being frowned at in disapproval.

This was becoming her Paris.

Another bridge crossed and she reached the partly concealed narrow stairs between high walls leading down to the tip of the island. Stepping tentatively through the darkness, not a place to venture at night, even less so when unaccompanied. Emerging into the shadowy light reflecting up from the river and a pocked half moon bathing it in a curtain of clouds. The narrow pathways almost merging at this late hour into the lapping waters of the surrounding streams of the river, the abbreviated garden at the centre of the brief promontory. Giselle walked down the path, her mind blank. A whisper, a movement to her left. Two shapes by a tree, a man on his knees, his face obscured, sucking another. Giselle moved on, even though deep down she would have liked to watch. She arrived at the tip of the island, the panorama of the river merging again, extending into the night towards the Eiffel Tower shrouded in a tapestry of darkness and the western reaches of the city. She stood on the very edge, savouring the silence and the void below, drinking in the night, a cool breeze running through her hair, communing, imagining herself at the prow of a ship.

Indistinct sounds behind her. Her heart jumped. She swiftly turned round. Squinted, her eyes getting accustomed to the darkness. A woman's muffled cry. There, on the thin grass, shadows in the shadow of a leafless tree, a couple fucking. Clothed, just his pale buttocks exposed, thrusting down on a shapeless form from which now recognisable, staccato sounds of pleasure emerged. Giselle blushed. Again, she was tempted to move nearer and watch, but there would be little to see, and she knew the lovers would most likely object to her presence. She stepped back and rushed towards the stairs that led to the bridge, and hurried towards the apartment. She didn't sleep any the better for her aimless walk and fortuitous encounters.

She swore she would not return to the edge of the Ile de la Cité should William give her a sign of life over the next twenty-four hours, but he didn't. The following night, a faint drizzle crisscrossing the 2 a.m. sky, she found herself back on the island, sitting with legs dangling into the water, momentarily shoeless, gazing at the occasional barge sliding past the promontory and being swallowed up by the river's darkness. She was, for now, the only person on this side of the bridge. But, instinct warned her, this might not be for long.

She closed her eyes, pulled her collar tight around her throat to hold the creeping cold at bay.

Right now, she imagined, William was somewhere exotic, immersed in a life dripping with colours, acute sensations, and surrounded by images of beauty. While she lingered, craving for things unexpressed, alone, shivering, miles away, a prey to all her uncertainties and fear. Was he even thinking of her?

She pulled her feet out of the water, wiped them dry with her ragged woollen imitation Burberry scarf, put her shoes back on, but kept sitting by the edge of the half-submerged quay. Muffled sounds — the rising breeze? careful steps? — reached her from the perimeter of the long, narrow parc that formed the island tip's central aisle. Night creatures coming out to play, maybe? Giselle closed her eyes.

A disturbance in the air, like a page being turned, a weak source of heat behind her back, a murmur, a breath exhaled. She was like a living statue, the curve of her back a solid wall confronting the stranger. The sound of steps dying in the gravel. Strangers.

Giselle remained immobile.

A hand on her shoulder. A questioning touch.

She did not react, sat frozen and glued to the spot, the

inert coldness of the stone quay on which she was sitting seeping through the stretched denim of her jeans.

Encouraged by her passive response, the hand descended.

Fingers grazed her nape. Swept across her hair, pinched the lobe of one ear, testing her reactions. Giselle gritted her teeth, her heart beating faster.

Behind her closed eyelids, she felt the texture of the darkness ahead of her, previously filled by the quiet, flowing expanse of the river, change, now shadowed by more solid shapes, blotting out the copper sky. A distant whiff of cheap cologne and strong coffee.

The initial hand still lingering in her hair, threading its way through her straight folds, almost combing her, caressing her gloss and then another hand, gloved this time, taking hold of hers and, imperatively pulling it away from her lap and towards a body which Giselle still wished to remain unseen. The earthy solidity of a leather belt. Her fingers were shocked by the arctic freeze of the belt's metal buckle.

Still willingly blind, she manoeuvred her fingers by memory and managed to unbuckle the belt, located the zip. Slid it down. Pulled out the heavy penis, its earthy warmth a stark contrast with the belt buckle she had just played with.

The man sighed.

As she took him between her fingers, the other man

standing behind her finally came to neglect her hair and moved around to place himself in front of her, she perceived. He took her free hand and dragged it upwards until she felt his cock also offered, already liberated from his trousers and underwear. It felt even hotter than the other man's.

The men were silent.

As was Giselle.

As if this was a ritual in the dark whose outcome was written in the night and words were unnecessary.

Both cocks throbbed in her hands, the silky skin of the strangers' lengths like a soothing talisman she had been entrusted to worship. She held them cocooned inside the hollows of her palms, tugging, squeezing, adjusting the precision of her movements to what she imagined was the electrical pulse running through them, keeping their blood flow steady and at an even temperature to maintain the rage of their erections.

One of the men was silent, just the exhale of his breath bursting out in rapid spurts, halting, desirous.

The other man swore under his breath, indistinct obscenities to either encourage her ministrations or soothe his inner anger.

Giselle, arms aloft, balancing the two cocks between her hands, orchestrating their pleasure, exploring the rhythm, felt in control and surprisingly lucid. She knew that by coming to the tip of the island in the darkest hours of the night, she had been seeking something, although she was unsure whether this problematic adventure was the beginning or end of some subterranean craving or just a twisted reaction to William's absence and recent attitude.

The man to her left, the silent one, shuddered, his whole body shaking suddenly with almost epileptic fervour, a deep roar dying inside his throat and she felt his boiling cum flooding her hand. The other man was still hard as rock, his skin sliding up and down under the steady movement she was directing around his stem, as if refusing to give in to his orgasm, wanting to make this last forever. Giselle felt an impulse to drop to her knees and take him inside her mouth instead but it was as if his stone-like rigidity was holding her bound to the vigorous hand job she was administering. Finally, he came, a thin stream of ejaculate dripping over her hand and down her raised arm. '*Putain*,' he whispered.

Both strangers were now drained, their cocks growing limper, still in her hold. One pulled back, soon followed by the other.

How could she wipe her hands, Giselle wondered, her eyes still deliberately closed? Now she wanted the men to just disappear and never to have to see their faces. Because, she knew, if she did set eyes on them, they would become human, not just incorporeal cocks and, inevitably, she would end up succumbing to her own desires and the powerful calls of pleasure and would want to take them – or anyone new who arrived on the scene, no doubt attracted, alerted by the odour of her want, the out of control aura that now emanated from her – into her mouth or open her legs for them. Something she was positive she was not yet ready to do.

As if they could read her thoughts, the two strangers stepped back and melted silently into the darkness and once again Giselle became aware of the creeping cold. Once ten minutes had passed and she felt secure that they were no longer on the island, she finally opened her eyes and rose unsteadily, a touch of dizziness invading her stiff limbs, and made her way back to the apartment and fell asleep within an instant.

When she woke, the acrid smell of the men that still lingered across her now dry hands felt as if it was surrounding her and she retched and rushed to wash. But that night, still without news of William's return, she was back wandering the Paris streets and the often carless paths and alleys. She journeyed across the Louvre perimeter at a brisk pace, getting lost in the narrow streets around the Montparnasse station, flipping a mental coin on every corner and somehow always ending back on the Boulevard Raspail, like a tourist. She slalomed between the columns holding up the Odéon Theatre, dipping between pools of lights, her eyes periscopes exploring the tilted emptiness of the Place then, like a ghost, circled the perimeter of the Luxembourg Gardens past the imposing bulk of the Senate building with no wish to even enter the empty gardens, became a shadow moving across the stone walls of the Saint Sulpice church before retracing her steps and walking across the river to the Marais, where sounds of laughter travelled between first-floor windows and underground cellars reminding her she was not the only inhabitant of this ghostly city she was discovering in her walkabouts. But not once did she stop, as if by doing so she would attract the wrong attention. Or would it have been the right attention and the dubious comfort of strangers?

Giselle walked at night and then slept throughout the day. She ignored messages from the few friends she had made here and forgot to call Beth back and only later found out her friend from ballet days had in the meantime returned to London.

This only served to remind her how much she had enjoyed dancing as she came to realise that it had now been almost two years since she had danced last, whether just for the fun of it or to exercise her body.

She missed it.

Giselle woke at last from the depths of the despair that had her seeking comfort in the arms of the night. Memories of music and of movement drove her to the city streets again but this time not in search of sexual escapism. She wanted to dance, to feel that fire in her soul that she had seen displayed in the bodies of others. Why not her too? She wanted to let go, to let the melody take her. And so she rose, as had become her habit, in the late afternoon, and pushed William's shirts aside and rummaged through the back of the closet until she found something that would do, a light summer dress in thin white cotton with cap sleeves and a boat neck that just skimmed the top of her knees. A waist tie accentuated her curves, and though the dress was perfectly modest in cut, the nearly sheer fabric and girlish style gave it a sexy look that had thus far caused Giselle to avoid wearing it. She had bought it while shopping with Beth, who had egged her on, but it had ended up buried in her wardrobe, brand new with the tags still on.

Giselle slipped the frock straight over her head without bothering with either a bra or knickers. She felt a strong sense of freedom and did not want to feel anything constricting cutting into her flesh. A pair of plain gold sandals with a low wedge, a coating of bright red lipstick and a spritz of perfume were all she added. She glanced in the mirror before she left, and at the last moment decided to pull her hair out of its slick bun and arrange her locks loosely around her shoulders. Over the course of the past few months she had worn more daring outfits than this, yet she

now saw something reflected in the glass that had not previously been visible. There was a sparkle in her eye and a
steely resolve bubbling inside her that showed in the upright
slant of her shoulders and the tilt of her jaw. A new Giselle
was ready to be born.

A light rain was falling, and had Giselle been wearing
anything other than white, she probably would have ignored
it. Modesty and the thought of how her pale, sheer dress
would cling to her form once she was thoroughly wet made
her race breathlessly back up the stairs to fetch the pocket-
sized umbrella she knew was resting just inside the front
door. She hesitated there for a moment, thinking of whether
or not to go hunting for her coat, but decided against it. She
feared that if she were to walk back into the apartment
proper she might lose her nerve and end up staying in all
evening.

As she walked, the rain became heavier and gusts of wind
blowing from all directions pushed the droplets in sideways
and horizontally, wetting her even beneath the protection
of her brolly. She huddled in against a wall and gazed around
her, trying to find her bearings and mentally locate the
nearest club or bar, somewhere dark and anonymous where
she could dance unnoticed in the shadows. Giselle had
begun her journey with no particular destination in mind,
just following both her nose and the bustle of light and noise
that would lead her, she hoped, to a party, but at the rate

that the weather was turning she would be soaked by the time she arrived if she didn't stop now.

She was just a block from the Rue Saint André des Arts, where she knew she would find people, cafés and restaurants, so she hurried on. Thunder rumbled in the distance. Her feet slid inside her shoes and her shoes slid against the uneven pavement. A bolt of lightning crackled in the sky overhead just as she turned into the usually busy street only to find it empty, since the entire population of the Left Bank was apparently sheltering indoors already. She rushed into the first door that she spotted, arched, painted green with a brass knocker on the front and a light and bar stools visible through the window.

It was a café, though nearly empty, probably because it was the habit of people to saunter along down the lane at least part-way before deciding where to eat rather than stopping at the first establishment. She approached the counter and ordered a hot chocolate.

'There's a heater there. Stand and dry yourself,' the patronne, behind her zinc counter, said, pointing to a radiator, after sweeping up the coins Giselle had proffered. 'I'll bring your drink over.'

Giselle stood against the wall as directed and let the warmth dry her. She slipped off her wedges. The linoleum floor felt pleasant against her bare feet where the slippery soles of her shoes had begun to rub at her skin. The café décor was worn, as though the owner had not had the money to renovate for twenty years. The counter top was chequered black and white like a chessboard and the bar stools were tall, metal-legged and covered with black and red vinyl. The walls were painted white and were chipped in places. Light fittings hung low on worn-out wiring that probably would not pass a fire safety inspection. The menu offered milkshakes and flapjacks, along with the typical selection of omelettes. It was more American than French, and reminded Giselle of the café in Notting Hill in which she had shared a final espresso with Olen.

A couple of good-looking young men were leaning against the far end of the counter, sipping cream-covered shakes from tall glasses. They were both watching Giselle. One was dark haired and the other ginger, but in other respects they might have been brothers, equal in height and stature with the same full lips and bright blue eyes. The brunette was slim and rangy and the red-head broad and muscular. They were in their early twenties, she guessed, but might have been as young as eighteen.

Near the window, three middle-aged women sat around a small table. They had positioned their seats, Giselle thought, so that they had a good view of the pert backsides belonging to the young men. The women sipped honey-coloured liquid, probably schnapps or calvados. Two of them were playing a card game. All three were smartly dressed, with cropped haircuts and rouged lips. The one nearest to Giselle wore black patent mules on her feet. Her legs were crossed under the table and she had slipped her heel out from one of the shoes so that it hung from her toes. They looked like Pan-Am air hostesses out of uniform.

A cold breeze chilled Giselle's skin as the door swung open and another customer entered. This one a man in a pin-striped business suit. He wore a tan felt hat but carried no umbrella so was soaked through, his hat being of little help against the downpour that now raged outside.

Giselle began to move away from the heater so that he could take her place, since she was dry now and had finished her drink. She bent down to pick up her shoes, and just as she did so, music began to play. She looked up – the woman with the black mules had dropped some coins into the red and silver jukebox. The song was 'Hit the Road Jack', though not the original Ray Charles version. It was sung by a chorus of full-lunged women, she didn't know the name of the group. Without thinking, Giselle began to swing her hips, and then her feet.

'Go on girl, you can move,' said the woman who had picked the tune. She was clicking her fingers in time and clacking her heels against the floor.

Giselle responded to the compliment by shimmying even more, and lifting her skirt up to reveal her thighs as she did so. The pair of women still sitting put their cards down on the table and cheered in encouragement. The men were silent but Giselle was aware of them watching. She could feel their eyes on her long legs, probably wondering if she was wearing any underwear beneath her dress since there was no seam visible. Her nipples were hard and undoubtedly obvious through the fabric of her dress.

The song was short, yet it was long enough for Giselle to lose herself. Something shifted inside her as though a weight had been lifted from her chest and she no longer cared what other people thought of her. Not her parents, and not her teachers, not even William, who was hardly around these days anyway, and certainly not these strangers. She danced with all of her heart and soul along with her body, and when she had finished the handful of patrons in the bar roared for her. Even the businessman in his suit clapped.

'Thank you,' Giselle said, proudly, and gave a bow, before picking up her things and heading out again onto the street. The storm outside had passed, but inside Giselle another was raging and she needed more. More music, more dancing. She folded up her umbrella and ran barefoot down the Rue Saint André des Arts, in search of a larger party.

Once again, Giselle had been up all night but this time as she crossed the Boulevard Saint Germain in the pale light of dawn zigzagging between the street cleaners and rubbish collection carts, she was determined not to compensate by wasting the coming day sleeping. She was determined to enquire where and how she could resume dance classes. Her mind was still buzzing, her body electric, as if suspended between euphoria and yearning.

The first thing she noticed when she walked in to the apartment was William's suitcase sitting in the corridor that led to the rooms.

Her heart skipped a beat.

She then ran to the bedroom, expecting to find him there, sprawled out like a lumbering starfish across their bed, resting from the probably long journey that had brought him home.

It was empty. No bedcover or sheet was out of place, just as she had left it the previous evening. Not even the clothes he had travelled in hung over a chair or left scattered by the laundry basket.

The rest of the flat was similarly empty, just the lone suitcase a witness to his passage.

The only place he could have gone to was his studio, Giselle reckoned. Maybe an idea had dawned out of the blue while he was journeying back to Paris, or inspiration had struck. She couldn't think where else he could have gone straight off the road.

On the way back out, Giselle caught a brief sight of her

face in the mirror. Her eyes were drawn, dark half-circles supporting them in place. She appeared haunted. She felt sorry he would see her this way after a few weeks apart, but there was nothing she could do to repair the damage; the handful of sleepless nights were lost to her forever, she knew.

Sounds were returning to the city as she made her way across the Latin Quartier.

She anxiously walked up the stairs, her spare key to William's studio clutched in the palm of her hand. She stopped in front of the door. No sounds reached her.

The key slid into the lock and she pushed the door open with the tip of her toes.

The main skylight had been opened wide, a growing cone of stark illumination bathing the cavernous loft-like room in an eerie unnatural glow. The coffee machine was bubbling away in one corner while lounging across the divan as if she owned the place was Flick, her urchin features frozen into a blank smile, her pale, short hair spiky like a crown of thorns. She had her back to Giselle. William was nowhere to be seen.

Just as Giselle was about to catch the attention of the young model and enquire about her presence in the studio, William erupted from the changing area. He was shirtless, his barrel chest still wet, his abundant hair stuck to his skin, his hair unkempt and wild. Had he just taken a shower? Had he and Flick been having sex? Giselle was bursting with questions. William initially didn't notice her. Flick was wearing a tight pair of velvet hotpants and a black T-shirt. Surely, they couldn't have fucked yet?

Giselle, by the door, stood rooted to the spot.

William held a half-smoked cigarette dangling from his mouth and a towel in his hand.

He stopped in his tracks.

'Giselle!' He beamed.

Flick turned her head. Blushed.

Giselle's lips felt dry, glued together.

He opened his arms to her.

'Come here.'

Then read the uncertainty in her eyes.

'You were not home, and I had all these ideas bubbling inside my head. Just had to come here. After days of just doing sketches, I wanted to paint so much. Missed its smell, the feeling of colours and canvas under my fingers. I'm so glad to be back.'

'You could have waited.' Giselle indicated Flick.

'I needed a model. And you weren't around . . .'

'I'm here now. Send her away.'

'But . . .'

Sensing the tension rise between Giselle and William, Flick rose from the sofa and offered to leave.

'It's okay with me,' she said. 'If you no longer require me . . .'

'No,' William hissed. 'There's no need. I'd like to work with the both of you.'

Giselle was unhappy with the outcome, but too shy to make a scene. All she could do was recall the last time the three of them had been together, posing for Mandel, and the inevitable outcome fuelled by alcohol and lust and the sight of Flick's tiny frame squeezed beneath the bulk of William's body, how she had loudly moaned with fake pleasure as he had moved inside Flick just a few metres away from Giselle and the photographer whose embrace and cock she had then felt too helpless to refuse.

Giselle was determined not to allow herself to prove weak this way again.

Flick sat herself down.

Giselle kept on standing.

'So, what's the idea, today?' the other girl asked.

'I'll improvise,' William said. 'But first I have to mix my paints, prepare them. I need a new batch.'

He gave Giselle an irritable look, well aware of the jealousy streaming across her mind. She stared back at him, unable to control her rage.

She was as angry with him as she was with herself. She had never thought of herself as possessive before. Yes, she had cravings and sometimes they dominated her thoughts, but she had rationalised that it was a physical form of need, not something sentimental. But William's absences had hardened her senses and feelings. So, this was love, was it? Wanting all of him, being unwilling to share. She had read somewhere that love was a thing of pain, and not just joy. And was displeased to find this out for herself. *Oh William, how can you be doing this to me?*

Ash dangling from his precariously balanced cigarette, William threw her a look of annoyance. Not of guilt. He moved behind the hanging carpets and frayed drapes that separated the main area of the studio from his work preparation area. The two women faced each other. Flick attempted a smile. She radiated both innocence and a canny form of mischief. Maybe it was her diminutive size and the studied way she had her hair cut. A pocket-sized temptress. But right now Giselle was in no way tempted and more inclined to kick the other girl's butt straight out of the studio.

A heavy silence hung between Flick and Giselle.

'I'll go and help him,' Giselle suggested, and went to join William behind the improvised curtains. He acknowledged her arrival with a grunt, hands busy emptying sachets of pigment and pouring water and oil into a variety of ceramic bowls. Giselle's lips opened.

'Not now,' he whispered.

'Missed you,' she nevertheless said, a feeble attempt at peace.

'So why did you give me such dirty looks, out there?'

'I was surprised to see her here.'

'Flick?'

'Yes.'

'So what?'

He began mixing the materials he had been adding to one of the mortars, carefully grinding down on the mixture with a pestle. He dipped a finger in, assessing the consistency.

'Listen, can we talk about this later?' he suggested.

Giselle was hypnotised by the sticky wetness now hanging from his fingers, a lively torrent of obscene images that might have served as a prelude to the image, involving Flick and her openings prior to her arrival, unavoidably racing through her mind. She was finding it difficult to breathe.

William pulled his fingers out of the bowl and wiped them against his corduroy trousers, leaving a thin trail of prominent blue pigment across their light brown surface.

'It's too thick,' he remarked. 'Can you hand me some water?'

Still trying to raise herself from the red fog clouding her mind, Giselle looked down at the nearby worktop laden with brushes, bottles, tubes and powder sachets, and her eyes alighted on the first of a dozen or so bottles in various shades of green full to the brim with liquid. She picked it up without thinking and passed it along to William. Still busy stirring materials into a trio of bowls, his shoulders bent, his hands moving swiftly from one to another, without raising his eyes to her, he took hold of it and, on automatic pilot, began pouring the water into the first bowl the consistency of which was not yet to his liking.

He sniffed. Stopped pouring. Brought the bottle to his nose. Swore under his breath. Turned to Giselle.

'Damn, you've given me solvent. It's the wrong stuff. Don't you know by now: we keep the water in the paler green bottles. It's always been that way ... Damn, damn, damn ...'

Just then, perturbed by his sudden movement, the length of ash poised at the end of his partly consumed cigarette detached itself and floated down, as if in slow motion like a mote of dust finally struck by gravity, skipping over the pitted surface of the muddy blueish concoction he had been mixing.

The world slowed down.

As the ash cascaded across the still unfinished mud of the paint and its wet layer of solvent, there was a savage flare of light, and a naked flame rose upwards.

There was a loud shriek. Giselle didn't even notice it was her own voice.

The flame, thin and malevolent, ran across William's naked chest, spreading fast, eating itself as it did so, but still advancing.

'FUCK!' William brought the flat of his hands down against his chest in an attempt to choke the small fire now attacking his abundant hair. 'Giselle ... water ... quick ... grab some water. I ...'

Giselle was nearest to the worktop and, without thinking, grabbed another bottle and frantically threw its contents towards William with all the strength and speed she could summon. It was only as the liquid splashed across his chest that, to her dismay, she realised that in her panic, she had taken hold of yet again the wrong kind of bottle. Her heart dropped.

The extra solvent splattered against William's body, renewing the fire, flames now rising towards his face. Alerted by the affray, Flick had rushed towards them and screamed.

By now, the deadly liquid pouring down from his chest had reawakened the fire simmering in the bowl below and spread across the rest of the work area and a corner of one of the drapes was already prey to flames.

Giselle felt as if she was trudging through quicksand and her hands felt disconnected from her brain as she floundered as to what she could possibly do, even though she realised the situation was getting more desperate by the second. William's head was engulfed in flames, his head a halo of light, his mad hair an exploding sun, his cries deafening, as he stood in place, nailed to the spot in a wall of fire. A separate fire was spreading along the table and moving up the drapes.

She caught sight of the other bottles. Paler green. Taller. So different from the two squatter, darker ones which had contained the solvent and which she had mistakenly grabbed. She picked one up and threw its contents over William's head. He had slipped to the ground, now on his knees, his hands flying around, as if fighting off a swarm of bees. Then another bottle. Drenching him with water. And another. Then yet another.

Flick had calmed down and was now copying her, grabbing the remaining bottles of water and pouring them over William's hunched and sobbing figure and the other areas still on fire.

There had been ten bottles of water and only two of solvent. And yet she had initially taken the solvent. How could she? The smell of scorched flesh and the acrid odour of burning organic matter flooded her senses. The fire was now out. William was down on the floor, lying on his stomach, his once leonine head of hair now an ugly desert of red, burned skin and incongruous patches of shorn curls. The flesh on the back of his neck was still bubbling.

As a tear took birth in the corner of one of her eyes and pain enveloped her, Giselle felt time returning to normal.

Her face a picture of total and utter dismay, Flick stood by, paralysed, rooted to the spot.

'I'll phone for an ambulance?' she blurted out, her voice a thin trickle of vanishing sounds.

'Yes, please.' Giselle's quiet voice was incongruous in context, politeness coming to her instinctively despite the despair and unadulterated panic washing over her.

6

In Shades of Darkness

'Come nearer,' William asked.

Beyond him, the freshly mown garden lawn extended endlessly, with a panorama of snowcapped peaks dominating the valley. Giselle had journeyed to the convalescence clinic by train and found a pre-booked taxi waiting for her at Geneva station. The journey onwards had taken just under an hour, through empty roads, winding hills and sharp turns, and finally the dark maw of the tunnel under the Mont Blanc.

It was a nice day and William had not been in his room. The attendant had led her to the communal room and beyond the sliding doors that opened on to the gardens.

'He likes to stay there for ages when the weather is mild enough to allow it.'

Winter

The sky was a deep blue, cloudless, the air crisp and pure. William was sitting in the shadow of a tall, expansive oak tree, turned towards the diorama of the mountains, contemplating their fixed majesty, deep in thought. He wore dark glasses. His hair had grown back, thick and curly and unkempt, and he now sported a full beard, speckled with white, no longer the neglectful arty stubble she had previously known. It did make him look older, but concealed any possible permanent scars caused by the accident. His shirt was buttoned at the collar, so it was impossible to know what sort of marks had been left on his upper chest. It was almost as if nothing bad had happened.

The soft grass cushioned her steps.

His words of welcome were warm, banishing in an instant all the myriad fears she had struggled to contain during the train journey. There was nothing resentful, or angry, in his tone.

She approached. Took a deep breath.

Stood at his shoulder.

'You smell nice,' William said.

Before the train's arrival at the station, Giselle had wetted her face and, as an afterthought, dabbed a finger of perfume behind her ears. Chanel No. 5. He had bought her the expensive scent for her previous birthday. She had argued the fragrance was maybe too middle-aged for her, but had since grown accustomed to it. 'You're a woman, now,' he had insisted.

His sense of smell was still acute, it appeared, pinpointing the distinctive whiff of her scent through the layered crowd of other stimuli Giselle could herself recognise about her person and close by: the distinctive odour of newly mown grass, the crystal-clear sharpness of the mountain air, the lingering trace of the fear filtering through her pores. She remembered reading somewhere how other senses often grew stronger to compensate for blindness.

'It's the perfume you bought me.'

'I know.'

He didn't turn to look at her.

'I'm sorry. So sorry,' Giselle said.

He reached out for her with his hand.

'It's the past,' he said.

She choked back tears, trying to be cheerful for him, but it was impossible.

Knowing how she had been partly responsible for William losing his sight in the accident.

For being jealous, for being thoughtless and clumsy.

Over the past weeks, she kept on thinking back to the dreadful day and what she could possibly have done differently. Would he have retreated to the work area so rapidly had she not been so distant and vindictive because of Flick's presence that morning? Had her handing William the wrong bottles been deliberate, her subconscious reacting with anger to the situation, or just a terrible mistake? Giselle was weighed down by the burden of guilt.

'I know how you must feel,' William said. 'But you mustn't allow it to ruin your life and ...'

'How can you say that? Because of me, you have lost the ability to paint. I've ruined yours.'

'It's happened. We have to draw a line under it. Nothing will change now. I'll find another way to express myself through art. I know I will,' William insisted.

A faint breeze was rising across the valley, running down from the Alpine peaks. William shivered. He was wearing a checked shirt with his usual brown corduroy trousers.

'It's going to get colder,' he said. 'Shall we move inside?'

She took his hand and helped him out of the chair and guided him along the grass to the warmth of the convalescence clinic and his own quarters, which they reached through a narrow, rickety elevator.

He had a private room, but there was a white bleakness about it, a lack of colour, despite the obligatory hospital iconography of prints of landscapes and flowers hanging on the far wall and above the bed. Which only served to remind Giselle of the fact that this no longer bothered William, as he had no leisure to set his sight on the boring images.

Giselle wanted to ask him how long he was planning to

stay here and recuperate, and how expensive it was proving, but he beat her to it.

'The folks at the Ball have been kind enough to pay for the room. They've been so terribly good,' he said. 'And when I leave, we've agreed I'll be off to join them on a permanent basis and work with them for a while. They say that my becoming blind should not prove a drawback. They will find ways to harness my talent. Oh, Giselle, if only you knew ... Once the initial shock of knowing I'm forever to be plunged in darkness had faded, how the ideas, the possibilities have been boiling away in my mind. Somehow I feel as if I'm more creative than ever, pregnant with so many possibilities. Raring to get started again. It's such an incredible feeling ...'

A nurse brought them plates of scrambled egg, cold cuts and fruit and they ate together in William's room, as outside his window the moon began to rise in the sky beyond the rugged mountain line, like a stop-motion movie. Every time Giselle noticed the sheer savage beauty of the landscape, her heart seized as she was reminded of William's inability now to be able to share any of this with her any longer. It made the food tasteless, contaminated by the bile of her guilt. Giselle couldn't help noticing how tentative his movements were, his spoon clumsily scooping up food from the plate more in hope than with confidence that he could guide it back to his lips bearing enough of a mouthful. Even though she was starving from her train journey, she deliberately slowed down to allow William to keep up with her. He didn't eat much. He did appear thinner.

'Will you stay the night?' William asked.

His request took her by surprise.

'Won't they mind?' She was thinking of the convalescence house's possible rules.

'Of course not.'

A thin stream of moonlight barely illuminated the room, its shimmer interrupted every time a cloud shadowed the moon. William requested Giselle to stand before him in the flickering darkness.

She felt uneasy. Even as a child, the presence of blind people used to unsettle her. Now that it happened to be a man she knew, and intimately so, the sensation was even more disturbing. As if this was no longer the same man who knew her, had held her, entered her, but his phantom, a ghostly presence whose thoughts she could no longer read, held at a distance by invisible curtains now permanently immobilised in place separating light and dark.

'This will be our last night, Giselle. I'm setting you free ...'

His declaration came as no surprise, but it felt like a knife cutting through her nonetheless. But Giselle knew not to protest or plead.

'I understand.'

'Were we to return to Paris together once I'm healed, you'd have to live with sorrow on a daily basis, and I have no wish to either destroy your life or be a burden to you. You're so wonderfully young still, and you have so much ahead of you. I'd hold you back. It's better to make a clean break,' William said.

She could have asked him to at least give things a try, in the hope that it would work out, but deep down Giselle also knew he was right. Even honeymoons come to an end.

His room at the sanatorium was on the top floor, over-looking the valley, away from Via Roma, the town's main road, with its array of bars, pizzerias and luxury gift shops geared to the ski set. It overlooked a wood mill.

William searched for her hand, found it and guided her towards the bay window and slid its door open and they stepped onto the balcony. Should she not be the one guiding him?

The night was cool, a faint breeze stirring. The silence was deep, so unlike the empty sounds of the city.

'Undress,' William ordered her.

She'd been wearing a simple old-fashioned summer dress with a flowery pattern dotted across a field of white. It reached down to her knees, where it flared. Had she danced with it, she knew it would have flown up and around of its own accord, baring the rest of her legs, revealing her white cotton panties. She'd slipped on a coarse knitted sunflower yellow cardigan to cover her bare shoulders and the dress's narrow straps.

She unbuttoned the cardigan.

William stood facing her. Watching.

Seeing her through the filter of his surviving memories, his painter's gaze so accustomed to hunting for the manifold manifestations of beauty.

The moment she dropped the heavy cardigan to the wooden slats of the balcony's sturdy floor, she felt the cold run across her body, a shroud of night and discomfort that brought goose-pimples cascading across her skin.

She hesitated.

William kept on waiting, his face rapt with attention.

'I know it's cold, Giselle. But I want you naked. Fully.'

How would a blind man even know the difference without touching her? Somehow she knew he would, if she didn't bare all.

She moved her hand to the dress's straps and pulled the garment up and above her head, leaving her in just her smalls. Then swiftly unclasped her bra and pulled her knickers down.

Shivered.

William remained immobile.

She knew he couldn't see her, of course, but wondered whether the distinctive scent of her body was now reaching him through the cold air, her particular odours and the heat she generated.

She stepped from foot to foot to hold the cold at bay. Realised she was still wearing her flat-heeled shoes.

'Come to me,' William said.

She moved nearer.

His hand swept her forehead and then his fingers slowly dragged through her hair. She drew a deep breath, stabbed by the electric immediacy of the contact, the rough touch of his fingertips, and a deep well of longing opened inside her. Remembered the way he used to touch her in bed, the delicacy with which those large, artist's hands would open her up, fill her, worship her, and how her own body inevitably reacted, ceaselessly welcoming him time and again.

Giselle closed her eyes. Imagining herself in darkness with him, two travellers floating through the night together. She forgot the cold.

Another hand moved from her shoulder, drawing a line between the cleft of her breasts, darted sideways, cupping her mounds, a finger then a nail grazing a nipple, transforming it into a hard nub. His other hand was now dancing across her stomach, an orphaned finger exploring the minuscule crevice of her navel then fading downwards to her cunt. She was now unkempt there, stubbly, not having bothered since the accident to shave again, tired of the inevitable rash caused by the thick follicles pushing through her delicate skin but now feeling a pang of guilt for the untidiness and rough landscape William's fingers were journeying over. A dip inside her, testing her wetness. A finger drawing back and William tasting her on his lips. A sigh of greedy appreciation. Both his hands now waltzing around her body. Here, there, everywhere. Weighing the heft and firmness of her arse cheeks, navigating between the line of the buttocks, mapping her external geography like some sex-mad surveyor. Brushing against the small of her back, the terribly sensitive underside of her thighs, circling her ankles then rising high again, swivelling her body with a gentle nudge to her shoulders and waist. Touching, exploring, appreciating.

She now knew what he was doing.

He was collecting data, storing every single detail of her body, processing her essence by touch, filing the sensations, the memories away, so that they would remain with him forever after they had parted.

Armed with this material, locked away in the stronghold of his brain cells, next week, the following year or even in ten years, William would be able to sculpt her in the air, revive her form, the feel of her out of sheer nothingness, recreate her.

Her heart melted at the thought.

Time flew.

Her body aglow she imagined she was being X-rayed, scanned, immortalised.

Her sigh lasted centuries.

Finally, his hands left her, retreated and she felt neglected. Empty. Unfulfilled.

They walked back into the room, closing the balcony door.

His hands now guiding him by touch, William stepped over to the bed and lay down, fully clothed.

Giselle joined him and spooned against him.

'I will always be able to see you,' he said.

They did not make love and fell asleep quickly. As her conscious thoughts receded, Giselle hoped that maybe in the morning when they awoke together he might fuck her, a final moment of madness, a last hurrah, but when she opened her eyes and light flooded the room, pouring over the mountain peaks and catching her pale, naked body in its fiery glare, she was alone. She rose, heavy under the weight of her sadness, and looked out from the balcony. William was in the garden, sitting in the same place as before in the shadow of the oak tree, as if watching the jagged edge of the Alpine peaks cut ribbons into the sky.

He couldn't actually see the mountains, Giselle knew, but hoped that right now he could see her, somewhere on some screen in the back of his mind.

'*Remember me.*'

She did not say goodbye and took the midday train.

★   ★   ★

Her shift at the flower shop had come to an end. Freya today had been working the same hours.

'I'm going dancing tonight,' her workmate said. 'Why don't you come? I do think you need cheering up.'

'Alright then,' Giselle replied. 'I will.' Why not? She had been doing nothing but mope for weeks. Finding her own place and moving out of William's apartment had distracted her for a time. None of their furniture was hers, and she had gathered few possessions besides her clothes. She had never wanted to take advantage of his superior income and so had deliberately lived on a tight budget, contributing to household expenses as much as she could, which left her little over from her own pocket for herself and consequently her shoes, handbags and toiletry items barely even filled one bag. Her books, piled into a large cardboard box, were the heaviest thing she had to carry, but nonetheless she managed it all in the back of a taxi with the help of the driver, who on seeing Giselle struggling up and down the stairs had volunteered his assistance.

The flat that she had moved into was run down, tiny and depressing to be inside. It reflected Giselle's mood perfectly and so she had taken it. Located near the Bastille, it was part of a block that had been converted into a series of tiny rooms, each with a single bed, a wardrobe that by necessity was so close to the bed that the door only opened part-way, a small, round stainless steel sink, a refrigerator that reached only to her knees and a single electric hob standing on top that functioned as the kitchen. The bathroom was across the hall, shared by two others. The building's other residents were all either students, most of them foreign, or a varied mix of down-and-outers who were either in the process of scraping themselves up from an even worse situation, or who had plummeted from a better one. Occasionally she bumped into one of her neighbours, walking down the gloomy, blue-green-painted corridor that was like a mix between a hospital and a swimming pool changing room, but they never exchanged more than a nod or muffled grunt in greeting. It was as though all of the residents were embarrassed to be there.

Giselle had, with Freya's permission, taken to storing some of her stuff at the flower shop, partly because even though she had few possessions, she still had trouble fitting everything into the space available, and partly because she disliked returning to her cramped apartment with its small window, damp walls, and the prevalent air of hopelessness that hung around the place. She'd taken on more shifts, as many as Freya could offer her, so spent more time at work. In the small space out back that served as both staff room and office, Freya had installed a rack where Giselle hung a few dresses and beneath that had a couple of pairs of shoes stored.

They brought the sign in and locked up the shop ten minutes early.

'It's been dead quiet all day,' Freya muttered as she turned the key in the lock. 'No one will know.' Had Giselle been the manager, she wouldn't have dreamed of closing early without the proper authorisation, but Freya did not have the same work ethic. Which was lucky for Giselle, she mused, since it meant that the Swedish woman was relaxed about many things that made Giselle's life easier, like turning a blind eye to the many times over the past few weeks that Giselle had been uncharacteristically late, and arrived red eyed, since after William's accident she had not been able to stop crying.

'Do you mind if I borrow one of your dresses, Gizzy?' Freya asked. 'Then we can both change here, and grab a bite on the way.'

Privately, Giselle could not imagine how Freya would fit into any of her clothes, but she politely agreed, and somehow Freya managed to get into one of Giselle's floral printed dresses with a wide flared skirt, although it was nearly impossible to zip up at the back and Giselle feared that the garment might rip apart at any time. Freya's large bosoms strained against the fabric and created creases that made it obvious the frock was too small.

Giselle wore a pair of trousers, so tight they were closer to leggings, and a pleated vest top with a faux collar trimmed with stiff lace. She slicked her hair back as tightly as she could manage without a set of hot irons and coated her lips bright red. It was a different look for her, and had her bust not been so prominent might have appeared quite masculine. With her height, and Freya like a wider version of Marilyn Monroe, they could have passed for boyfriend and girlfriend from behind rather than two women.

They stopped for a crêpe and a glass of wine at a little café just a few blocks down from the flower shop where the owner knew them and so filled their glasses far more generously than the bill suggested. He was a stocky Italian man with particularly hairy arms, who spoke poor French and only a little English, and always greeted them with an enthusiastic 'Bella!' as they entered. He had other staff who worked the tables and bar but he always came out to serve them personally. Giselle suspected that he had a crush on Freya, or at the very least admired the size and fullness of Freya's breasts, which he did not seem able to take his eyes off, barely encased as they were in her too small dress.

After they had eaten they walked out of the city centre to an area that Giselle didn't usually frequent close by the Porte de Versailles, a gateway to southern suburbs of tower blocks where, increasingly, immigrants tended to live. The streets were poorly lit and not populated with the usual Friday-night crowd, just the odd drunk stumbling by and the occasional frightened pedestrian hurrying along.

'Are you sure you know where you're taking us, Freya?' Giselle asked. Maybe it was just a sign of her depression, being spooked by her own shadow, but she didn't like the feel of the place. A morbidity hung around in the thick darkness of the stone walls that loomed around them, as though the air hadn't moved through these lanes for a long time.

'I'm sure,' she said. 'Trust me. It's a small spot, not well known, but busy on a Friday. A good place to dance. The people who come here aren't the regular sorts. You'll like it.'

Giselle was silent after that, until they arrived. She was using all of her energy just living; she didn't have anything extra left over to argue with.

Freya stopped all of a sudden outside a flight of concrete steps that led down from the pavement, underground. A dim light shone at the bottom, illuminating the metal bars that served as a handhold but looked a bit like the gate of a prison. A sign was bolted to the wall at the bottom but it was so faded that it was illegible, just a blurred, chipped mess of once bright, pink and purple painted lettering.

A female bouncer stood in front of the door. She was as tall as Giselle, beefy and dressed in full leather, with her hair cut short at the sides and long on top, styled into a high, bleached quiff. She nodded at Freya, intimating that they knew each other, and indicated that the girls could go through.

They entered through a corridor, painted deep red.

Strident and aggressive punk music with a loud bass played so loudly that it felt to Giselle as though the walls around them were thumping. The bar was through a side door at the end, and Freya was right, the place was heaving. There was no dance floor set aside for the purpose, but all across the room individuals were gyrating, some in time to the music and others to another beat, as if an invisible orchestra played inside their minds. Around the dancers other patrons milled, chatting, drinking, or watching those who writhed on alone. Perfume hung in the still air, along with whiffs of sweat, the sour scent of spilled drinks and cigarette smoke.

'Drink?' Freya asked.

'Sure,' Giselle said. 'Whatever you're having.' She hadn't drunk, really, since the time that she and William had got together with Flick. Alcohol reminded her of that night, and that night reminded her of Flick, which in turn made her think of William's accident. So she'd since avoided booze. Secretly, too, she harboured a fear that she was the sort of person who might take drinking too far. She was a passionate person, an all or nothing kind, not someone who fared well with moderation. Tonight, though, she wanted to forget all of her worries and dance the hours away, and if a drink would help her to trip over that line into forgetting then she would have one, or two, or as many as it took.

Freya was served quickly, since she pushed her way to the front of the line, and she returned with two squat glasses filled with clear liquid in which a lemon wedge floated and ice cubes clinked.

'Gin and tonic,' Freya said. 'It's Happy Hour for another forty-five minutes, so drink it quick.'

Giselle obliged, throwing the drink back in a couple of mouthfuls with a quick turn of her wrist although the bitter tang of the quinine and the sourness of the lemon made her wince. Once empty, Freya took the glass from her hand and set it down somewhere then pulled her away from the bar and into a gaggle of dancers, bodies all jostling against one another as though they were at an orgy albeit with all of their clothes on. Freya lifted her arms overhead and swung her large hips, causing her skirt to ride up so high that a flash of her mint-green frilled panties occasionally peeped out from underneath.

'Freya,' Giselle hissed into her friend's ear, trying to be discreet but audible over the music, 'is this a gay bar? There's no men here.'

Freya shrugged. 'It's where I come when I just want to dance,' she replied, and then she closed her eyes and continued to gyrate, grinding her hips and twisting down to the floor like a go-go dancer.

Giselle felt a pair of hands resting on either side of her hips and the slight brush of a body not quite pressing against her. The touch was tentative, questioning. She tensed, and then relaxed, and began to sway to the rhythm of her

Vina Jackson

mystery dance partner. The pressure became firmer and the unknown hands began to move over her covered thighs as she and her companion swayed and twisted as though they were one, joined together like Siamese twins. Giselle let the other woman carry her. Fingertips lifted her shirt and traced a faint pattern on her torso before running over her breasts and then her upper arms, directing her hands into the air.

She felt as though she were flying, gliding free on the wings of the heavy punk beat that thumped through the speakers around them. Her heart had been taken over by bass, her muscles were connected to the rhythm. Like a puppet, her body was just the shell around which the music vibrated. Giselle felt complete, as though she had finally found the crack that existed inside her and managed to repair it. She had discovered a new life force.

She hadn't even noticed that her dancing partner had faded away into the shadows and abandoned her to join someone else on the dance floor. Giselle was too enamoured with her own body and spirit to be enticed by anyone else, or even distracted by the prospect of queuing at the bar and pursuing drunkenness a step further to help her forget her sorrows.

For the first time in her life she felt truly satisfied within herself. Longing for William and times past that they shared still possessed her, but she left the bar with Freya holding onto the grain of hope that she could be happy again, without him, though she missed him still. And she thought of her old friend Beth, who had been assiduously sending her bright and breezy postcards from London via the flower shop for weeks since word of William's accident had reached her, probably through a modelling contact in the art world they inhabited. Giselle had barely glanced at them, never mind replied. She had wanted to be left alone with her misery, but now she felt that, all of a sudden, the cloud had lifted, and let a bright beam of light shine through where before there had only been darkness.

Giselle firmly resolved to return to dance lessons. For pleasure, this time. She would dance for the love of it, and damn whether or not anybody thought she was good enough.

When the letter arrived, it carried with it the weight of the unexpected. Giselle recognised William's scrawl immediately. She had seen it enough times, decorating the bottom right-hand edge of his paintings, the W beginning narrow and merging into a set of wide, arching loops that had always reminded her of a heavy woman's buttocks. He had a way of doing things backwards. He was not purposefully contrary, but an original, someone who did things the way that suited him regardless of the fashion.

She felt a lump rise in her throat. More than a lump, she just about couldn't breathe for the sheer strength of emotion that threatened to overwhelm her entirely. Giselle took a breath, and sipped her espresso to calm herself. The small china cup that held her coffee clattered against the saucer as she set it down, her fingers shaking so badly she nearly splashed the drink over the table.

Giselle was sitting outside at a café at the foot of Montmartre. She loved the maze of winding, cobbled streets here, and the sharp rise of the hill on which the imposing mass of the Sacré Coeur stood, overlooking the village within the city. There was a majesty in the church that extended far wider than the shadow of the building itself, spreading over the whole area like an oversized cassock. Giselle had never felt the pull of religion in her heart, but she appreciated the grandeur and solemnity of its monuments, and she often found peace being close to them, particularly on quiet, still days like this one. It was still early, and a chilly morning. She was so far the only customer.

The lone waiter had been friendly to her and looked her over with curious eyes, probably assessing why an attractive young woman in a lemon yellow cardigan and neatly pressed cream skirt was out alone so early on a Saturday morning without a coat, her bright, dark, raisin eyes deep wells of sadness but no longer red with tears. He brought her a plate of tiny shortbread biscuits, cut into star shapes, that she had not ordered. Giselle felt his eyes drawn inevitably to her cleavage as he set them down.

The letter was still sealed. She hadn't wanted to open it under the prying gaze of Freya, when it had arrived. Or in her bedsit, with its gloomy interior that made any other emotion besides sadness almost impossible to achieve. She had carried it with her, still sealed, in her purse, for over a week. More than once she had nearly dropped it into a garbage can as she had with Olen's correspondence, not wanting to sully the memory of their time together or draw out the knife edge of her pain any further by digging up old wounds. But each time she had tried, she had been unable to bring herself to let go of the envelope. Her fingers had clung to the plain white paper as though it were made of gold, far too precious to be tossed into the trash.

Finally she ran her thumb under the seal and carefully pulled it open. She withdrew the folded piece of paper within. It was just a single sheet of unlined art vellum, torn down one side. A page from one of his sketchbooks. He had written on both sides, and the letters were etched so deeply onto the page that the ballpoint had indented the paper. Giselle imagined him writing it. Pressing so fiercely against the pen he held in his left hand that when she ran her fingertips over the sheet it felt like Braille. She could not read the words by feeling them, but she could sense the fraught state he must have been in when he wrote them.

Dearest Giselle, it began. They had never been one of those couples who used nicknames for each other or terms of endearment. She had always been Giselle, and he William. Even their names were well suited, she had once thought, though quickly dismissed the idea as the sort of foolishness that schoolgirls come up with in the playground. It didn't matter a jot what their names were.

I hesitated a long while before writing this to you, as I am sure you can well imagine. You know how I railed against the thought of us staying together. Me growing older every day while you are so young and beautiful, and have so much life in you. More life than I have ever had.

I wanted to set you free.

But I can't. I remain your captive. We are wedded, in soul, if not by law. I belong to you.

Does that make me a bad person? Or just a silly old man? I don't know. I only know that I love you more, every day. And in a strange way, I feel as though I am getting to know you better, even with what feels like the whole world between us.

Do you remember the Ball we attended in that odd twilight zone beyond Long Island that I never even thought was on the map? Of course you do, though I hadn't told you really what it was. There was so much more I should have told you. I wanted to protect your innocence in some way. I should have known, though, that your core of goodness could never be corrupted, no matter what perversions I exposed your body to.

Giselle paused. Yes, she remembered, she thought, with bitter irony. She remembered every moment that they had spent together as though she had recorded their relationship somehow and was able to play it back in full colour, three dimensional cinemascape in her mind.

An African flower seller walking by on the road, preparing to accost unsuspecting tourists with roses at extortionate prices, stopped and offered one to her and she took it and paid him the fee, just so that she could feel the thorns and the silky sweep of the petals against her skin. She needed something familiar, something that she didn't just associate with William, to bring her back to the present. Having only just recovered her equilibrium, she refused to lose it again. She popped a piece of the shortbread into her mouth and continued to read. The sweetness and the crunch of pistachio fragments in the biscuit mix reminded her that she was here, in Montmartre, and not outside New York as fleeting memories of the Ball drifted by in her mind, triggered by the letter. All she had to do was close her eyes for a moment and she could see him as though he were really there, feel him behind her.

She snapped her eyes open and continued to read.

We stood near a sculpture, a water fountain, in the parking lot. A man and woman embracing. Tightly. The way I wish I could embrace you now. And you asked me if I had considered sculpting. I told you 'no', that I preferred the medium of paint, that I wished to record my subjects draped in light, not carved from stone. Hard, cold. At least that's what I thought, then. I was wrong.

You won't believe it, Giselle, but there is another blind man with the Ball. Walter is his name. We are two! Which explains why the Ball was so kind, and so keen, to have me, when I am next to useless now, as an artist. He sculpts. And is teaching me. I have not touched any clay yet, or other material. So far, all he asks me to do is sit with him, and bring an image to my mind, and dissect it to the last millimetre. Touch, taste, colour, the precise geometry of each curve. To trace it into the air with my hands.

Of course, I use you for my inspiration. Ever in my mind. I hope you don't object, my darling, being used in this way. You are the only memory that I have potent enough with life for this task. Everything else in my memories has begun to fade away, to lose its gloss. I can see nothing but you now, in my mind. And so every day I sit and I sculpt you in my imagination.

One day I will bring you to life, I hope, though I will never do you justice. I am grateful, that at least I will not be able to see whatever ill representation of you I cast with my hands!

The last line caused Giselle to weep. She recognised straight away his odd brand of dark humour, and his optimism, making a joke even now of his condition, as if there could ever be anything positive in the fact that he had been blinded. *That she had inadvertently blinded him.* The thought wrenched at her, repeatedly, and she pushed it from her mind. She knew that William did not want her to think that, and she felt she owed it to him to try, at least.

She dashed the tears away from her eyes with the back of her hand. Her coffee was cold, she ordered another.

'Can I get you anything else, Miss? A tissue, a glass of water?' the waiter asked her, concern in his eyes mingled with desire. Giselle had seen that look on the faces of enough men to know it when she saw it. She shook her head, and replied, 'No, thank you.'

She had come to the last few lines on the page, and almost wanted to put the letter down again. To pause once more and return to it later so that she could make it last longer. While she was reading his words, she could almost hear William's voice in her mind. She could see his face, feel the coarseness of his rough beard against her cheek as he kissed her. She would give anything now, to feel him inside her. To have him pin her down, to chain her as he once had when she had craved to be his own Joan of Arc.

But she knew it was not to be. Giselle was pragmatic. A realist. She knew in her heart of hearts that no matter how painful this was, it couldn't last. His memory of her would fade. And so would hers of him. Wouldn't it?

You are the only thing I see.

I will hold you in my heart and mind forever.

I love you.

Yours,

William.

Even after she had read it, she could not bring herself to

throw the letter away. She was disciplined enough to stop herself from reading it over and over again. That, she knew, would just drive her crazy. But discipline didn't stop her from thinking of it, from knowing that the letter was there, folded neatly inside its original envelope and resting inside the cover of one of her favourite books. She had put it inside *The Great Gatsby*, because ever since the party off Long Island, where nobody knew the host, that book had reminded her of William.

Soon, she would have a collection of them, for that was not to be her last letter from him.

He never left a forwarding address, so even if she had wanted to reply, she would not know where to send it.

William's notes from overseas, even though there was only so much words could do to soothe her conscience and her sense of loss, helped a little. But soon even the words became more infrequent, like a lifeline being stretched until it snapped. A few paragraphs here, barely twice a year, a post-card with an exotic stamp from a surprising location there, presumably wherever the Ball had pitched its tents. The intervals grew longer, the letting go a mathematical progression engineered to alleviate the pain of separation and the emptiness.

One day, Giselle neglected a lecture at the Censier-Daubenton campus, then another and again as she felt too bone tired to raise herself from her bed following nights of energetic dancing and manic socialising in night clubs stretching from Neuilly to the Montparnasse boulevards, dizzy immersions in a world of flickering strobe lights, fierce neon kingdoms and the roar of stoned crowds. Soon several months had passed and Giselle realised she had given up on her studies. It hadn't been a deliberate decision, more a sort of fading away of her free will and determination. But she no longer missed the classes. Her appetite for the life that lived in books had faded.

The intermittent job at the flower store also came to an end, following a row with Freya about a guy Giselle had picked up in a club and returned home with. How could she have known Freya was sweet on the man? They'd all been pretty drunk and it felt as if Freya was open to any-thing on those boozy nights of dance and joviality. Within a week, she had even forgotten the man's name, or even how expertly he had mounted her or not. But the hurt in Freya's eyes survived and working together proved increas-ingly fraught as a result.

Her father had died, just a few days after William's acci-dent, and left her a small sum of money, which she supplemented with her modelling for artists, photographers and still life classes at the Ecole des Beaux-Arts on the Rue Bonaparte. Somehow the grief of his passing had mingled with her loss of William. She and her father had never been close, anyway. She knew that she ought to spend more time with her mother, now that she was alone, but Giselle could not bear the deep sense of absence that hung around her family home, as though her father's death had cut a hole right through the living room. She stayed away.

There were men.

A tutor at the art school, who had asked her to model privately. He was William's age, or maybe even older, but his total opposite, small, wiry, hair impeccably groomed, attire always carefully ironed and spotless. Initially, she had reckoned Stephane was gay, but the gleam in his eyes when he had invited her out following their first session had quickly put paid to that assumption. It was the lusty look of a man who desired her, and not the detached gaze of an admiring artist. She hadn't played too hard to get and became his mistress. He also happened to be married. He was an attentive, if unimaginative, lover but the affair was also frustrating. Even though her heart still confusingly appeared to be in thrall to memories of William and his rough and wanton ways, in her mind she also craved a normal relationship, the sort of situation where she could phone a boyfriend at any time of day and night and suggest having a coffee in a bistro, or going out to see a movie together or, at the last minute, decide to go dancing or travelling to the coast for a weekend of frolics and relaxation. Married men were not available and on call at short notice.

So, she embarked on a parallel affair with Robert, one of Stephane's students, yet another man who knew every contour of her body, the geometry of her curves and the shades of her pallor long before she even slept with him, having sketched, drawn and painted her in a variety of brightly lit amphitheatres and lecture halls at the art school on various occasions, alongside a few dozen other fine art students in his second-year class. In bed, he was as unimaginative as Stephane, and sometimes blushed when Giselle would take the lead in her search for pleasure, drawing him away from his missionary standards and introducing more dangerous variations to their lovemaking. Even though she was only five years older than him, it made her feel like something of a cradle snatcher, a scarlet woman debauching youth with her unspeakable needs and a knowledge of sex and its delightful extremes William had given her a greedy taste for.

Stephane knew of Robert and didn't appear to mind. Married men know they have no right to be possessive. Throughout the few months when she was sleeping separately with both men, Giselle often fantasised on the prospect of bringing them both together with her between the sheets for some special occasion, engineering the feat if only to confirm in her mind that she was no longer a fool for romance, and that only the flesh mattered. And pleasure. Both selfish and rewarding.

But it never came to pass.

And time passed.

Robert moved on. No doubt to someone his own age, or maybe less demanding and cold-hearted. Stopped answering Giselle's phone calls. She understood why.

Then Stephane left Paris to take up a residency in Rome at the Villa Medici. He promised that, once he had settled in, he would be in touch and they would arrange for Giselle to fly down for a week or so – his teaching obligations were minimal – when they could spend time together travelling in the Lazio region. He'd been advised by a previous artist who had resided at the Villa that there was a lake north of the city which was ideal for a tryst. Lake Bracciano, it was called. With a castle overlooking the waters. Apparently a major celebrity had got married nearby. And then there was the medieval village of Calcata, which was being transformed into an artist's colony where you could rent an isolated stone-built house for a weekend. Giselle looked the places up on maps but the call from Stephane never came. No doubt Italian models were a new attraction, more exotic, closer to hand.

Men.

While she was still sleeping with Stephane and Robert. In between. After.

Men with no names picked up in the dizziness of clubs under the sway of the music's beat, or in a bar. Their hardy, sometimes sweating hands travelling at light speed across her shoulders or the thin material of her skirt on the dance floor or under the table in an expensive restaurant, the Procope or a gourmet joint by the Champs Elysées, an area she detested, digits inching past her stocking tops.

She would let them fuck her in toilets, in cars or in the dark, sheltered safety of the Bois de Boulogne, or they would take her to cheap hotel rooms rented for the afternoon close by the railway stations. Now, the one place she never took men back to was her small apartment near the Bastille. It became a rule, even if it meant not sleeping with a particular man.

Some were talkative and others silent. Giselle preferred those who didn't speak much. Who would order her around once they were alone, sometimes skirt the edges of roughness and change her fear into a thing of excitement.

Days turned into weeks that turned into months that turned into several years, flowing with the impetus of inaction.

A photographer called David took her to Bali, where she made love on a beach for the first time. The sand everywhere was an unpleasant irritation she hadn't previously conceived of.

An airline pilot she met in a hotel bar took her to Tokyo, where she gorged on sashimi and miso soup. She stayed behind when it was time to return to Paris and found a short-term gig in a hostess bar where local clients paid fortunes to be flattered by foreign women, mostly Eastern European, and never even required sex. In a dance club in Shinjuku, she witnessed dancers in cages transformed into epileptic skeletons by the strobe lighting and, later the same evening, watched in terrible fascination a demonstration of rope bondage led by a tiny little man with a bald pate and a flowing white stream of a beard that made her think of Don Quixote. She returned there a week later and introduced herself to him and asked whether he would be willing to bind her too. She left his studio some hours later in a state of extreme exhilaration, buzzing with the romance of the rope, every nerve in her body sitting on a cliff edge and yearning to be tamed, completed. She made a beeline for the first bar and seduced a bemused company executive who couldn't believe his luck and took her to a love hotel nearby. His body was totally hairless. He left her behind in the room, post-sex, while she was still showering, as if embarrassed by the whole episode, bequeathing a handful of banknotes on the dressing table.

She returned to Europe, settled back into her modelling, letting off steam dancing at least two nights a week, collecting men as you do butterflies. Transient men, invisible bodies, men with cocks, voices with hands and sweet words and sometimes foul breath.

Modelling assignments became sparser. It didn't happen

overnight, more of a gradual thing, with artists and photographers slowly moving on to other models, new faces
and bodies, having maybe exhausted the possibilities, the
dreams she could offer and seeking renewed inspiration
with others. In truth, Giselle knew that for some time now
her heart had not been in it: she stood in studios, sets and
fields suspended between worlds past and future, her mood
indifferent and aimless and, no doubt, the artists could sense
this. It was only with William that she had been transformed
into a full-fledged muse.

Her funds were becoming problematic, with even rent
payments a monthly strain.

The call came.

She'd been thinking for some time that maybe she should
sign up with an agency to find extra modelling work, relying
as she had until now on word of mouth between potential
employers and less than a handful of art schools dating back
to the days when she had begun posing for William and his
circle of acquaintances had taken note of her.

The approach from the talent company – one she had
never heard of previously – came at the right time. It made
Giselle feel as if someone was looking after her from afar,
aware of the turn in her circumstances. The company's
name was L'Or du Temps, *Time's Gold*. From the outset,
the name had intrigued her.

Their offices were situated on the first floor of an *hôtel particulier* on the Rue de Verneuil, all polished mirrors, dark wood fittings and discreet furnishings. The woman who had contacted her was prim and tanned, her fading auburn hair held back in a tight bun, wearing a grey business suit, a formal white blouse and a single string of pearls. Her name was Madame Fur.

'We've heard good reports about you,' she said. 'You come highly recommended . . .'

'May I ask who brought me to your attention?' Giselle asked.

The woman ignored her question.

'I gather you have a background in dance?'

'Yes. But it's been some time since I've properly practised,' Giselle said.

'I understand.'

Giselle had the feeling this woman knew far more about her than she let on, aware of the amount of dancing she did in clubs on wild nights, the fact that she did so on her own and often without an actual dancing partner, suspended in sound and in a world of her own, the solitary centre of attraction on a crowded floor. Also how she met men there, whored herself for the sake of pleasure. The secret life she had carved out in the heart of her solitude.

The woman's eyes were steely green. She held Giselle's gaze.

'We can offer you work. Well paid. Regular.'

'Modelling?'

'Sometimes.'

'I'm not an escort, if that's what you had in mind.'

'Absolutely not,' Madame Fur said. 'Your experience is as an artist's model, and you have experience of dance. We know.'

'What else, then?' Giselle enquired.

'It would also involve dancing. Of a particular nature,' the woman added, her features still unreadable.

'I have no wish to become a stripper,' Giselle insisted.

'Indeed. We are more interested about the artistic side of things,' she was told.

Giselle was intrigued, asked for more details.

'After a suitable training period, it would involve you relocating to the United States,' she was informed. The last postcard, birthday wishes bordering on clichés, she had received from William a couple of years back had been posted from San Francisco. Madame Fur now had her full attention.

Sensing Giselle's interest, Madame Fur visibly relaxed and offered her coffee, suggesting they repair to the white leather sofa rather than sit either side of her desk in a formal interview situation.

L'Or du Temps was the Paris branch of a large international organisation with fingers in many areas of the entertainment and arts world, she explained. They pursued a strictly low profile in view of the sometimes particular, although never illegal, nature of the activities they organised.

The shocking if fascinating spectacle she had witnessed at the Ball on Long Island came to mind and Giselle couldn't help questioning her interlocutor.

'That large, wild party, all those years ago outside New York, on the island, was it something you were involved in?'

'The Ball?'

'Yes, that's what it was referred to as. A close friend of mine later worked for it. For you?'

'Not me personally, but yes, we are connected. There are many things we get involved in.'

'Did William put you in touch with me, by any chance?'

'Would it matter if he did?'

Giselle reflected. No, it wouldn't. But still the connection between L'Or du Temps and William and the Ball was more than a coincidence. In her mind, the loop was closing again, as if another chapter in the book of her life was ending and she was about to embark on something new and inevitable.

'I'll do it,' she said. 'The training you mention, the work . . .'

Madame Fur's smile was enigmatic, her distant eyes knowing as if she had expected this response.

'I haven't yet provided you with much in the way of details . . .'

'It doesn't matter,' Giselle said. 'I will do it all. I'm on board. Definitely.'

7

The Mississippi Waltz

Just under fifteen years later, Giselle was interviewing a new dancer in her study at The Place, a discreet property hidden behind high walls and fragrant magnolia-scented gardens near the eastern edges of Bourbon Street and Esplanade Avenue.

She had sat for well over an hour earlier that morning at her dressing table gazing at herself in the mirror. It wasn't as if it had happened overnight. It had been progressive in the way that you don't notice the changes from day to day – like a child growing up – but all of a sudden she was now faced with the incontrovertible evidence: her hair had turned grey.

It was still long and silky thanks to hours of brushing and care and the expensive shampoos and conditioners she treated herself to, had not become dry and brittle as she thought it might have, but the grey strands dominated nonetheless.

Giselle had sighed. But it had not been in sadness, just a reflection of calm acceptance.

As long as she remembered, her mother had also had grey hair, even in the dim past days of Orléans. But even though she'd also worn it long in style, her mother's hair had not been as dark as hers and somehow the effect had not been as striking.

It was now Giselle's turn to assume her genetic inheritance.

She knew two things for sure: she did not wish to cut her hair, and neither did she plan to colour it, and revert to her original ebony shade, or for that matter any other. She had never been one for artifice.

Back in Paris, she would occasionally come across a few new white strands and had never been overly concerned by their often overnight appearance and somehow, over the years, her indifference had failed to note how they had spread. This early greying was something common to women in her family. As if in contemplating her features she had been half blind, or her subconscious had engineered her to ignore what was happening.

Tonight, she decided, after the club closed its doors, she would go out and roam the Vieux Carré streets, ambling towards Jackson Square and, if she did not attract attention before, would end up at the Café du Monde where a lone woman in the dark of the night sitting at a corner table facing Decatur, sipping her coffee in a stance of expectation and availability, would find it easy to connect with a man. She would smile, hope that the stranger had a modicum of wit and didn't reek of booze, and then follow him to his hotel room and sleep with him. Be fucked. And slip out of the room at dawn on tiptoe, quietly, like the dancer she was at heart, and return to the peace of her own bed several blocks away close by the Louisiana State Museum in the Old Mint building, secure in the knowledge that she was still attractive and beddable.

She lived in a small one-storey building, once the slaves' quarters but long since renovated to modern standards, hidden behind the lush vegetation of the club's grounds. She had never brought a man back there. Many had asked, but she always made it clear that this was a deal-breaker and would never happen. They quickly capitulated.

The new applicant had been referred to Giselle by the Network so, for once, she knew the young woman was unlikely to be unduly surprised by certain aspects of the job. Giselle wouldn't have to wear kid gloves when explaining what the gig would sometimes entail. Total newcomers would sometimes recoil in surprise and, on occasion, walk out, albeit not before Giselle had to remind them of the non-disclosure agreement they had signed prior to the interview.

The organisation had no wish to attract unwanted publicity or notoriety.

'So where do you come from?'

'Portland in Oregon.'

Giselle had a slight preference for employing dancers and performers from foreign places, mostly Europe or Eastern Europe. They were somehow more worldly. American women lacked a sense of what she liked to call 'poetry' even when their bone structure happened to be drop-dead gorgeous and their skin unblemished, although some had proved outstanding, wonderfully wanton and knowing in a way foreign women who lacked the necessary guile did not. American-born girls also seemed to learn the more unusual routines faster and with more ease, although their performances were also a tad more mechanical and unfeeling whereas the foreign ones invested not just their bodies but also their hearts in the chosen act.

Giselle looked down at the opening page of the portfolio the dancer had brought along to the audition.

'Deborah?'

'People call me Debb . . .'

The young woman appeared nervous.

How much had she been told? What did she expect?

All those years back, when Giselle had found herself in

the same situation, how much had she hesitated when everything had been explained? Had she been shocked? Or taken back? Or had she fatalistically taken it in her stride? It was not easy to remember her then state of mind. So much had occurred since.

There had been a lengthy assessment of her dancing abilities, her physical fitness and her general state of health, which had been followed by a series of sessions with a psychologist in front of whom she'd had to reveal all her sexual tastes and quirks. The interrogator had probed deep, uncovering her disturbing fixation on Joan of Arc, torture, her hidden streak of masochism and the way it expressed itself in her approach to men and, as the conversations continued over several weeks, how her exhibitionist nature lurked skin-deep below the surface of her personality, the mask she wore, something she still found difficult to accept about herself.

But none of these revelations appeared to disturb her potential new employers, and soon she appeared to have successfully passed all the tests, the barrage of questions had ceased and her turn had come to learn what was actually on offer and why the interview process was so elaborate and probing.

'And you have no problem with being naked in public situations?'

'Not at all,' Debb answered. She nodded to the portfolio

Giselle was still holding in her hands. 'When I was a student, I did some stripping and lap dancing. But they were very reputable places; everything was above board; no funny business allowed.'

'And how did you feel about that?' Giselle asked.

'A bit flushed initially, but I quickly got used to it. Then ...' she hesitated briefly, ' ... then it got to the point where I actually looked forward to those nights and it got me excited. Sexually. The power it gave me over the men watching me. Being in control.'

'Good,' Giselle said.

After the Paris office of the Network had been satisfied Giselle was on the right track and could fulfil her potential, they had flown her to New York where she had lodged in a small Upper West Side walk-up with two other new dancers, one of whom was male, an impossibly handsome if dim brute called Pietr who'd been brought in from Latvia and would, she knew, function as a stud for the special sessions she would one day have to perform at. He was a physically perfect example of the male of the species and knew it, parading nude around the small communal apartment whenever it wasn't too cold, which in a Manhattan summer meant most days, his erection seldom faltering. His English was still halting, so any further social interaction with him was an uphill struggle though. Both Giselle and the other dancer sharing the second bedroom with her, an

Australian girl named Joy, tried their best to ignore him, although back in their room together they could barely repress their laughter as they gossiped and speculated as to how his physical beauty would translate into the nitty-gritty of sex. Or how he would feel about it as he was visibly so enamoured with his own appearance to the exclusion of all else. He never missed an opportunity to gaze appreciatively at himself in the mirrors scattered around the lodgings, flexing a muscle, holding in his stomach or even casually passing a neglectful hand over his hard cock as if testing its unyielding rigidity, oblivious to the fact that one or the other young woman was present.

'And you like men?'

'Well, yes,' Debb replied. 'Of course. But, I assume it's in my file, I am not averse to women. Bisexual, some would say.' She gave Giselle a querying look, as if trying to determine the nature of her interviewer's personal tastes.

In fact, Giselle, although open-minded and appreciative of women's looks, had only occasionally been attracted to others of her gender. There had been Beth, her friend from ballet school with whom she had maintained a correspondence for years but heard from only rarely these days. Flick, the woman that she and William had once fucked together on camera. She'd had sex with some others on stage, but only few in her bed of her own free will. The aesthetics were pleasant but the act did not raise her pleasure from its dormant pit somehow in the same way as it did with men.

'Good,' Giselle concluded.

In New York, she'd been assigned to a private club owned by the organisation situated close to Columbus Circle, where she would dance up to four times a week. Discreetly hidden down a cross street, the brownstone from the outside resembled a perfectly normal residential house. The activities the dancers were engaged in took place on the ground floor, with the upper level occupied by offices she never set foot in. The club had no name, something the Network, she would learn over the years, was in the habit of doing. It was just known as a number; in this case Nr. 19.

Membership was very exclusive and by invitation only.

To the unsophisticated, it might have been considered a strip club, albeit a classy one. But, as Giselle knew, it was much more than that. In Paris, when she had still been training and refining her dance skills, she had been taken as part of her learning curve to a succession of establishments from a basic Pigalle strip joint, dripping with vulgarity and the unsound odour of commercial sex, to a more upper-class place where the seats were cleaner and the dancers prettier and less used in appearance, their eyes not completely blank and absent, and then to the Crazy Horse and another more upmarket club actually controlled by the

Network. This had demonstrated to her the degrees of skill, engagement and quality that could separate a mere strip joint from the grace and delicacy and innate cultivation of sexual arousal an upper class club could offer. She had been unable to suppress an initial feeling of reluctance when she had first been informed that one of the aspects of the job would consist of dancing nude for paying customers, having initially protested at the prospect of stripping.

'Imagine you are dancing in the privacy of your own bedroom for a man you desire and who wants you,' her instructor had suggested. 'It's a whole different experience . . .'

'But . . . ?'

'Don't think of the money involved. That's beside the point. Remember the Ball you attended, and the beauty of the dancing, the nudity, the sheer joy of it all. You provide visual pleasure and please yourself in the process. It's as much in the mind as it is in the flesh. Don't think of it as a monetary transaction.'

Visiting the successive clubs had proved her instructor right. She had observed with terrible fascination how dancing nude could be a thing of beauty and how at the same time it could reconcile all the contradictory streams flowing inside her own mind and body. Just as much as posing for artists could result in incomparable art, so could this. There was no difference. She had warmed to the idea.

'Have you ever knowingly been watched by strangers while having sex?' Giselle asked Debb.

The young woman blushed.

'Yes,' she whispered, as if being quieter made it more confidential.

'Tell me about it.'

There was a long pause as Debb gathered her thoughts. Giselle had been in this situation many times before. She was not tempted to fill in the conversational gap with her own words, or to move on to another topic to make things easier. She knew that if she waited long enough, Debb would talk.

'I was on vacation in the Caribbean with a couple of girlfriends. We'd met these two guys at a night disco, made out, fooled around a little and agreed to join them the following day to spend time on a different beach nearby. We were staying at an all-inclusive resort and had grown frustrated at being cooped up within its grounds and were in the mood to explore the island more. We walked for under an hour and came across a narrow beach shielded by outlying rocks. You could only reach it by first walking into the sea, waist high, and bypassing the rock formations. It looked idyllic, and although it was still quite early in the morning there were already dozens of folk scattered across the sands. All butt naked. We followed suit. It's such a great feeling to be nude on a beach surrounded by others, isn't it ... ?' Debb now smiled, as her recollection flowed freely. 'To cut a long story short, I quickly dozed off, all terribly hot and sweaty from the walk along the coastline. When I half woke up, drowsily opening my eyes, I saw that the beach was now even more crowded and one of the men from the previous evening, lying on his back just inches away from me had a huge boner, which one my girlfriends was stroking. At first, I was taken back but then noticed similar scenes were happening here and there further down the beach. And no one seemed to care. It all looked quite innocent. Then the guy with whom I'd made out at the disco began caressing my breasts. I hadn't slept with him the night before as I knew I was a bit drunk and always made it a rule never to mix sex and booze, you know. His touch was indolent, as if his attraction to me was merely casual, weakened by the heat of the sun beating down on us. I remember squirming, and ...'

Giselle watched the young woman's face with rapt attention, observing the currents of awakened lust course silently beneath the sharp lines of her cheekbones and her eyes cloud. She knew from experience what to seek out in her dancers. Whoever at the Network had sent Debb to New Orleans had chosen well.

' ... willing him to move his hands further down and finger me and damn the fact we were not alone, and surrounded by strangers. It all happened in a daze. He pulled me to my feet and a circle opened up around us as others made space and watched as I kneeled down on all fours and he fucked me in full public view. It felt like a dream. I was on fire, switched on, and the more witnesses and set of eyes fixed on me, the more excited I felt. Later, on the walk back to the resort, neither of my girlfriends would speak to me ...'

Giselle moved on to other questions but it was now all a bit of a formality. Debb would certainly be a useful addition to her team.

At Nr. 19, Giselle had perfected her dancing. Noting how every new variation affected the way customers in the sparse audience reacted. How it was not a matter of teasing and mischievous provocation that always triggered the best appreciation of her art. She watched the other dancers with whom she shared shifts, learning what not to do, what didn't suit her and what did. Soon, she was the one who was being sent the largest bouquets of flowers in the shared dressing room, or bottles of vintage champagne and cognac and envelopes with polite and elegantly scripted invitations to dinner or more, which she was taught to ignore. She wanted to be the best. Lived for her time on the small stage.

Until the day Rosalia arrived in New York. Her fame preceded her: Giselle knew she had once been a renowned classical ballet choreographer who had worked for both Sadler's Wells and the Scala in Milan. Rosalia was tiny. Too small to have been a proper ballet dancer, Giselle thought. She also remembered reading somewhere that Rosalia's public career had come to a halt in murky circumstances. Some sort of sex scandal involving politicians. It seemed she was now also employed by the Network.

'I'm told you are good,' the older, diminutive woman dressed all in black said. Her Italian accent was pronounced.

Giselle had mumbled some words of thanks, which the choreographer had blankly ignored.

'Tomorrow morning in the practice studio. Early,' Rosalia had ordered. 'Get a good night's sleep. You will need all your energy, young lady. We only have two weeks to perfect the routine you will be performing at the next Ball.'

Giselle had caught her breath. She would at last attend another Ball. Maybe see William again?

What she didn't know that night of a hundred dreams was that the dance Rosalia had in mind would involve her dancing with Pietr and end up with her being mounted by him. It was a dance of sex. Explicit, choreographed to the inch, excruciatingly precise and lustful. It would become the first of several routines she would perform with the dim but reliable Latvian, first at the Ball then on occasions at private parties around the globe, which the Network organized for a fee for those who could afford it. At first, Giselle was in two minds about this new, totally perverse direction in her dancing, but soon grew to enjoy it, if only for the pleasure it gave others (although seldom her male partners, who were more preoccupied by the assigned clockwork precision of their steps, movements and positions and the sustainability of their sexual performance) and the majesty she felt running through her when everything came together just right, dance and music, music and sex, bodies and epiphanies, mind and soul and cunt merging in perfect harmony, leaving her invisible audience silent and breathless; and Giselle panting but triumphant.

Debb coughed, and the past retreated. Giselle looked down at the young woman sitting on the cloth couch. Her gaze was quizzical, uncertain of the nature of Giselle's prolonged silence triggered by the memories.

'As I was saying,' Giselle said.

But her mind kept flitting back to the past, panning over her previous experiences without judgement. Just remembering.

On the occasions that she performed at parties arranged by the Network, or the far larger but irregular Balls that occurred only every year or two, Giselle rarely had a chance to mix with the guests. This was partly because the organisers preferred it that way, and Giselle grew to appreciate this as she became more experienced. She was taught that the performers should be like ghosts, retreating into the shadows after their time in the limelight. It helped them retain a sense of aloofness. Like stars, they could be gazed at and admired but not touched. If they mingled with the guests, they would lose their shine as well as their mystery.

She always thought of William as she danced. Did he attend the shows? He couldn't see the performances, she knew that, so could think of no reason why he would sit in the audience. He had never been a great fan of music for its own sake. More likely, he worked directly with the Network behind the scenes along with the other artists who put together the set, designed the ornate and often bizarre costumes and props to go along with the themes for the events that were planned over months or even years in advance. The whole affair was a massive enterprise and must have hundreds beavering away in the shadows to make it always look so entrancing and perfect. And lip-smackingly erotic.

Gossip of Walter reached her; the man that she knew had been, at least for a period of time, William's mentor. The other blind man who worked with the Ball and could apparently 'see' despite his loss of traditional sight. She had been told of bizarre spectacles that he orchestrated, dances that he choreographed where the performers were chained together or pierced, instances where he appeared to control their movements with a kind of magical wizardry like some sort of supernatural puppet master. Giselle was now accustomed to the workings of the Network, and she understood that virtually any illusion could be pulled off with cleverness and enough money. Yet the fact that one of the men behind all this was actually blind did not escape her, and she could not rid herself of the idea that Walter's methods and his apparent talents were not just a trick and that he had taught his skill of 'seeing' without sight to William wherever he now might be.

It became Giselle's habit to hurriedly fix her hair, make-up and any costume she was required to wear and creep to the stage wings early and take up a position somewhere so that she could scan the crowd. Then, until the moment of her cue to perform, when she had to rush to the stage, she would let her eyes cruise along each and every guest in the hope that she might see William. Each of these sessions was always accompanied by an acute, wrenching fear of what she would discover. Would he have retained his bear-like bulk? His shaggy mop of dark hair? Or would his disability have caused him to age young, to become frail? Would she even recognise him? The thought that she might not was almost too much for Giselle to bear. She was possessed by a kind of predetermined guilt, the worry that if she saw him now, she might not be able to love him. Not in the same way that she once had, when they were both young and beautiful together.

One time, she had been in the dressing room at Nr. 19 when one of the bar staff had burst in and called for her to answer the phone in the office. Giselle was so used to being nude that she hurried along in just the gold-coloured thong that she was wearing, without bothering to throw a robe over the top. She was barefoot, since the first thing she did once she finished her set was remove the shoes that she was wearing, if any. That night she had worn a pair of sky-high, glittering strappy sandals that had bit into her skin terribly, and it had been a blessed relief to slip them off when the curtain came down. Gladys, the then manager covering the evening shift, a buxom woman in her fifties who lacked the glamour of most of the women who worked for the Network, was sitting at a desk covered in papers and scraps of receipts and handed Giselle the receiver. The phone was sitting on the far end of the table and the cord stretched only a short way so that Giselle was forced to stand nearer to Gladys than she found comfortable in her nude state, with the older woman unashamedly staring at her breasts. Whether in lust, or envy, Giselle wasn't sure.

It was Rosalia. 'They want you for a solo piece,' she said, her thick Italian voice blurring the words so it took Giselle a moment to comprehend. 'The next Ball. You will be choreographing yourself.' It was a major honour.

'The theme?' Giselle whispered.

'The senses. Everything besides sight. It will be magnificent, unusual, different, all sound and touch and scent – plan something wonderful. You must, I know you will.'

Excitement was plain in Rosalia's voice, and the words erupted from her mouth without a pause between them.

'Yes,' Giselle said, 'yes I will,' and Gladys took the receiver from her hand and hung it back on the cradle before Giselle dropped it.

She ran back to the dressing room where now a couple of other dancers had completed their sets and were standing near the mirror, brushing or scraping glitter from their skin, removing nipple pasties and wiping make-up off with cotton-wool pads. Usually she would stay and chat. Tonight she shimmied into her jeans and jacket and stuffed her minimal stage belongings into her rucksack and headed straight for the subway home with barely a word to anyone.

Giselle found the work she did to be a strangely solitary activity. Though she opened herself to strangers in arguably the most intimate way possible by baring her skin and giving the illusion of even more, the wall that the stage created was impenetrable. Her role as entertainer made building any real relationship with members of the audience impossible, and few people outside of her field could ever understand the beauty and the fragility of what she did, and the temporal nature of performance. What it did to a person's soul to reveal themselves so utterly night after night for these brief spans of time that existed in the bubble of the dance and then faded away as the lights dimmed. It was hard work, tiring for both the body and the mind, and yet it nourished her as well as draining her, the constant tail-chasing of the creative soul, the ones who perpetually hungered for the very thing that ate them up. A nourishment that was both spiritual and physical, in the absence of more concrete forms of personal satisfaction.

She didn't tell her roommate, Joy, about the assignment. Didn't want to risk her jealousy, or her questions. It consumed Giselle, thereafter, planning her sequence for the Ball of the Senses. She knew that Walter, or William, or both of them, must be behind it. Perhaps now William had learned to see with his fingertips, to deduce the form of a body in a room by noticing the particular pull of air currents around a form, a waft of scent, or some other indefinable quality of an individual's presence that could not be explained. Perhaps William would finally be able to see her again. Touched by magic. Would he recognise her now? It had been a few years, and there was no denying the fact that she had changed. Ever since she had passed the milestone of twenty-five she had noticed a slight decline in the quality of her skin, and mourned the loss of her ability to eat whatever she liked without thinking about it. Even with a schedule as rigorous as hers was, she had to work now to keep her stomach as taut as it was, and her long legs as lean. There was no holding back the passage of time, even for someone still as relatively young and athletic as Giselle.

Then there was the concern of entertaining a whole

crowd of people by dancing in the dark. Could such a thing be done? Of course it could. The Network had made an art out of it, and she had never known them to fail, artistically. But whether or not their creative ventures would succeed was an easier argument to mull over when she was not the one on stage juggling success with failure in some outlandish performance that would mark her as either the one who managed to pull it off or the one who didn't. At least no one would see her fail, she mused, smiling internally at the irony of it.

By the time she had reached the stage that night she was in such a state of overdrive that she could hardly bring herself to focus on her surroundings at all. The Network had been true to their word. All light was banned, and instead performers and guests relied on an army of sight-impaired staff who knew every inch of the layout and seemed to possess some kind of extra sense that the sighted lacked and that enabled them to lead individuals through the crowd and to their destination. Giselle found, once she had settled in, that her hearing and sense of touch became keener so even without this assistance she could manage to find her way from the bar to the dressing room and stage. The pay-off for her temporarily heightened abilities was that every nerve ending was firing on red alert, her body coiled like a spring, each noise and smell threatened to overwhelm her. The only solitude that she could find was deep in her own core.

There was the knowledge that she knew her routine so well the steps might as well have been etched into her muscles. She knew she could perform it without any thought at all, and in this physical display she would find peace.

But she was unable to find William.

Under cover of darkness she had felt anonymous, and so free to ask any and all that she could if they knew of him. But nobody did. The best she could do was ask after a man who lost his sight in an accident, a painter, an artist. But they kept telling her, 'Walter?' Few even knew that name. The guests were oblivious to what had gone on behind the scenes to arrange the evening and the blind staff had been recruited through a Ball intermediary, just as she had been. The identities of those who worked with the Network on an ongoing basis were closely guarded.

The best that she could do was throw everything she had into her dance, and she did. After playing with the idea of synchronising every movement to a different sound, and so creating a type of orchestral dance, she had decided instead to have no sound to accompany her at all. Instead she requested the audience to remain utterly silent. Barely a breath could be heard besides her own. And she performed the most energetic routine she had ever choreographed, with the audience 'seeing' her steps only by virtue of the thud and slide of her feet, the noise of her exhalations, the whisper of her loose hair freely whipping round as she leapt. There was something else too. The overwhelming presence of her desire. The strength of Giselle's need to find William somewhere in the crowd, and her disappointment at having realised that this was an impossible task, virtually bled from her pores.

When finally she reached the end of her routine and stopped, still, the audience burst into rapturous applause. After the preceding quiet, the noise was deafening, but Giselle waited politely for it to end before dashing behind the curtain and fleeing for the relative comfort of the dressing room. Tears streamed down her face. In her hurry, she forgot to take extra care, though she knew the way, and she hit her foot, hard, against a free-standing mirror and cursed loudly. She cursed the dark, she cursed the Ball, she cursed whatever foolhardy, masochistic part of her still longed for a man whom she didn't even know any more. And had likely already forgotten her.

But no matter how much time passed, she was unable to forget him.

After Debb had departed and all the necessary paperwork had been properly completed – the Network was most meticulous when it came to administrative matters – Giselle took herself to the garden. Navigated through the tangle of bushes and flower beds to her favourite bench, white wood tinged by decay, scarred slats marked by the assault of passing seasons and the whims of the local weather.

The spring afternoon heat was mild with a strong touch of humidity that clung to the breeze breathing down on the city's streets from the nearby Mississippi river. The fragrances rose from the soil, like invisible coils, birthing at ground level, a cocktail of rotting leaves, magnolia blossom in full flower, Louisiana irises, bougainvillea and the invasive spread of wild hibiscus on the rampage.

She sat. Pulled a delicately embroidered silk fan from the deep pocket of the shapeless velvet dress she was wearing. She had been gifted it in Spain ten years or so ago. Don Gerard was a Catalan grandee, his white hair unkempt, his frame cadaverous, his posture stooped, the ghost of the man he had once been, but still handsome despite his years. He had assiduously courted her at the Segovia Ball and extravagantly complimented her on the daring performance she had been encouraged to devise; on previous occasions others had choreographed the proceedings and it had been a sign of her seniority and, she hoped, talent, that she had finally been allowed to offer her own twist on the lasciviousness of the post-midnight celebrations. His old world charm was fastidious but endearing. It was obvious he was dying. Gerard sought no pity, making it clear that it had been a life enjoyed to the full and that all that was now left were small epiphanies which he intended to celebrate without reservation, and one of those epiphanies was Giselle. In any ordinary circumstance he was too old to be a lover of Giselle's by far, but she could not find it within herself to reject him. Denying anyone because of age or some physical imperfection reminded her only of William, and how she had allowed him to unilaterally end their relationship in order to set her free. She would never allow that to happen again. Gerard was a good man, and she felt pity for him, and was happy to play the courtesan. He had taken her out to dinner to a restaurant perched precariously on a high cliff overlooking the greenest of seas and watched with a wry smile as she gorged herself on seafood and the finest of white wines, outrageously flirting with her as if he was still in the prime of youth and intent on seducing her with his wit and wealth. Giselle would have willingly offered herself to him, but realised that even sex was beyond him now, his frailty all too evident. He had surprisingly invited her back to his hotel suite, where she had danced for him and felt a tightness in her throat as he shed a discreet tear watching her in sinuous motion.

'I can't . . .' Gerard had said.

'I know.' Giselle could see the regret in his eyes, how his desire tore him apart and he raged against the failings of his body.

'Will you return tomorrow?' he had asked, after ordering a car for her. Giselle had agreed. She was in town for another few days although she doubted the old man would ever overcome his frailty, even with chemical stimulants, let alone by the following evening.

Don Gerard's suite was bathed in a dim red light and the table laden with oysters, succulent razor clams soaking in melted butter and garlic jus next to a towering platter of marine delicacies. In a corner of the room, a guitar player was softly picking out a mournful flamenco dirge. The musician's eyes were obscured by a tight black piece of cloth so he could see neither her nor anything else in the room.

'Dance for me again,' the old man had asked her, once they had finished their meal. He'd barely eaten. 'As you did at the Ball. Just for me.'

Giselle had undressed.

Don Gerard had sat motionless throughout, his eyes fixed on her as she had danced at her most sensual and enticing, conjugating her bare flesh to the sounds of the nearby guitar and its blinded player.

She danced for ages, as the guitar never tired of its melancholy lamentation. Finally, pearls of sweat dripping across the waterfall slope of her breasts, her skin a brilliant sheen, Giselle had to stop. As if sensing her lack of movement, the guitar player also stopped.

'That was still beautiful,' Don Gerard remarked, a note of yearning in his voice.

Giselle was catching her breath.

'One more thing . . .' he said.

'Yes?'

'Would you ... ?'

'Anything, Gerard ...'

He approached Giselle and took her by the hand and they stepped over to the now statue-like flamenco guitar player. Don Gerard whispered something in Spanish in the man's ears. The man set his instrument down.

Giselle understood.

She unbuttoned the musician's tight white silk shirt then loosened his cummerbund and freed his manhood. She knelt down. Don Gerard led the guitar player's hands down to her breasts.

'Make love to her,' he ordered gently.

All he wanted was to watch. Did he imagine it was him touching her, spreading her, fucking her and not this blind stranger who would never even know what she looked like and would be summarily dismissed from the room after he had taken his pleasure? As the younger man thrust energetically inside her, Giselle couldn't take her eyes off Gerard's face as he gazed down at the spectacle he had organised, his face an enigma beneath which a million thoughts and feelings ran wild. She wanted to read him but couldn't, distracted by the inevitable arousal spreading like a creeping vine inside her.

Was this the way William now pictured her, thought of her, locked inside his darkness? Did he remember what she felt like, the touch of her skin, the sound of her halting breath in the joy and agony of lovemaking?

The next morning, looking more frail than ever, Don Gerard had given her the fan as a parting gift. It was an exquisite piece of workmanship, the handle intricately carved out of ivory, the silk sensuous to the touch. Sometimes the smallest gifts are the best.

At the next Ball, a year later on another continent, she never came across Don Gerard. In her heart, she knew he must be dead.

Shortly after, she was given the opportunity to hang up on her actual dancing and offered the management of The Place, the Network's New Orleans club. It had felt like a sign of the gods, finally landing in the French Quarter, after all the dreams of her youth, as if the city was where her destiny was, the locale she was intended to live in, where her DNA had been knitted together. Within a few months here, she had fallen in love with the city with a vengeance.

A shift in the late afternoon breeze, the flow of humid air now racing towards Lake Pontchartrain and away from the muddy nearby river. Giselle fingered the fan, sensuously enjoying the smoothness of the ivory and confusedly deciphering the Rosetta stone of its delicate carvings with her fingertips.

The temperature dropped a few degrees in an instant, the sun disappearing behind a blanket of grey clouds. Maybe it would rain, often a torrent-like tropical shower of biblical proportions where the water would splash against walls, wash across the streets and pavements only to evaporate within minutes, a phenomenon she never tired of. Here nature had its own set of rules. Just like this garden she had slowly assembled in an amateur way within the walls of the club's grounds, her bare knowledge of flora restricted to the brief time spent working at the store in Paris on the Rue de Buci, random, wild, experimental, managing to get flowers and plants that should never theoretically coexist to live together in her garden, luxuriant here, Zen-like in its economy there, seeds acquired on her travels, from the flower market on the banks of the main Amsterdam canal, to cacti purchased as a last-minute impulse at Phoenix Airport in Arizona on the edge of an arid desert, to local varieties that had grown from cuttings stealthily stolen from behind Garden District walls and fences, the woods near Metairie, ghostly cemeteries or the gardens of suburban antebellum houses when she drove out to the bayous or the countryside.

It was a place where she now felt at peace.

She screened the new dancers, oversaw their work, organised their travel and assignments, sometimes helped choreograph new routines for either the club or the secret engagements the Network put her way. It had become an ordered life, an undemanding one where only the calls of the flesh sometimes interrupted the quiet flow of her days. She had recently entered her fifth decade and finally had attained a level of serenity she hadn't thought possible. All that was left were the regrets. Those, of course, never went away.

But anonymous sex helped. No strings, no names, passion within a veil of darkness. Feeding an appetite, no more, no less.

Yes, tonight, she would go out cruising. In yet another hopeless attempt at banishing the ghosts of yesterday. Of William. The more she went with other men, the more she realised how much he had meant to her. Her first teacher and real lover, the wild man who had sculpted her soul into what it was now.

She left the garden and walked to her room. What should she wear tonight?

Management came easily to Giselle. Her height and quiet, firm demeanour made her an imposing figure. She took advantage of that fact by dressing in formal, floor-length velvet gowns which marked her out in The Place as someone who was more than a dancer, or one of the bar staff, when she stalked through the rooms. There was the added benefit of the cut flattering her figure.

Giselle was determined that under her leadership The Place would thrive and become known as a rare gem among dancing clubs, both retaining its exclusivity and still turning a profit without resorting to cheap tricks or encouraging crowds of uncouth men who would ruin the atmosphere even if their dollar was as good as anyone else's. By keeping The Place upmarket, she could encourage a select clientele who would pay more for the privilege, and justify a hefty door fee, which would counter the relatively low takings at the bar.

But all of this rested on her ability to find the right girls.

Right now, she had a reasonable crew. Sofia wasn't bad, and there was Pinnie, short and voluptuous, unusual qualities in themselves in a dancer – most were tall and thin, these days, often to the detriment of their breasts. Pinnie was even more irregular than most, since instead of covering the large mole that sat in the centre of her forehead she cut her hair into a blunt fringe that swept above it, making a feature of this flaw.

'If you can't find the beauty in yourself, you shouldn't expect others to. That's what I think, anyway, madame,' Pinnie had said to her during the audition, when Giselle had queried her motivation, if any, for not growing the fringe just a little longer. Giselle had hired her on the spot.

Yes, the girls were good. But Giselle had felt for some time now that The Place needed something more. Someone more. A star. Previously, she had been the dancer who had that little bit extra the other girls lacked. An indefinable quality that, in Giselle's experience, went hand in hand with the experience of harsh times. Giselle needed someone who had been broken down, and risen up again, and made themselves new. She was looking for the diamond in the rough, and she couldn't advertise for that. So instead she made it part of her routine to go on the road looking for it, frequenting circus shows, strip bars and even beauty pageants in the belief that what she was seeking could be found anywhere. Giselle didn't know it, but she was becoming somewhat of a legend among performers, this woman in her floor-length velvet gown who would slide into a show and out again like a ghost, never accompanied by another.

California was last on her list of places to visit, and had it not been for the storm that kept her stranded at LAX she would never have stumbled upon the biker bar in an industrial part of town near the hotel her airline had put her up in until the weather cleared. For want of anything better to do, Giselle sat at one of the tall stools sipping a rare bourbon and wondering what had possessed her to even bother travelling all this way to check out the high-heeled, silicone-breasted and, for the most part, wholly unimaginative dancers of Beverly Hills and Hollywood. Girls trying to claw their way out of Orange County and doing so with fake nails as long as talons that lent a hint of desperation to their shimmies.

She wasn't even watching the stage when she heard the

Russian girl's soft drawl over the Tannoy. Giselle knew, without turning to see her, that she had found what she was looking for.

'My name is Luba,' said the recording.

There was a long pause, and then the strained sounds of a Debussy piece filtered through the sound system, all the more provocative for being totally out of place in a run-down boozer that was only half full and populated entirely by ageing surfers, lower-league businessmen on a downward spiral and motorcyclists.

Luba's turn on stage was truly hypnotic and seductive. Giselle had heard of this girl before. A dim memory began to resurface in her mind. Bianca, who ran one of the Network's clubs in New York, had once mentioned a woman who refused to dance to anything but classical music. 'Ethereal' was how Bianca had described her, blonde but not in the typically hometown American way nor in the vapid style the LA girls favoured.

She looked like a surfer girl when she appeared twenty minutes later, clad in denim cut-offs and an old T-shirt with an ancient rucksack slung over one shoulder. Giselle prepared her pitch. First rule of managing dancers: never show your own weakness. Don't let on too much about yourself. And so she purported to be fifth-generation Cajun, a proper New Orleans Madame. The French, broken-hearted former dancer was only allowed to surface when Giselle was alone.

Giselle straightened her shoulders and puffed out her chest.

'Hey,' she cried.

The girl turned.

'You're Luba,' Giselle continued, outwardly not emitting even a shadow of a smile. Inwardly though, she grinned.

The Russian girl was perfect.

Giselle was content. More so than she had felt in ages. She felt settled in New Orleans now. She'd even planted trees in her private garden in the grounds of The Place and could feel her own roots spreading along with them. She remembered William still, but the ache that her memories of him carried was more sweet these days than bitter.

Still, when the parcel arrived without a note attached, she immediately thought of him. It had been years since they had corresponded, but his was the only mail she ever received that came without a return address.

Eric, a beautiful Japanese man who looked barely out of his teens and was Giselle's latest addition to the bar staff, had been polishing glasses and readying The Place for the first show of the evening when a courier delivered the parcel. Giselle thanked him politely when he brought it in to her, and made a mental note to encourage him to bare the tattoos that he usually kept covered at work, a stylised dragon the colour of a peacock that spanned the length of his left arm from his wrist to his shoulder.

She was in her office, attending to the staff roster and monthly accounts. Initially she had found the paperwork associated with running a business a chore, but over time she had developed an appreciation for the order that she was able to apply to her working life, and the signs of success that were evident in the ever growing profit margin on her balance sheet.

Giselle could feel Luba's eyes on her, watching her carefully as she weighed the parcel in her hand and took note of the typed address label that did not give any clues to the sender's identity. The Russian girl had been a major part of Giselle's success at The Place. It had been a quiet growth, since Giselle believed shouting about such things to be vulgar. But there was no denying that her takings had nearly doubled since Luba had appeared with her wraith-like set, Debussy overture, and the pre-recorded intro that she insisted on playing every night to announce her arrival on stage. She was a class act, not that Giselle would ever let on to her, in case Luba's ego got too big for her high-heeled shoes and her awareness of her own popularity upset the other dancers. The business of managing people was a tenuous one and required the smooth touch of an expert politician to keep conversation civil backstage.

She had a soft spot for the tall Eastern European girl

though, and so had allowed Luba's habit of quietly entering her office to sit and drink her iced tea in peace, away from the chatter of the other dancers in the dressing room. They shared a bond of unspoken recognition, the older and the younger woman who were separated by two decades but joined in matters of the heart.

Giselle slit the envelope with her letter opener, withdrew the package inside and then set it aside on a pile of wage slips that were waiting to be filed. She carried on with her work as if she hadn't given a second thought to what might be inside the box or who had sent it to her. The contents were heavy. Whatever it was, it was closer to a paperweight than an item of clothing or jewellery. As she totted up the previous week's miscellaneous expenses and set the receipts aside her mind ran on, seeking some remembrance of an internet order she might have placed and forgotten about or a recent conquest who seemed the sort to track her down and send her a gift.

But all she could think of was William and his unmarked post.

She asked Pinnie to stay later and lock up the principal building which housed the actual club for the night, claiming a headache. The first time that she had left work early since she had begun running The Place, and her absence did not go unnoticed, although her staff were all too polite and well looked after to comment on it.

Emerging in the grounds, she took the narrow path that slithered between the wild array of plants and led to her quarters. She looked up.

It was a full moon, and the streets of New Orleans were alive with the promise of hedonism. Giselle wondered what unknown sins were taking place all around her, in alleyways that she hurried past, behind the closed doors of bars and houses, and down by the banks of the Mississippi river that still gleamed in the half light of a bright night. She loved this city with its bloom of magic and its lusty soul that stirred beneath an imperfect exterior, gutters that ran with beer and rubbish and air that smelled of fish and sweat and spices.

She often took a walk to clear her head before and after her shift. Holding the heavy carton, she knew she would not do so today.

Once in her kitchen, she switched on the kettle and opened the wide French doors that led to the garden to let the still warm night air wash over her. She left the lights off and undressed, slipping out of her knickers and tossing them into the wash basket, removing her bra and draping it from the bedroom doorknob and carefully brushing her velvet gown and setting it on a hanger in the closet. Those small chores finished, she padded, still nude, into the kitchen and made a hot cocoa, picked the box up from the side table and carried both outside to the garden where she sat down, resting her naked backside on the smooth wooden bench seat that faced her flower pots. It was nearly too dark to see as she flipped one end of the box open and carefully slid the contents onto the palm of one hand.

The object was heavy and cool, even through the thin layer of tissue paper wrapped around it. She peeled the tissue away, and ran her fingertips slowly along the surface of the gift. It was some type of stone, she guessed, from the weight of it, but polished so perfectly smooth that it felt a little like glass. The stone piece was cylindrical and ran the length of her hand, from her wrist to the tip of her middle finger. It was slightly wider than the gap left when she touched the pad of her forefinger to her thumb. The end of it curved up slightly and flattened into a nub.

Someone had sent her a dildo. The thought of an anonymous donor sending her sex objects through the mail tapped immediately into the river of lust that ran deep through Giselle's core. It was truly exquisite, the dark green material at first cold to the touch but as soon as her fingers roamed across its smoother than smooth surface, it appeared to warm up, heat transferring from body to stone in an instant. The workmanship involved was delicate and subtle. More of an objet d'art designed to sit on a shelf in a gallery than a sex aid. Her nipples hardened, caressed by the gentle gusts of wind that periodically swept over her. She spread her knees apart, lifted her heels so that her feet balanced on the points of her toes and she hunched her back, thrusting her pelvis higher into the air. Wetness began to seep inside her cunt, her sex lips becoming slick with arousal. The flat end of the stone dildo slid between her folds easily, but Giselle was in no hurry to quicken her pleasure. She wanted it to last. She drew the smooth cock across her pussy over and over again, faster and faster until she was dripping and longing to feel the stone's firm touch inside her, filling her hole. Finally, she slipped it inside her entrance and thrust, hard, and almost cried out, so wonderful was the sensation. The dildo fitted her perfectly, as if it had been manufactured to suit her precise dimensions and taste. The nub of it pressed against her G-spot when she applied even the slightest pressure.

Giselle came out there in her garden, and shuddered as the tides of her orgasm rolled through her. She thought of William, and imagined that it was his cock inside her, instead of the polished edge of stone.

She wished that she could know for sure if it was him who had sent her the sculpture, and find some way to thank him for pleasuring her despite the years and the distance that separated them.

Giselle dreamed of him that night, and woke feeling empty, and lost.

8

Dancing in Another Book

Time never stands still.

For Giselle, it felt all too often as if it just repeated itself, waking each morning as she did to the familiar sounds of the New Orleans birds twittering as they flitted between the branches of trees, seagulls swooping along the nearby river diving below the arches of the bridge, breaking the heavy silence of the night. The passing of years orchestrated by the reassuring lullaby of birdsong and the slow inexorable growth of flora beyond her window.

Or, when she had not slept in her own bed, trapped against the flesh of yet another stranger, heavy with regret, the lust ebbing slowly away, the weight of reality waking her mind, every face a blur, every new male body in close contact with hers a deliberate instrument of pleasure, every breath another page turned, another day punctuating the book of her life.

How had the years swept by so slowly? Or was it too fast? Her mind could sometimes not even properly grasp the concept of time. It was only when she faced the mirror naked in the small hours of the morning, her mind tired, her spirit low, that she could note its passage in the new lines imprinted on her body, the almost imperceptible loosening of the skin, the lack of sheen in her hair, the dullness in the depth of her eyes, the lack of sharpness in the curve of her breast or hip. She wondered if, had she remained against all odds with William in that unalterable past that still shone like a diamond, the attacks of time would have been lessened, if still being in the orbit of his love would have muted the ravages of days?

She had never been one to keep a diary. Had no need for pen and paper to list the men she had known since William, the minor but transient epiphanies they afforded her, the dancers she had trained and sent on their way, the exquisite and complicated partitions she had constructed of skin, music and pornographic movement for the performances at the club, on highly paid outside assignments for her employers and, yearly, for the Ball.

Once, she had been one of the dancers, and now she was the mistress of ceremonies, basking in the spectacle of the beauty of lust unfurling as her lithe and fiery protégés danced and fucked, their public but nonetheless intimate ceremonies of the flesh a glorious celebration which still pulled on Giselle's heart and cunt strings, evoking memories of her own past and the intensity of physical love.

Inspiring her own night encounters.

On the upper floor of the redbrick Lower Pontalba Building fronting Rue St Ann and Jackson Square, pinned against the wall, every thrust by the Spanish man from Gijon piercing her deeply while his hand circled her throat and she struggled for breath, her vision clouding and then, out of nowhere, the painful release, the nuclear impact of her orgasm and a scream of release that resonated all the way to the nearby Mississippi shore.

On a Carnival night, in a dark alley in the Vieux Carré, sounds of drunken laughter echoing through her head, bent over, necklaces of colourful beads hanging from her neck, swaying under the impact of low hanging balls smacking against her bared rump, hands cruelly twisting her hard nipples and others smacking her arse cheeks to the accompaniment of whispered obscenities, aware that several men were taking turns with her and relishing the excess.

Tied to a tree at night in the darkness of Audubon Park, her mouth gagged by her own silk scarf, a stranger's tongue insistently delving between her thighs, licking, biting, teasing, digging, her own wave surge rising inside, out of control and silently begging the man to fuck her. But he didn't, satisfied at the outcome of their tryst to just come across her face, dripping belatedly against the front of her thin cream-coloured cotton dress, a stain she later would be unable to get rid of.

Hotels.

Balconies.

Streets.

In Algiers, by the river bank, a couple visiting from New York's Upper East Side sharing her. He, inside her, thick, brutal, vigorous; she, with lips of velvet soothing her senses and caressing her breasts, fingers threaded like a comb between the silk of her long hair.

In a minimalist backroom of a run-down Garden District house, the Russian twins with vague Mafia connections, all three of them high on poppers, surfing a wave of temporary insanity.

Straddling a long-haired teenager less than half her age on the steel balcony of a two-storeyed bed and breakfast joint down the unfashionable end of Royal Street, impaling herself on his youthful hardness. He'd even bought her flowers and taken her out to an expensive meal at Tujague's first in his unnecessary attempt at seduction.

In the back seats of a street car on the St Charles Avenue Line, being fingered by a football player from Cedar Rapids on the eve of the Sugar Bowl.

Locals. Visitors. Tourists. Expatriates. Drifters. Vagrants

even, unwashed and wild. Men. Women. Giselle had willingly sampled the whole menu that the Crescent City could offer.

But gazing at the pale, bare skin that faced her in the mirror today, it was all a blur. Felt pointless.

Giselle sighed.

There was a knock at the door.

'Yes?'

'It's me, Luba . . .'

'Come in, the door is not locked.'

Giselle pulled a kimono wrap from the chair facing the dresser. She wasn't shy about being seen naked, but then Luba was so inch-perfect and statuesque herself that she preferred to avoid the comparison.

The tall Russian dancer walked into the room. She was wearing a pair of denim hotpants that skilfully showed off her bronzed, unending legs and a body-hugging Fruit of the Loom white T-shirt. She was, as ever, braless, her prominent nipples visible pressing against the stretch of the fabric. Her gold sandals a bright spot of colour in the diffuse light of early morning.

'Welcome back,' Giselle greeted her, tightening the kimono's broad belt.

Luba had been away at a private show in Seattle. It had been her initial gig outside New Orleans since she had joined Giselle's team. It was also the first time she had been partnered in a public performance outside of rehearsals; in New Orleans, for obvious reasons, the club's fare was restricted to nude dancing and there was never any actual sex involved.

She had been paired with a male Spanish dancer with whom she had been trained to perform a carefully choreographed tango which was to artistically culminate with actual sex. Giselle had initially been hesitant to send her to Oregon, unsure as to whether Luba was in fact ready for this inevitable next step in her career with the organisation, despite the fact that it was Luba who had broached the subject of her dissatisfaction with just dancing at The Place and her desire to spread her wings and do something more. She was not only Giselle's favourite and most accomplished dancer but also something of a novice and still nervous about this rather particular aspect of the job. Even though skilful in the sexual arts, Luba was also still under the spell of an unsuccessful love affair she refused to discuss with Giselle, a sign if any of inner vulnerability. Giselle sympathised: she was also one who retreated behind the walls of silence to protect her privacy and secrets.

'You did great in Portland,' Giselle said. She'd had a highly favourable report on Luba's performance.

Luba's eyes widened and an enigmatic smile moved across her lips.

'I'm glad the clients appreciated us.'

'They did. I hope you felt comfortable.'

Luba imperceptibly nodded in response, an indication she was not yet fully reconciled to this specific side of her job. There were some girls, Giselle knew, who though they expressed themselves without inhibitions when they danced and performed at private functions also carried an underlying stream of sadness as they did so. Luba was one of these, and Giselle knew it had been her own case too. The body excelled but the heart, the mind, somehow retreated elsewhere. It made for a form of poignancy which the majority of the customers perceived and appreciated, mistakenly interpreting it as unattainability, a lost puppy syndrome which, combined with the overt sexuality of the act, made them desire the object of their gaze so much more than if she was openly provocative and available.

They took tea together and then walked over to the club's principal building and the large upstairs converted attic which served as a rehearsal room, all polished sprung wooden floors, a three-sided hall of mirrors and bars, sound-proofed and brightly lit.

Giselle opened the windows wide, allowing all the morning scents of New Orleans to rush in and fragrantly colour the room. It was coming to the end of September and soon it would be too cold to air the room in such a manner. Dark, heady scents of sweet, half-rotten flowers and plants, spices rising from the narrow streets of the Quarter's hundreds of restaurants where crawfish boiled in vats, gumbos simmered in pots alongside arrays of indulgent sauces, all the diverse notes blending like an invisible jigsaw, invading the room, banishing its sterility and bringing it to life.

Other dancers joined them.

The tango routine that Luba and her male partner had performed was one of Giselle's earliest pieces of choreography, and the tall Russian dancer was not the first of her motley troupe she had drilled in its fluid complexities. It had been inspired in her by one of her first individual visits to the Ball, just a few years after her parting with William. It had been an unusual Ball, which had taken place in an old palazzo in the hills of Mondello, near Palermo in Sicily. In contrast to other Balls she had attended or heard of, it had been a bare Ball: empty, unfurnished rooms, a total lack of decorations and lighting, blank terracotta walls with plaster crumbling, unkempt gardens with sparse vegetation growing in irregular patches and just an open night full of naked stars. Similarly, the guests had not been allowed costumes, no Harlequin tunics or crinoline dresses or extravagant confections in hundreds of diverse fabrics, or body paint, glitter or sparkling jewellery. The austere, enforced nudity had at first appeared something of a distraction from the tense, sexual atmosphere surrounding the participants but, soon enough, the mounting accumulation of barer than bare skin and unveiled bodies in all their natural splendour and imperfections had witnessed a steady rise of desire as hands wandered over foreign skin, alien parts, fingers, the geometrical alignment of fine muscles, the softness of liberated curves and a slow dance had begun in part darkness, and mouths, tongues had met, a delicate balance of lust and stillness. The music playing from invisible speakers hidden among the high cornices bordering the ballroom's patchy ceiling had been classical and all of a sudden, from a part of her memory Giselle had long buried, she had recognised the strains of a melody from Tchaikovsky's *Swan Lake*, a repertoire piece she had always had difficulties mastering back at the London academy in her youth. The music and the way the stylised decor highlighted the persistent strands of lust that hung in the air at the Ball had stuck in Giselle's mind ever since. She was now intent on devising a new dance that could eventually be performed by Luba, either on an occasion of limited bookings or even, one coming day, at the Ball. She was such a graceful dancer and her solo act against the phosphorescent strains of Debussy's *La Mer* was a thing of beauty, and she truly deserved a new showpiece, Giselle felt.

Part shards of memory, part shapeless filaments of dreams on sleepless nights, the Tchaikovsky ballet dominated her thoughts and, for the past few days, while Luba had been away on assignment, she had been sketching ideas, steps, movements, a whirlwind of shimmering action rising from her once blank page of notes and patterns into some form of reality.

In her mind, Luba would be the white swan, pirouetting with abandon and grace, drawn into the orbit of the black swan. She had no male partner available in New Orleans – the men her dancers were partnered with for their specific activities were under contract with the Network and flown in for training and rehearsal only when the dance was fully devised – so another of the club's performers would, for now, have to stand in. Giselle's gaze was drawn to the fierce stone toy she had been keeping on her desk and wondered again who had sent it to her and the reasons behind the anonymity. Observing its girth and hardness made her throat go dry.

The climax of the dance would culminate with the white swan succumbing to the manly thrusts of the black swan, once its gender had been spectacularly revealed. Luba was tall, and she would need whoever partnered her in the dance of death to also be significantly taller.

'Luba,' she called out. 'Can you find yourself a white leotard? I have something in mind I'd like to try out.'

She picked out Maria, one of her more experienced dancers, an equally Amazonian performer with a definite streak of mischief offstage, and suggested she should wear black and dismissed the two other dancers present. The three of them began rehearsing the steps and movements after the orchestral music had been switched on, all glissandos and pizzicati and swooping, melancholy melodies. It would take months to perfect, Giselle knew, lots of time still to think of the costumes, as she positioned Luba at one end of the room in a prone position and ordered Maria to circle her with intent, in an attempt to bring the visions she carried to life. Turning a mental image into the stuff of life.

First the young women would have to master the proposed dance's technical aspects; the passion and the sex would come later, often of their own accord.

Within an hour they were all exhausted and a pause was agreed. But Giselle could perceive a glimmer of what could be achieved. Immediate matters for tonight's more mundane performances at the club had to be addressed. An hour a day was allocated for the project, to which the two dancers agreed.

It would take time, Giselle was aware, but it would be a hundred times worthwhile.

The second sculptured object that arrived for Giselle was wooden, and carved into the shape of a bear, though of course proportionally longer, cylindrical and designed to fit inside her. It was slightly larger than the first, and took Giselle's breath away when she fucked herself with it, this time in the dark shelter of Pirate's Alley at night by the Faulkner House where she hid, waiting for a brief rainstorm to pass after her day at The Place where the package had been delivered earlier.

Once home she had flicked her bedroom lamp on and studied it, marvelling at the shape that both stimulated her so cleverly and also carried so much detail and life. The line of the bear's shoulders suggested tension and a simmering violence, as did the cut of its head and the deep grooves that outlined the face of the creature that had only a short while ago brought her to orgasm as she stood with her legs apart, her skirts hitched up and her back pressed against a stone wall, desperately trying to close her nostrils against the inevitable smell of piss that lingered on the path at her feet.

She'd found the idea of penetrating herself with the likeness of an animal strange at first, but that moment quickly passed. Now she thought not of the beast, but of the qualities that the sculptures possessed. The other that she had, which she often used, perversely, as a paperweight in her office, carried the features of a bird. She hadn't noticed, the night that she'd buried it inside her cunt in the relative privacy of her garden, but the next day, she'd kept gazing at it, the deep multi-shaded green jade with the flattened beak at the end and the almond-shaped bird's eyes so neatly etched into the head.

The one reminded her of freedom, and the other of the sort of tearing lust that she so longed for and rarely experienced. She'd tried to find that sensation of being near or torn apart by a lover in the casual encounters she sought in the darkness of the French Quarter as she roamed the city streets and bars looking for someone to satisfy her. Eventually, she'd realised that what she wanted could be provided only by someone she loved, and who loved her. The arms of strangers could be a poisoned chalice, sometimes.

She slept fitfully.

She had not suffered through dreams like these since she had first met William, and he had asked her to be his Joan, and from then until the day he chained her she had been possessed by night-time visions of her torture. Now, she was accosted in turns by images equally as vivid yet different in their subject. In some, she was penetrated by beasts, or turned into a beast herself, like some kind of supernatural monster, roaming the Quarter on all fours in search of sex, a voodoo-infused ectoplasm or creature, snarling until she was satisfied. Never was Giselle satisfied. In others she dreamed of William sculpting her, blindly.

In her dreams she posed for him in an enormous wooden-floored room that was empty apart from the two of them and a white sheet that she held over her body until he wrenched it away.

'But you can't see me anyway,' her dream-self whispered to him.

'Yes I can,' he replied.

And then she watched him as his hands flew over a piece of marble, working with it as if it were clay, and from the inanimate lump of rock her likeness appeared with the speed of a sunrise appearing in a darkened sky, one moment just a flicker of light, the next moment dawn. When she touched her doppelganger, the marble was warm, and soft, like her own flesh, and carried all of her flaws as well as her perfections. Her long, slim neck. Her full breasts, even heavier now than they once were. Her still firm thighs. The rounded curve of her belly. The straight edge of her cheekbones, the upward slant of her eyes. The particular press of her lips when she smiled at a joke that had significance only between her and William.

When she woke, inevitably her cheeks were wet with tears.

Oh, how she missed him.

It was that strange stretch of days between Christmas and New Year's Eve, stuck between celebratory nights, a semi-permanent buzz in the air, the comedown of excess balancing with the anticipation of more revels.

You couldn't just wander off the streets and attend The Place; it wasn't open to the general public. One had to not only be aware of its existence and whereabouts but also have a form of introduction. To many, its existence was something of a legend.

Folk who had attended Balls or had connections with the Network might mention The Place to others in confidence, and the trusty concierges of the high-class hotels of Canal Street and the Quarter served to vet the curious and, somehow, the system worked. There was only seating for fifty guests at most in the small main room which served as the club's focal point.

Most of the dancers had returned home for a vacation and Giselle had been unsure whether to open the club over the period. Only Luba and one other dancer were available, but a group of wealthy industrialists here in advance of the big January ball game at the Superdome had booked ahead, although right now they appeared more intent on drinking than watching a show.

Giselle was in her office when the front door chime sounded. She hadn't been expecting anyone else. Her contact at the Sonesta had recommended the club to a tourist couple who fitted the right criteria, she knew, but they had not rung ahead to book. This must be them. Her shaven-headed and tuxedoed security operative had gone to fetch the newcomers. They were English, it appeared. He was serving them champagne and asked for her instructions. She could have asked him to take them straight to a table by the diminutive stage, but felt curious. She slipped on her white carnival mask. It was a ritual. Tonight she was wearing a vintage red velvet gown she had found years before in a now long gone store by the French Market. She had, for the first time, dyed her hair this morning to eliminate the invasion of grey and had a kick in her step. A desire to avoid artificial enhancements to her looks had been easier to stick to when she was young enough not to require any.

She walked down to the salon.

'I'm your hostess for the evening. This way, please,' she introduced herself, and led the couple upstairs.

There was something out of the ordinary about them.

There was a dark, febrile intensity about the casually attired man. He was in his late thirties, Giselle guessed, dressed in a black, waist-length thin leather jacket, a pale blue button-down shirt and designer jeans, with well-polished brogues. His eyes were dark brown, as was his slightly unruly hair. He wore glasses. His English was accentless, unburdened of any regional lilt, the sort of voice she remembered from her time in London, a radio voice with a sensual warmth to it. He radiated a distinctive form of danger, Giselle reckoned. But he only had eyes for the woman who accompanied him.

She was also remarkable. A little younger than the man,

of medium height and average curves, with towering Medusa-like auburn curls falling all the way to her shoulders. She had a look of strong determination, a living fire burning deep in the pit of her eyes, a look Giselle knew all too well. The one that stamped her as one of the possessed, the type of person who lived a double life, outwardly quite normal and even conservative but inside a cauldron of desires, ambitions and cravings. Once, Giselle had been the same. She still was the same now, but her fire was better concealed under the mantle of middle age and she had learned how to tend to it herself, without the uncontrolled urges that had filled her when she was in her twenties and led her too frequently into the beds of the wrong men.

The red-haired woman wore a thin cream-coloured linen two-piece outfit and thin-soled golden sandals. The jacket buttoned tight across her thin waist, cinching her modest opulence tight, and the matching skirt fell to just above her knees. Apart from a prominent scarlet line of lipstick, she wore no other make-up. As soon as they entered the club's main room, the eyes of the young woman darted frantically to and fro with curiosity and appetite, rapidly imbibing the sights and atmosphere, her hand clutching her male companion's. There was a feverish appetite to her.

Giselle seated the couple just in time before the lights dimmed and the strains of the Debussy music began, the accompaniment to Luba's preferred dance.

'I am Luba.' The whispered, sultry Russian voice came over the speakers, foreshadowing the theatrical tone of the performance.

Throughout the Russian dancer's number, Giselle's eyes were drawn to the table where the English couple was sitting, fascinated by the posture, reactions and body language of the young red-haired woman sitting there, weaving a fantasy about her, what she did, sought in life, had previously been involved with. Giselle guessed there were many stories to tell about her, felt a sense of familiarity connecting her with this uncommonly beautiful stranger.

The shine and pout of her coloured lips in which the angled offstage light barely reflected, the tremor in her shoulder, the way she would at times dig her nails into the thigh of her man, the nervousness with which she watched Luba's studied and dramatic disrobing and the way it emerged from the impressionistic background of the classical music, as if she identified with the flamboyant performer, even wanted to be on stage with her.

Her name was Summer, she knew. The security guard who had let them in had overheard the man talking to her.

Giselle's attention was torn yet again between the compulsive vision of Luba's teasing dance of sex and the invisible tempest running behind the young, watching woman's features as she communed so intimately with the spectacle. Her male companion was impassive, eyes firmly on Luba, the bare hint of a smile crossing his lips.

'Show your appreciation for Luba ...' The spectacle came to a lingering end and the lighting changed. Giselle observed Summer inhaling deeply, as if only now remembering she was allowed to breathe.

Giselle made her way to the table to ask the couple if they had enjoyed the show. Ravel's *Bolero* played on the sound system.

They had. 'Greatly,' said Summer, sitting there still transfixed. Without glancing at his partner, the man enquired whether the club accepted private hires. The other customers were beginning to drift away. There was an air of quiet authority and determination about the Englishman.

Giselle thought. They had a dinner planned for New Year's Eve, just her and the staff, an old tradition. He appeared disappointed. Following the dinner, she then suggested to the man. Maybe around one in the morning? She assumed he would ask for Luba's participation, but he didn't. He intended for Summer to dance instead. For him or any selected audience Giselle might care to invite. Next to him, his girlfriend evaded Giselle's gaze, squirming in place as he outlined his plan, her pale features ever so slightly blushing as he hinted at her possibly more than just dancing, the acceptance in her eyes a blend of nervous expectation and challenge.

The negotiation was brief and to the point. The club would provide an appropriate costume for Summer and the music for the occasion was chosen: Vivaldi's *Four Seasons*. He also had one further and rather particular stipulation, which he was careful to communicate to Giselle while Summer had moved away to use the washroom. Giselle was taken back, but excited by the man's imagination. The professorial-like Englishman handed over his credit card to secure the booking and the couple soon left, hand in hand. It was difficult to know who was leading whom.

Giselle's sleep, that night, was full of troublesome dreams.

In her visions she was the one dancing under the fierce heat of the spotlight to a surrealist audience of dark-sunglasses-adorned long-beaked birds, wearing just ornaments cruelly attached to her nipples and labia, steel stigmata generating a maelstrom of welcoming, life-affirming if localised pain, circling around the polished floor like a spinning wheel until her mind was drowning in a sea of desire. Followed by darkness and then finding herself looking down on the scene from a terrible vertigo-inducing height and realising she was no longer the dancer, but had been replaced on the proscenium by the red-haired woman who would be returning to the club in the small hours of tomorrow morning. At which point Giselle woke up with a start. It was too early to rise, the scents of the French Quarter streamed along the ceiling of her bedroom, the window open on to the wild garden, echoes of paddleboat calls fading in the distance. She recalled the man's final demand.

In the dark she tiptoed to her dresser and, almost blind, once again picked up the sculpted objects she had been sent, feeling their intoxicating smoothness under the pads of her fingers, drawing paths along their surface, her mind attempting to decipher their significance, as if the contact she was making now would miraculously project her thoughts, her words towards the mysterious person who had sent them. She had received half a dozen packages by courier now. Carved objects, birds, beasts, horns, cocks, toys, talismans. Shaped to within an atom of perfection. For her. Always in darkness, she regularly used them for the purpose they had been created for.

Spreading her thighs wide open.

Inserting the jade bird.

Carefully relaxing her sphincter and completing the double penetration. Smooth, warm wood of the carved bear stretching her hole. Filling her.

Now the scents of the night were blending ineffably with the strong, musky notes of her juices. She felt herself becoming drowsy. Giselle lay down, still holding the two phallic objects tight between her openings. And, at peace, fell asleep.

That night, the couple returned.

Summer was visibly nervous but also a touch defiant and was reluctant to wear the revealing dress Giselle had laid on. Maybe she felt there was something more natural in dancing naked than having to humiliate herself by stripping in front of what was to be a very select audience. But her benefactor had been clear about his intentions and what he had in mind and instead Giselle, as a form of exquisite punishment he had suggested to her, attached a pair of fierce-looking clip-on nipple rings, with rust-red jewels dangling heavily from their extremity, to her slight but high breasts and matching attachments onto each of her outer labia that bit into her flesh. Summer winced. She completed the sweet torture by inserting a glass butt plug into the young woman and led her past the velvet curtains, through the club to the actual stage where she would have to dance. Throughout in the dimly lit changing room, unsettling the young woman even more, the whole scene had been observed by Luba, who was lounging in a bird cage suspended from the ceiling, clad all in white and masked, adding a disturbing sense of the bizarre to the preparations.

Summer arrived on the stage in utter darkness. When Giselle switched the lights on, she knew the younger woman would initially be blinded and dazed.

The music began and Summer stood fixed to the spot, visibly torn between the humiliation of staying still, or moving and exposing her utter nudity and vulnerability even further by sketching the initial movements of a slow dance. Giselle leaned at the bar counter at the far end of the intimate salon and watched her, remembering in a rush of images swirling across her mind the first time she had similarly danced naked for others and without the comfort blanket of a rehearsal space or her own room where somehow it had felt more natural. Or how, in her early modelling days, she had posed in the altogether, the highways of desire rumbling inside her, hesitantly attempting to reach a precarious balance between the nascent rumble of her sexuality and the undeniable craving to provoke, be liked, an equilibrium that shifted under her feet like sand.

She shuddered.

Recalled the lines she had mapped across her face the other morning, the evanescent wrinkles at the corner of her mouth, the grey hairs she had since concealed. Wishing she was still young and desirable enough to be doing what Summer would be doing now, to offer herself so completely just because a man had so ordered.

Sleeping with a pleasant stranger, anonymously fucking in darkness with no strings attached, just ticking another notch on her sexual book of days, were all actions that any woman could indulge in. A wave of intense sadness washed over Giselle as she wondered whether she would ever again have the will, the power, the occasion to offer herself so openly the way she used to and as Summer was doing now. What had she become but a pimp, gratifying the desires of others, ruling the roost over her feisty, assorted troupe of sensual dancers and not even finding any pleasure in their activities aside from the satisfaction of a job well done? A distant mistress of ceremonies. How had she become that way? Lost her fire? Deadened her soul?

Summer finally began to dance.

At first she was clumsy, then rapidly drifted into the folds of the melody, her bare skin lighting up in the spotlight, a sheen of sweat from nervousness and her exertions highlighting her nudity. She visibly had no training in dance but there was something organic about the way she understood the music, how even the mad curls of her red hair moved to the inner life of the raging violins, like tree leaves in a heavy breeze.

By the time the brief dance ended, Summer had transformed. She had become more flexible, daring, wanton, exposing her hidden appetites, her inner lust in ways that Giselle recognised, the vocabulary of sex expressing itself with full abandon. Giselle looked in the sparse audience for the man who had brought Summer here and organised the exhibition and imagined how he would fuck her later in their hotel room, tame her, ravage her in the sweetest of ways, cementing yet another unforgettable bond between the visiting couple.

Soon enough, the performance was over and the couple were gone, and it fell to Giselle to switch off the lights, tidy the place up and close the club following the private hire. The security guard had the evening off and Luba was sleeping in a room in the upper wing.

Who were they?

The man, whom Summer had on a single occasion referred to as Dominik, was English but the young red-haired woman was not, although Giselle was unable to recognize her accent. English-speaking at any rate.

She guessed what they were doing now, in some hotel room close by, extending the craziness of this night to further levels of lust. Summer had departed still wearing the ornaments – he had insisted she do so (and had paid for them); the cold steel clip-ons now bruising her delicate flesh, imprinting marks deep down through the layers of her skin which he would likely keep on teasing, twisting, biting, playing with, extracting every degree of pain and pleasure from her in his studied assaults.

Giselle sighed. How long had it been since a man had managed to make her moan, let alone make her cry?

And tomorrow, no doubt, they would leave New Orleans. Never to be seen or heard of again.

Her throat felt tight, a powerful sense of longing invading her thoughts. What would happen to the couple? Summer and Dominik? Would she ever know anything about the rest of their life? Before and after their New Orleans intermezzo?

Or would they be faces passing in the night, like characters in a book whose ending you were not allowed to read, only to haunt her dreams and sleepless nights? Like so many others: William, Beth, Olen, Flick ... She had turned the page on them, left them lost inside their respective novels, adrift.

She unzipped the heavy velvet gown and stepped out of it. Lay on her bed, and finally the tears came, abundant, fertile, warm. She cried for those she had lost along the way.

When she woke, Giselle had reached a decision. She would take a leave of absence from The Place. Pinnie was capable enough of managing without her, and ambitious enough to jump at the chance. The curvaceous brunette with the blunt fringe, heavy breasts and large nipples was canny, but honest with it, and would not think twice before taking advantage of a financially prudent opportunity. She would call an agent and rent out her private quarters. There was always a demand from tourists looking for something more homely than a hotel.

She pushed the covers aside, showered and brewed an espresso, which she sipped as she paced through the house nude, collecting up the things that she would need for her trip. Her case was the same one that she'd had for years.

William had bought it for her when they planned their inaugural holiday abroad together, that weekend beyond Long Island that now felt like a lifetime ago. It was designed for carry-on, and only had space for a few changes of clothes and one or two pairs of shoes, but that was enough for Giselle. She'd never got over the habit of packing light, nor was she one for possessions. She tucked her passport inside, just in case, though she intended to remain based in the US.

The card was white, with a name and phone number in simple black font, and it had been sitting inside her dressing table drawer for the duration of her time in New Orleans, and slipped inside her pocket long before that.

Giselle picked it up, brushed her thumb and forefinger over the smooth paper and fading lettering and let the memories of her final days in Paris wash over her, but only briefly. The time for reminiscing had passed. She was now ready for action.

She dialled the number. If it had been connected to any organisation besides the Network, she would have expected an error tone, but of course, it rang, and after a few seconds, a woman picked up.

'Madame Fur?' Giselle asked.

'Yes?'

'I need your help,' Giselle said. Her voice faltered. She had not spoken French for many years, and the words came back to her slowly, travelling through the long corridor of years in her mind before emerging on the tip of her tongue. Cajun French was rare in New Orleans these days and even then it was not the language of her native tongue.

Madame Fur chuckled, as Giselle explained her situation.

'Oh, I'm not laughing at you, my dear,' she said. 'The roads that lead to the Network are littered with broken hearts. All of us have a story like yours to tell.'

Giselle leaned forward, drew the blind and pushed the window open. Outside, a grackle rasped, or it might have been a starling. Giselle had always preferred plants to animals, and had still not entirely familiarised herself with the local bird life, or learned the knack of recognising one species from another, just from the sounds of their cries.

Eventually, Madame Fur continued. Giselle smiled inwardly. Allowing a silence to linger was an artful form of negotiating that was often underestimated and seldom implemented. Giselle had won an awful lot of arguments by simply waiting for her conversational counterpart to fill in a pregnant pause.

'My answer is yes, I will help you. Let me make a few calls and phone you back.'

Giselle called out her number, repeated it twice, then hung up the receiver. She mentally totted up the passage of time and deduced that Madame Fur was probably in her seventies now, although since she had been so elegantly dressed and well made up when they first met, it was difficult to guess her age. She wondered if she still ran the Parisian branch of L'Or du Temps, and whether she was still recruiting handsome and emotionally fragile young men and women to perform for the Network. Giselle knew, though, that she was in no position to judge. She had made her livelihood doing the very same thing. She was convinced, too, that women like Luba and Pinnie were far better off working at The Place than they had been in the ramshackle bars they'd been dirty dancing in before she recruited them. None of the girls who worked for Giselle were cut out for the Royal Ballet, and neither had any of them articulated a desire to work as lawyers or bankers or secretaries instead of as erotic performers.

No, there was a reason for The Place, and for the Network, and Giselle regretted nothing. She had enjoyed herself in her employ, and had enough set aside to live cheaply without working for many months.

Her nest egg had been largely unintentional. She simply didn't need or use much, and consequently had managed to save the majority of her income, which had grown exponentially in recent times as a result of her savvy recruiting of dancers like Luba and her refusal to in any way downgrade the bar's reputation as a destination for an elite brand of pleasure seekers by trying to attract more punters and lowering standards in the process.

Giselle had always been good at switching off, at drawing a line between one life and the next. She made decisions quickly, and rarely regretted the actions she based on her intuition. By the time she had filled her small suitcase and dressed, her home in New Orleans no longer felt like hers any more. She suffered barely a pang of emotion as she pulled the French doors to her garden closed and turned the key. In all likelihood, she would be back before long, and in any case she would recommend to Pinnie to find green-fingered tenants to look after the place in her absence.

Her velvet gowns she had covered with plastic bags from past dry cleaning visits and decided to store at the club, in the large changing area out the back which was already filled with rows and rows of costumes. For the trip, she wore a linen pantsuit that she hadn't tried on in ages, and was pleased to discover that it still fitted her.

When she glanced in the mirror, she was no longer a Madame, but a sleek, sophisticated woman preparing to embark on a new adventure. With her hair pulled back, a pair of gold studs decorating her ear lobes and low-heeled mules on her feet, she was another Giselle altogether.

She had always been intrigued by the way that she and others used their outer selves as an expression of their inner lives. The secrets that a wardrobe could tell.

Just as it occurred to her that Madame Fur had not

specified whether she intended to call back later that morning, or later that week, the phone rang.

'He's in Portland,' she said. 'Oregon.'

'Oh,' Giselle replied. 'Thank you.' She had never really thought to guess at William's location, but if she had, she probably would have come up with somewhere more romantic than Portland. It made sense, though. The Ball had a large office there, where Luba had recently been stationed, and she suspected that he still discreetly worked for them.

'If I might give you a word of advice, though?' Madame Fur continued.

'Of course.'

'Things change. People change. He's not the same man that you left behind, and neither are you the same woman. The passage of time leaves a rosy tint on everything, especially old lovers.' This time her laugh was closer to a witch's cackle.

'I know that,' Giselle replied. 'But I must search for him. Or I will die wondering what might have been.'

At the last moment, Giselle slipped two of her sculpted toys into her baggage, the first two that she had been sent. Her favourites. The rest went into a box of personal things that she would leave at the club. She could always check her case in to save the risk of airport security turning her away at the screening gate when they discovered the carved, phallic objects that were certainly heavy enough to be used as weapons.

Winter

She arrived in Portland on a sunny, clear day that belied the tide of nervous emotion that had possessed her ever since the pilot announced the aircraft would be landing shortly. If real life was anything like fiction, Giselle mused as she slipped her jacket off and let the warm breeze caress her skin, it would be raining. A taxi pulled into the cab rank and Giselle climbed in and instructed the driver to take her to the cheap, chain brand hotel she had booked online that promised to be within easy walking distance of the city centre. It was close to Powell's, a bookshop she had always wanted to visit.

Madame Fur had been rigorous as well as swift in her investigation, and discovered that William now lived and worked in the North East neighbourhood, owning a small gallery off Alberta Street, where he had grown quite a following with his work. He was still employed by the Network, but also sold his pieces to the public, and conducted workshops. Armed with her laptop and the name of William's shop, *L'Art des Sens*, The Art of Senses, Giselle had discovered that he had an exhibition and open evening scheduled, and she had booked her flight in time to attend. She had avoided tracking him down before now, feeling that doing so might become the start of an obsession with following him and his artistic progress and that such a habit would do her no good. Now that she was here, following him in real life, Googling his name seemed a perfectly reasonable thing to do. He now called himself William Tee.

There wasn't much more than the name and address of his gallery and a sparse handful of reviews. His disability had attracted attention, as had the erotic nature of his work. Giselle was certain that whatever stuff he put on display was nothing in comparison to the perverse creations that he dreamed up for the Network. She wondered, suddenly, if he made dildos for others, or if hers were the only ones of their kind. His lessons were popular, and all of the advertised classes for the rest of this year were already sold out. The course notes were brief, but comments from past students indicated that attendees learned more than just art. 'A place to practise another kind of seeing,' read the blurb.

Giselle stretched out on the small double bed. She had been lying there, typing William's new name into search engines for so long that night had fallen and her muscles were cramped. Her stomach rumbled. She flipped her laptop closed and carefully fitted it into the hotel room safe, not so much for security but to stop herself from staying up till dawn trying to uncover more snippets of news about her old lover.

On the streets of Portland, everyone fitted in, it seemed to Giselle, as she roamed downtown in search of some comfort food. She passed kids with spiky gelled-up hairstyles, long shorts and skateboards, mom-types buttoned up in shades of pastel, dreadlocked Rastas in long, bright sarong

326

skirts, city types who still visibly carried the weight of their corporate working week even though it was a Sunday night. She had packed an umbrella, but hadn't needed it, and was still warm even with her legs uncovered in a knee-length white dress with a scoop neck and a lemon yellow cardigan that she had worn all the way back when she lived in Paris. In the end she ordered a slice of pizza from a street vendor and ate it as she walked back to her hotel room, ignoring the pull she felt deep inside to find a bar somewhere, pick up a man and fuck him, to drown the shadows of her loneliness in lust.

The open evening and preview for the exhibition was being held late the following afternoon and would also feature a workshop, to give potential buyers ample time to cruise the gallery floor and hopefully decide to part with a substantial amount of cash to procure one of the items on display. None of the objects were visibly priced, which in Giselle's experience meant that they were sure to be expensive. She arrived about an hour into the show, partly to ensure that she could mingle unnoticed within what she hoped would be a crowd, and partly because she had lingered over getting ready, putting on a necklace and removing it again, tying her hair up and then arranging it loose, trying her outfit with one set of shoes and then another, before finally telling herself firmly that she was being silly. William was blind. He wouldn't even know that she was there, never mind pay the least attention at all to what she was wearing.

An attendant carrying a plate of canapés stopped and offered her a thin slice of sourdough bread with a sliver of salmon and an even smaller speck of sour cream on top and she popped it into her mouth. She was standing in front of a wall display that was covered in sculpted vulvas, each of them so extraordinarily lifelike that they surely could not be the product of imagination. Women must have posed for these. They were made from marble, so the detail must have been carved by hand, rather than poured from a mould. Giselle imagined William carefully – almost medically – examining the women's vaginas in order to recreate them in stone and felt herself moisten at the thought of it. She took a few steps back to view the display from another angle. They were like a glass–encased rose garden with petals of endless variation. Seized by a sudden impulse to own another of William's objects, Giselle caught the attention of one of the staff. She almost gasped at the price the attendant told her, but handed over her credit card and slipped the wrapped package into her shoulder bag. Had he sculpted her parts, by memory, she wondered? Perhaps there were bits of her in the homes of art lovers all over. The thought of it was a strange one. Could a person be reduced to their likeness? Could a likeness be greater than the person who had inspired it?

Still pondering the vagaries of artistic philosophy, she slowly made a circuit of the gallery again, soaking up as many details as she could, trying to get a measure of the man from his work. There was another wall of cocks, and Giselle could attest to their realism, having experienced the pleasure of so many different shapes and sizes herself. She saw none of the surrealism that she recognised in the dildos she had received in the mail, though, which pleased her. Perhaps he had made them especially for her. Or perhaps he was not even responsible for her anonymous phallic gifts. It was a strange coincidence, sure, but it was the sort of thing that might occur within the Network, prompted perhaps by an organisation-wide reminder that the purveyors of pleasure should regularly experience pleasure themselves, like the way employees of other enterprises might receive a bulk memo and a gift card of thanks or a leg of ham at Christmas.

The show did not contain any full-bodied works, or representations of penetration. Such works, Giselle guessed, would take many hours, perhaps even years, and might out of necessity only be created on receipt of a commission. She had no idea what the materials he now used cost, though she recalled that his canvases, brushes and paints had been expensive. She winced at the memory of William preparing his paints.

If only.

If only she hadn't ... if only she had ... Giselle had lost

count of the number of times that she had begun a thought with those words. But thoughts could not change the past. She sighed. Shook the cobwebs of regret from her mind. And filtered through from the front room of the gallery where William's pieces were for sale to the room behind, where a demonstration was taking place. She was careful to remain at the back of the small group in attendance. She could not shake the feeling that he might recognise her somehow. By her scent, perhaps. She still wore the same perfume that he had bought her once. Her hands shook and her breath quickened. She had put her job on hold, given instruction to Pinnie to rent out her quarters, flown all the way from New Orleans to Portland and yet she could not bear to reveal herself to him. Not in front of so many strangers. Not while he was working.

Instead she stood and watched, far out of the path of William's line of vision even if he had been able to see her. In fact, so trapped was she behind the wall of interested onlookers that she could not see him. She could hear him, though. The crowd was entirely silent and attentive and his voice, deep and rich, carried to her ears as though he was speaking just to her.

'Forget about seeing for a moment,' he instructed the onlookers, 'and think about perceiving. You take in far less information with your eyes than you think you do. Consider experiencing the world, instead of looking at it. Become part of it. Use your tongue and your hands to discover the person in front of you.'

Giselle could see now why his regular classes were so popular. His words were hypnotic. William was teaching his pupils more than the how-to of sculpture. He was instructing lovers how to learn the maps of each other's anatomy outside the boundaries of vision.

The talk was scheduled to run for another fifteen minutes, after which the audience would have the opportunity to watch William work with a model. Giselle could not bring herself to stay. She had seen and learned enough, for now. Hearing his voice and observing his work, this trajectory of his life without her, was all that she could stand, without breaking down into floods of tears and drawing attention to herself that she was not yet ready for. Walking into a room with William present, after all this time, made her feel like a drug addict exposed to a tiny taste of a forbidden substance. If she stayed for a moment longer, she feared that she might scream, or burst through the crowd and throw herself at him.

She walked all the way back to her hotel, although it was miles away and it no doubt would have been safer and swifter to catch a taxi. It was dark, but not too late yet. The cool night air helped to soothe her and bring her out of the funk that had settled over her mind and heart, so that she could think. What was she to do now? Probably, she could go straight back to New Orleans and pick up exactly where she had left off. It had only been a few days. It was highly doubtful that a new tenant had been found for her quarters yet. Pinnie would be disappointed to be demoted, but she would quickly get over that and Giselle would think of some way to sweeten the deal. She couldn't face the thought of going back to her old life, though, now that she had made the decision to break away, to try something new.

Perhaps she would travel, and properly, this time. Giselle had been all over America, but not much further, and almost without exception every trip had been in aid of either her own dancing or some business of the Network, and so she had seen more strip bars than monuments. She had spent most of her life as a tourist or a purveyor of the flesh.

Giselle had almost decided to throw caution to the wind, spin a globe of the world and set off into the unknown when she arrived back at her hotel and was informed that someone had left a message for her.

It was Madame Fur. How the hell had she tracked her down to her hotel?

She was irritated, initially, thinking that the older woman who had changed the entire course of her life with the single brief conversation that had led her into the path of the Network just wanted to feed on her heartbreak, and gossip; but she felt obliged to return her call, considering that without the information Madame Fur had provided her with she would never have tracked William down to Portland.

But the topic of her flight from New Orleans in search of rekindling an old love affair was not even mentioned.

'I have a proposal for you,' the Madame said. 'Stay in Portland. We have another event coming up, shortly. A private affair, naturally, and one that your particular expertise would suit. In addition, we could also use your invaluable talents as we near our next Ball. A troupe of new dancers who have to be moulded into shape.'

'For the event you mention, if you need a dancer, I'm well past that,' Giselle responded, amused.

'We don't need a dancer. But if we did, my dear, might I add that no one is ever past dancing. Dancing is life . . . but I digress. We need a choreographer. Someone to arrange something . . . spectacular.'

'What did you have in mind? Surely you must have specialists for the Ball already, more familiar with the dancers you have on file. Someone that you work with regularly.'

'Well yes, of course, but this isn't for the Ball. It's even more exclusive than that. A birthday party. A celebration that we have been asked to cater for, and the person in question has tastes that are beyond the imagination of our usual choreographers. Also, we wish for this event to remain totally private. All of our performers are discreet, of course, but we feel it prudent to arrange certain events separately. I'm sure you understand.'

Giselle nodded without thinking, although she was alone in the room and Madame Fur on the other end of the receiver somewhere else in the world. Perhaps she had now moved to the US.

Madame continued.

'You'll be paid, of course. All of your expenses covered. And a fee for the work itself that I'm sure you will find generous.'

'What kind of show, exactly, did you have in mind?'

'It's a little sensitive to explain over the phone. But since an ocean separates us, and our time is limited, we must do things this way. I hope you will forgive me for the intrusion, but in my investigation of your William I unearthed some of his earlier artwork.'

The phrase 'your William' rang in Giselle's ears, so that she did not guess ahead what Madame Fur was getting at until the words came from her mouth.

'The paintings are wonderful. You were beautiful in them. Luminous.'

'Thank you,' Giselle murmured politely, though she knew that the beauty was all in the artist who had captured the image.

'I particularly liked the pictures of you as Joan of Arc.'

Giselle nearly dropped the receiver as the memories of posing for those works burst forward in her mind, as vivid as the day when they were first imprinted.

But she agreed.

'Yes,' she said. 'I'll do it.'

A Ballet of Joan . . .

9

Save the Last Dance for Me

Giselle was given only a month to perfect the Joan Ballet, including selecting, hiring and training all of the dancers. Her contract specified that none of the performers be associated either with the Ball, or with any of the Network's clubs or other events.

'It's impossible,' she whispered, pale-faced, to Madame Fur as they discussed the arrangements. The older woman had flown from Paris to Portland to oversee the proceedings and was ensconced in a cavernous, pastel-pink, bucket-shaped armchair, staring at Giselle from across her hotel room through heavy-lidded, unblinking eyes. Her hair was cut into a short bob and dyed a brilliant midnight blue, an ironic twist on the pale-violet-tinged rinses often favoured by the aged. She wore a sleek black tailored suit and patent leather court shoes and sat with her legs firmly crossed and her chin resting on her entwined fingers.

Giselle was mesmerised by Madame Fur's fingernails, which had been sharpened into pointed, claw-like tips and painted the same deep, night sky shade as her hair. A large onyx pendant on a silver choker hung around her neck. She was still slim, but her skin hung in deep folds like a turkey's, as though her body had meant for her to have more flesh and her epidermis had expanded accordingly.

'There is no such thing as impossible, when it comes to dance,' Madame Fur replied. 'You must simply be more creative. You're not trying hard enough.'

Madame excused herself shortly after relaying this information, without leaving Giselle any further feedback, or even a scrap of guidance. It was apparent that she had come to Portland to keep an eye on the ultimate result before it was presented to the client, but did not plan on providing any help throughout the creative process, which had been entrusted entirely to Giselle.

The Network had shifted Giselle to the Nines, in a room on the penultimate floor overlooking the wide urban landscape of Pioneer Square. She was provided with every comfort. The bed was monstrous and the bedding luxurious.

And yet, Giselle was unable to sleep. She was possessed by the perpetually uncomfortable juxtaposition of the banal and the divine; reliving the minutiae of her life's greatest and harshest fantasy, and yet at the same time required to sit through auditions both beautiful and tedious, order pointe shoes, enter hardware stores and arrange for lengths of chain to be cut and trimmed and passed through the till at $5.99 per yard. She suffered the slow and constant torture of the artist, making something beautiful by wringing out the contents of her heart and soul, but doing so with the distant and critical eye of the uninvolved spectator, as if it were not her own life and dreams that she was cannibalising for fuel but someone else's altogether.

Translating the contents of her dreams to the stage seemed at first to be the easy part, but in practice proved much more troublesome than she had anticipated. The choreography of the Ballet itself she had thought would prove a simple task, since she had imagined in cinematic detail the story of Joan over and over from her childhood. Yet when she performed the steps exactly as she had seen them so many times in her visions, the lines of her body reflected in the large hotel mirror lacked all the depth and detail that the same movements possessed when she played them in her head. She was forced to confront the fact that everything looked different through the lens of reality than it did through the looking-glass of the imagination.

She mulled over what she had heard of William's brief lecture on perception and 'seeing' again and again, convinced that the answer lay there somewhere, and if only she could find it she could build a bridge between her fantasies and the stage that she planned to put them on and bring them to life.

She returned to William's gallery repeatedly over those few weeks, always careful to peer through the display glass before she entered to check that he wasn't present on the shop floor. Always, when she did this, her heart was in her mouth, both praying for and dreading a glimpse of him. She acquired more and more of his pieces, spending the generous advance that Madame Fur had transferred to her. Every surface in her hotel room was now home to one of his works.

He had created a series of semi-mythical creatures. A seahorse with the trunk and ears of an elephant. A hare with the long, slim legs of a giraffe. A squirrel with the head of a fox. They were imaginary and yet ultra real at the same time, evidence of a mind that now saw the world in a different way, and yet was still able to create a visual reality for others, one that touched the heart as well as the eyes. As though William were able to see the essence of a thing even if he could no longer see the thing itself, and was able to form it into an image that others could recognise.

There was another set that Giselle stood in front of each time she visited the gallery and could not tear herself away from, yet could not bring herself to own. Halves of faces, split from the forehead through the nose to the chin and melting like Dali's clocks with features too blurred to be distinguishable and yet undeniably human and masculine. They made Giselle think of that awful day when William had been burned and the scars that he bore because of it. Was this how he saw himself, William after the fire? And was the man he had been now so remote that he was forgotten entirely, cut off, just vanished into thin air?

Creating the Ballet and thinking of William were activities that Giselle was unable to separate. One could not exist without the other. Her heart was simultaneously breaking and soaring, and there was nothing that she could do about it but keep inching towards her deadline and hoping that by some miracle she could make something beautiful from the shattered pieces of her past, that she could thread together her desire for the man that she loved still and the twisted tangle of her darkest dreams, and enact in full public view thoughts that she had only ever shown to him.

She did not even know who her audience would be. Madame Fur declined to inform her and Giselle did not push for an answer. She had been working for the Network long enough to understand that she was merely another cog in their wheel and that they would take advantage of her talents for as long as she possessed them, reward her handsomely but never provide her with any scrap of further knowledge that might enable her to set up on her own. They held the purse strings and the power, yet Giselle also knew that the fog of ignorance she worked within would add something to the dance. There was an unstated but always present frisson between the audience and the performers that changed when the blanket of anonymity was removed.

Slowly, she recruited her dancers. She had visited all of the local dance schools, strip bars and clubs in the downtown area and well beyond in the first few days of taking up her assignment and quickly abandoned that track. She longed to break the terms of her agreement and fly in Pinnie or Luba or get a recommendation from Bianca at the Grand who had first discovered the Russian girl. It even crossed her mind to get in touch with her old friend Beth from her dance school days. But she discarded all of these thoughts.

Something more was needed here than talent or the ability to fill a hand gesture or the angle of a calf or the bend of a spine with life and emotion. She just had not yet worked out what it was. But she had faith that it would come, even if that faith was attached to the nagging panic that it might not, that one dreadful day her talents might desert her and leave her unable to even come up with the tenuous ghost of an idea.

Her first recruit was a young Italian named Antonio, a medical student, who worked at the hotel. She had spotted him in one of the long, carpeted corridors, pushing a laundry trolley piled high with fluffy white bath sheets. There was something in the turn of his hip that gave her pause, and she had followed him all the way down the hall before inviting him to audition for her. At first, she suspected that he thought her to be a little unhinged, and possibly believed that her invitation to work as a dancer was a loaded euphemism for another kind of job altogether and one that he would happily have undertaken, but he accepted her offer nonetheless.

Soon after she recruited one of the counter staff in a small clothing boutique close to William's gallery. She was short, in her early thirties and with enormous breasts, an atypical dancer in every respect. Her name tag read 'Lacey', and in Giselle's opinion it was a moniker that didn't suit her at all. Yet there was something in the sharp angle of Lacey's brow and the sardonic glimmer that flashed across her face as she served the line of customers at the register while Giselle browsed nearby that gave a hint to her inner core of rebellion. Purposefully, Giselle asked her to reach up to a crimson-coloured dress that was hanging on a hook halfway up the wall so that she could watch the way Lacey moved as she extended towards the hanger with a long hook on a pole to retrieve the item and bring it down. Yes, she would do.

Antonio suggested his girlfriend, Celia, for the role of Joan, a sturdy Canadian girl who had been a rower and had the broad shoulders and firm legs to show for it. She was proud and stood erect with her chin jutting out, bordering on arrogant, but with an inner vulnerability that became apparent when she stood alongside Antonio and demurred to him. There was a private fire in their relationship that Giselle instantly recognised. The signs were evident to the attentive and educated observer. The way that he instinctively directed her by applying gentle pressure to her elbow. How she ducked her head ever so slightly when she looked at him. The way the timbre of their voices changed when they spoke to each other. His deepened, hers purred.

Giselle experienced a white-hot, searing jealousy when she watched Antonio and Celia together. Not because she wanted to possess either of them herself, but because she wanted what they shared, what she had once had with William. She missed that power exchange, and she knew that it was something that came with time, and even then only existed in the most particular of circumstances when two people met and their stars aligned. It could not be faked, bought, sold or found propped up against a bar or in a dark room in a club.

But the more it hurt her to watch them, the more convinced she was that they were right for the job. The fiercer the fire in her heart burned, the sharper the cut of the knife that turned inside her as she created, the better her art would be. So she endured.

There were others. Only a handful by necessity. The best, the only thing that she could do, was bring them on raw, recruit those who possessed the same inner demons that she had. It might not be polished, but it would be real. It was the best that she could do. The nature of the performance she was inviting them to be involved in initially worried some of them, because of its explicitness and revealing aspects, but the cash on offer soon overtook their scruples.

Bringing Joan to life was more than a job to Giselle; it was an obsession. No doubt this was why Madame Fur had hired her to direct the piece. The individuals who could afford to commission the Network's events were a rare breed, wealthy and particular, and should they be left intrigued, delighted and impressed rather than merely satisfied; then they could usually be relied upon to return with further requests, and often paid a large premium on top of the already astronomical performance fee. The Network's reputation was built on legends based around carefully leaked truths, and keeping the upper echelons of their customer base happy with small, specialist orders like this was what elevated the regular Ball to something beyond an ordinary club night.

She considered a silent performance, like the one that she had undertaken many years ago at the Ball that had occurred entirely in the dark. But in the end, she felt that they needed music. Giselle downloaded and listened to thousands of songs. She walked the city streets at night with her headphones on trying to find exactly the right mix of dark and light instrumentation and in the end she found it, not online but in the form of a CD single in one of the few independent music shops still surviving. It was a violin solo, bleak and haunting, but with an underlying refrain of hope that lingered beyond the final fading chords. The artist was Summer Zahova, and the picture on the front showed a young woman's torso, partly covered by the body of her violin. A bunch of flame-red hair hung over each of her shoulders.

Madame Fur attended the final dress rehearsal and approved the piece with no particular comment, though Giselle thought she noted a gleam of satisfaction in the older woman's eye. She had no doubt that Madame would have made her displeasure apparent if she had not been content with the outcome.

The performance itself took place at the front of a small chapel attached to a stately home in Irvington. All but Madame Fur had been blindfolded once they were within a few blocks of their final destination, so Giselle was unsure as to the precise address but she recognised the style of the house from the steps that she had been guided up and the vast halls she was led through before reaching the chapel and having her sight restored.

Eight guests looked on, an even number of men and women, perched in one row at the front like a line of crows balanced on a telegraph wire. They all wore masks, so Giselle was not able to glean much from their appearance besides the wealth that was apparent in the cut of their clothing and the understated style of their watches and jewellery.

'Family money,' Madame Fur whispered to her. They were huddled in the wings, where the speaker would wait before approaching the lectern. Giselle nodded. Each of the individuals watching bore the mannerisms of one who had grown up with privilege. The spines of the women were bolt upright and did not touch the backs of the wooden pews that they sat on. The men bore the poised, open posture of well-fed young lions, aware of and luxuriating in their own power.

Giselle instinctively smoothed down her skirts, conscious suddenly of the comparative difference in her social status, something that rarely had any cause to cross her mind.

She had worn one of her old velvet gowns tonight. Madame Fur had arranged for it to be sent to her. The deep-green dress reached all the way to the floor, with a boned waist, low neckline that emphasised her cleavage and a lace collar that gave her the look of a nineteenth-century governess.

The lights were dimmed, and the first low keening sounds of the violin solo began, Celia's cue to take to the stage. It occurred to Giselle that others must be involved whom she had not even met. Lighting and sound technicians. Prop attendants. She dismissed the thought.

From her position in the wings, Giselle's view was limited. She could see only snatches of what was occurring. A flash of Celia's bare calf, her thigh, the curve of her buttocks. She closed her eyes and imagined it. Knowing that Celia was nude, and smeared already with smudges of dark red paint to signify blood, her hair matted and her eyes wide and wild with struggle. There was the sharp intake of breath from the small audience. The almost inaudible puffing as Celia and the other dancers who were now on stage began to move with more intensity, acting out the fight, the capture.

In Giselle's mind, it was her being dragged backwards and bound to the makeshift wooden stake that had been erected. But she was not about to be defiled by soldiers, but rather by William. She imagined the pull of long chains against her skin, running between her thighs, pressing deep into her flesh.

Giselle began to feel faint, and grasped the wall to aid her. She felt the gentle touch of Madame Fur's hand on her shoulder, an uncommon gesture of reassurance, but it was not enough to pull her from her flight of fancy. The current of memory and fantasy combined with reality was too strong; Giselle was drowning in the pull of it.

Her breathing quickened. Her hands shook. Her palms

began to sweat. The solidity of the walls around her and the floor beneath her feet receded as her reverie took over, punctuated with the sounds of the fantasies that she had translated into movement, now being enacted by others.

Her past and her present, her desire and her shame, set to steps and music and played out as she listened and remembered those very same actions performed on her by William, her lover, her love, as she willingly submitted to him.

She nearly fainted.

The last sweet sounds of Summer Zahova's bow on strings faded away.

Madame Fur squeezed her hand.

It was over.

Warm breath against her cheek. The brush of skin like paper. Madame Fur whispering in her ear.

'That was beautiful. There is someone else here, my dear, who would like you to be Joan.'

Giselle could not speak. 'Me?' she mouthed.

'Yes. Now. Will you?'

She nodded. What else could she do?

She kept her eyes closed and was led through further hallways, down stairs and out into the open space of another room. She could taste the faint lick of dust in the air, as if it had not been aired in a long time. Another tap on her arm as Madame Fur indicated she was letting her go, then the click and scrape of her heels and faint rustle of material as she turned and walked away. The sound of a door closing.

Giselle was not alone. She heard footsteps, soft and light, slow and deliberate, coming towards her. The tread was familiar, yet different, like the faint echo of a sound that she had heard before played with a different instrument. There was a scent that she knew, but couldn't place. A touch on her cheek, gentle. A finger running along her jaw, explorative.

A hand caressing her lips, and then covering her mouth, momentarily restricting her breathing.

She sighed, and felt her shoulders relax. The tension left her muscles. Giselle felt as though she had been away for a long time, and had finally come home.

The pads of fingers belonging to large, strong hands brushed against the nape of her neck. Cool air soothed her skin as her dress was pulled away. The folds of fabric swished as her gown fell to the floor, like the hush of heavy curtains being drawn. Air moved around her as her companion bent down to retrieve her outfit and stepped away, perhaps to hang it, then returned and briskly yanked down her panties, a lace-trimmed, dark green satin pair that matched her dress. The hand that tugged on the fabric knocked against the curve of her waist first, before moving lower and finding the elasticated band that sat low on her hips.

Her ankles were pulled apart and she nearly stumbled as she stepped out of the knickers pooled at her feet. A cupped palm caught her elbow, keeping her upright. Then as soon as she had regained her balance she was pushed down again. Just as she thought she would fall backwards she felt the prickling scratch of wood scrape against her buttocks. A stake. Unsanded, rough against her skin. Her wrists caught and lifted over her head, bound tightly to the timber.

A voice whispering, 'My Joan,' deep and husky, and her memories blooming again in vivid Technicolor, a fusion of thoughts and emotions that caused every one of her sexual switches to be turned on at once, like a lit spark dropping into a barrel of fireworks and all of them bursting together.

Her body shook uncontrollably as her nerve endings twitched. Her senses were nearly overpowered by the strength of her body's reaction to stimuli both past and present, physical and mental. Layers of immediate desire melded with yearning and produced something closer to frenzy than arousal.

Giselle was still dreaming, but her dream was also coming to life around her, happening to her. Reality and fantasy danced together in the long corridors of her mind.

Instinctively she kept her eyes clamped shut, not even opening them when the bonds on her wrists and ankles were tightened, nor when warm lips brushed over her nipples or sharp teeth grated against her skin. The fluid of her lust ran from her cunt and soaked the inside of her legs. Hands grasped her thighs and lifted her flesh aside and a tongue licked at the droplets that dripped from her opening, like a bee feeding from nectar.

Fingers explored the contours of her body as if every inch of her was being mapped, investigated, explored like uncharted territory traversed for the first time. The touch was soft and slow but in Giselle's visions she saw herself whipped and gagged by her captors and so the pressure of every gentle caress was multiplied a hundredfold and the stroke of a fingertip became a crushing blow.

She writhed but was barely able to move, so closely was she tied to the length of timber that held her.

'Joan,' the voice said again, a voice that she knew in every dimension of her being. It was the voice of her past and her future, the voice of her despair and her hope, the voice of her dreams and her reality.

She came.

Her orgasm grew from her depths, at first, a spark that simmered and seethed in her loins, and then accelerated through her whole being like a wild fire, a body-aching, back-arching climax that occurred in her heart and mind as well as her flesh.

Slowly the wracking jolts of her limbs' twitching subsided. The visions that had overpowered her mind faded away. And she knew that she had not been destroyed by the blaze that had burned through her, but born again, ready for new shoots to grow from the ashes.

Her bonds were loosened.

Giselle opened her eyes and the night in which she had willingly cast herself finally retreated.

A pale light spread across the room. It appeared to extend forever as her sight grew accustomed to her new surroundings, a room that reached as far as she could see, more of a stage, a cavern even.

Her breath still came in short, hungry bursts.

Her body was perilously teetering on the edge, balanced between agonies of pain, pleasure and terror. Her mind a cloudy jumble of thoughts and panic.

She blinked.

Emerged from the depths.

And there he was.

William.

Sitting in a thin pool of illumination, facing her, just a few steps away, his features fading into the ambient darkness.

No longer in her dreams. Here in real life.

She was nude, her hair dishevelled, uncomfortably sweaty, but it no longer mattered. After all, this was the man who had first taught her how to be both naked and innocent, to be proud of her body, how to fully assume the call of her senses and present herself to the world.

He was smiling, but there was also the trace of a tear in the corner of his blank eyes.

Which is when Giselle remembered he couldn't see her. He was still blind. There were no miracles, even in the phantasmagorical world of the Ball. Her heart dropped.

As if sensing she was now aware of his presence, he spoke. 'Giselle.'

His voice was the texture of coarse velvet, warm, solicitous, melancholy.

'It's you?'

'Yes. Had you expected anyone else?' A faint hint of irony in his words.

'No.' Even when she had been deep in the zone, floating along a storm of terrible emotions and utterly lost to reality, she had somehow known it could only be William orchestrating her ecstasy. No one else had the power. Ever had.

'I want to touch you,' he said and rose without awaiting her response, then steadily stepped towards her. Despite his infirmity, he knew exactly where she was standing, could sense that she hadn't moved.

'But you already have,' she replied, instinctively turning her head to check that yes, nobody else was present.

'Yes,' he said. 'I want to touch you as Giselle, not as Joan.'

Giselle's senses returned to her slowly and his face came into focus.

His hair was still wild, thick curls sprouting in every direction, untamed and now totally grey. His features bore the mark of ageing, though, deep lines cutting across his forehead, a spidery network of wrinkles nesting in the corner of his eyes. His beard now matched the colour of his hair, obscuring his scarred cheeks. A shadow ran across the bridge of his nose. But he still radiated the same animal energy that dissolved all form of resistance inside her.

A knot formed in Giselle's stomach.

As he neared, he towered a full head above her and he was so close that she could hear the sound of his breath and feel its warmth wash across her face. She almost fainted at the recognition of his distinct scent.

'May I?' he asked.

She was unsure what he was requesting. She wet her lips.

His dead eyes looked down at her and she could have sworn he could see every detail of her face, decipher the tremors of emotion racing across her damp skin, read the fear and expectation in her own gaze, trace the invisible scars that the passing years away from him had imprinted on her skin.

William raised his hands towards her face.

Time came to a standstill.

Caressing her cheek, hard calluses sweeping sensuously against her skin, dredging up so many memories, this time without the ghosts of her fantasies intruding. His fingers following the slope of her cheekbones, drawing the downward curve of her nose, fingerpads mapping the lush thickness of her lips, travelling with imperial languor, sculpting her contours in the minutest of detail, learning to read her again.

Giselle stood like a statue as William hovered around her, reacquainting himself with her shape and lines of softness, reinventing the past and conjuring it back into life in his own particular way. She was not his Joan any longer but his Giselle.

Hands lowered, grazing a nipple, weighing a breast with all the precise delicacy of a jeweller appraising a rare stone, drawing a line across the fragile valley separating her arse cheeks, dipping into the surging wetness between her thighs. Bringing his damp finger back to his mouth and greedily licking it, ending with a satisfied sigh, seemingly reassured by the fact she still tasted the same. A familiar ceremony of welcome unfolded in the hushed silence of the cavernous room.

Because of William's blindness, every gesture and movement seemed imbued with a charge of tenderness and a solemnity she had never previously experienced, turning the whole carnival of touch and feel into an almost religious celebration.

Giselle tried to clear her mind of any superfluous thoughts, just yearning to live in this unique moment of reunion.

Two of William's fingers squeezed her clit and she faltered and dug her nails into his back.

'Yes,' he sighed, withdrew his fingers from the cauldron of her cunt and took her by the waist, gently lifting her and lowered her to the floor.

They fucked.

And it was as if the decades in between had never even happened.

Washed away in their furious coupling.

They slowed down.

Then they made love. Moved to a more leisurely pace, having spent the hunger. With the ease of familiarity, hearts beating in harmony as each in turn remembered the gestures, the quirks that acted as triggers. William gently biting into the lobe of her ear and then sneakily tonguing the crease between her ear and her neck, an act that inexplicably turned Giselle to mush, while she remembered how he squirmed with unavoidable delight as she inserted a finger deep into his arse as he thrust inside her in a missionary position and she felt the ensuing tremor shake both their conjoined bodies.

They gasped.

Moaned.

And fucked again.

Bodies fighting, struggling, dancing a ballet of desire unleashed, skin against skin, juices mingling, wonderful cocktails of come, sweat, saliva and intimate secretions, games being played of power and domination, of submission and acceptance, flirting with the abyss in that eternal mad quest for nirvana and peace that never ends. Seeking shelter in the storm.

Made love.

Kissed.

Caressed.

Fucked, until they were raw, skin and emotions intricately linked, seared together, melded in intimacy.

Later, in the comfort of her hotel room.

'It was you, wasn't it?'

'Me?'

'The objects. In the post.'

'It was.'

'I thought so, but could never quite be sure. You could have sent a note with them. An explanation.'

He stretched a leg, catching the duvet between a toe and pulling it away, uncovering her chest. Instinctively, Giselle pulled it back to cover herself. It had been ages since she had slept with a man in a bed, and was no longer accustomed to sharing sheets or quilts, more used to sprawling unfettered like a spider across the softness of the mattress.

'I could,' he said and retreated back into silence.

'They are beautiful. You were always wonderful with your hands.'

'They're all I have now, since I lost the use of my eyes. I have to decrypt the world through touch. But it's okay, I've learned to like it, to appreciate the way objects and people feel under my fingers. Did you know that most things and human beings vibrate? It's strange. Being in darkness enhances so many things. You navigate between sounds and scents, you know.'

'Why did you stop writing? Never allowed me to answer by leaving no return address?'

'On one hand, I felt as if it was the wrong thing to do. Wanted you to have a new life, unencumbered by my presence. I didn't want you to become dependent on an invalid who also happened to be an older man . . .'

'Age never meant anything, even before the . . .' Giselle hesitated.

'The incident?'

'Yes.'

'I know, but one day I would have been so much older – as I am now – and you would still have been so much younger.'

'It's the same road down which we travel. I also have grey hair, now.'

'I suppose that's for you to know and me to guess. But I like that you have kept it long. Just running my fingers through it earlier made me so hard, Giselle . . .'

'Silver-tongued as ever.'

'And, anyway, even if I had provided an address you never would have answered my earlier letters.'

'I know.'

Because she'd felt too guilty, lost, angry.

Her hand moved between the sheets, grazed his dormant cock. It shuddered under her touch, as if it was alive, the beat of his heart coursing through its prominent veins. She gripped it. Felt it grow in rigidity. Again.

'It almost feels as if nothing has changed, has it?'

'I counted the years,' William said.

'Me too. I missed you every single day.'

'I tried not to, but I couldn't help thinking of you. So much. I often imagined I was a stranger meeting you for the first time, stealing a kiss, touching you for the first time, undressing you and what it would feel like being a new man for you. I realise you must have known other men during such a long interval. I wouldn't have wanted it any other way, but I was jealous of every single one, whether I knew their name or not, the way they looked or how they treated you. I wanted to be them. To be inside you, to be burned by your fire. It's why I eventually carved the toys, wood and stone, polishing them with a vengeance, measuring their length and girth, weighing them until I knew they were just right, secure in the knowledge that they would fill you, fit you perfectly. My way of knowing you again by proxy . . .'

Giselle sighed. Wanting to say that she now no longer remembered any of those men, their names, the way they looked or smiled, barely the diverse images of their jutting cocks lingering on a remote, indifferent screen at the back of her mind. Wanting to explain that each and every one of them had merely been a means to an end, an instrument, an excuse to feed her emptiness. She was briefly tempted to ask William about the women he had come to know in the same gulf of years, but then realised she had no wish to learn about them, wasn't even in the slightest way jealous.

She closed her eyes. She no longer knew whether it was day or night outside. They had been here so long. Time had been suspended while they embraced, been banished.

'Tell me about New Orleans,' William asked. 'Where you live?'

Giselle attempted to describe the city to him, its charms and atmosphere, but words failed her and she knew that her explanation was prosaic and uninspired, finding herself unable to properly encapsulate the essence of the place. She could have told him about the dozens of occasions when she had returned to the grounds of The Place in the early hours of morning after a mindless fuck or an assignation with yet another identikit lover and had imagined on her walk back that, waiting for her, sitting on the steps by the front gate, would be William, with tender words of forgiveness, his sight restored even, his presence a haven of peace. But there had never been anyone sitting there. It was just a recurring daydream with which she had tortured herself.

'I think you would like it,' she said. 'It's a very sensual place.' She was going to mention its palette of colours, but remembered that this was a sense he was now deprived of, and how excruciating this must be for a painter.

Sensing her growing discomfort, William cuddled up to her, his strong arms enveloping her, his natural warmth washing over her.

'Come,' he asked. And Giselle laid her head on his chest.

For a brief moment, she wondered whether in his constant state of darkness, he still pictured her as she was when he had first known her, young, unmarked, or whether his hands and fingers could now recognise the way she had changed as they roamed across her, aged. Probably a bit of both, she assumed.

Drained by their exertions, they finally both fell asleep, arm in arm.

The following morning, neither had any Ball duties and William asked Giselle to drive him to the nearby coast, which was just an hour or so away. One of the Ball riggers would agree to lend them his car, he said.

'I want to smell the sea air,' he said. He'd wanted to make the journey for ages, but the opportunity had never presented itself.

Oregon had been a fertile hotbed of Nordic immigration a century or more ago and the coastline north of Portland was rugged and rocky with deep, picturesque fjords cutting sharply into the land and a wild sea spuming below, mist rising slowly through the air, an aspect of the untamed landscape that had attracted so many visitors from Scandinavia after the legendary Gold Rush. Most had gone into logging while others had started wineries dotted across the Willamette Valley. Passing the vineyards, the road began to wind its way through thick pine forests that led to the coast. William sat in the passenger seat, impassive, impervious to the changing shades of autumn unfurling outside his window. As they approached the coast, he opened his window and took a long, deep breath.

Holding his hand in hers, unsure whether to grip it or just casually guide him along the path that snaked to the cliff, Giselle led William from the car park to the promontory that overlooked the raging ocean. When he was moving in an environment he knew well, he could navigate around with surprising ease in total denial of his blindness, but in a new place he was unfamiliar with, he did require help. He refused to use a cane. It was more than a question of principle, it was one of defiant pride.

There was a wooden bench on which they settled. The wood was damp from centuries of ocean wind. They sat.

The view was spectacular. Waves below crashing

thunderously against the rocks, the line of the horizon weighed down by a herd of grey mastodon clouds owning the sky, claiming its immensity, waving away onlooking human beings' right to their ownership of the planet.

Giselle wanted to describe what she saw through the wall of the mist to William, but the moment she opened her mouth he sensed it and patted her forearm and suggested silence instead.

Giselle, feeling the cold and not having brought along any warmer clothing, laid her head on his shoulder, seeking out his heat. He was wearing baggy jeans and a thick sweatshirt. It smelled of paint, tobacco and dry sweat. It smelled of him.

Yet again, she had a compulsion to speak out but William shushed her.

'Don't say anything that you might regret,' he told her. 'It's a moment, a lovely one, but it will pass. There is no need to talk about love, let alone tomorrow, Giselle.'

They contemplated the ocean.

That night they again stayed in the room Giselle had been allocated by the Network. He forgot the dimensions, having only had limited time to learn where the bed was positioned, and stumbled on his way back from the bathroom, catching his knee against a sharp corner of the bed. He had not yet offered to take her to the apartment that he lived in, attached to the gallery, claiming that it would be silly to cram themselves into a small room when she had all this luxury still available.

Annoyed, he waved her attention away as he rose to his feet.

'See,' he said. 'You don't want to become my nurse, do you? You have better things to do.'

Train other women into the subtle arts of seduction and dance? Despatch them on amoral assignments where they made love in public under pretence of artistry for the relish of rich voyeurs? Tend her garden? Punctuate the nightly emptiness with the comfort of strangers while she still retained the power to attract? Could she return to that life now that she had found him again and trembled under his touch, been filled by his power and despair? It seemed pointless.

Madame Fur had offered her more work on the next Ball, to be held somewhere in the far North. A complex performance was planned, dancers on ice, flitting across gigantic frozen expanses like sea birds. William was always welcome too. There were many objects, props and stages that needed to be carved and sculpted into things of beauty as well as function.

It was tempting. But all at the prototype stage. There was a place for them both with the Network, Madame Fur assured them, wherever they decided to go. There was no need to decide right now. They could take their time.

Winter

They found peace together.

Learning all over how to become a couple anew and banish the years of separation.

It was far from easy.

Avoiding any discussion of the future and what either of them might wish to do next.

Three o'clock in the morning; William in the clutches of a bad dream. The fire or another buried memory from before he had known Giselle? Gripping the sheets, febrile, vulnerable. Giselle, worried, cuddling up to him, taking his hand in hers, reassuring him, guilty once more about the darkness he was travelling through. Skin intimately layered against skin, triggering the synapses of desire, adjusting positions, docking gently into each other, slowly at first but then movements changing gears, lubrication born, parts merging, the familiar, exhilarating waltz of sex.

Another night; silence deeper than an ocean. Giselle caught in the net of her own madness, Joan again, imagining the pain, craving it against every ounce of rationality still persisting at the back of her mind, a battalion of faceless monks tearing her apart, stretching her on the wheel in a ceremony of confession, nipples being tortured by sharp blades and monstrous implements, her throat tightening under the pressure of a chafing rope until even her deep-lodged scream was unable to release itself. William's lips passing across her cheeks, lapping up her tears, pulling her into his arms, harbouring her and then the heavy mass of his body disappearing under the sheets, his tongue consoling her clit and expertly directing the nascent path of her lust. Later, his cock inside her mouth, velvet smooth and hard within its exquisite softness. Feeding her.

Nights.

Epilogue

It was New Year's Eve.

The crowds were milling around Jackson Square where a temporary stage had been built to host a succession of rock and jazz bands. They had booked a table on the upper floor for 10 p.m. at Tujague's on Decatur, facing the Café du Monde where long queues of revellers stood in line for beignets and coffee, while street artists shaping balloons into increasingly weird and often obscene shapes and blues singers selling their home-made CDs from their open guitar cases entertained them.

At midnight, the diners would be allowed onto the balcony where they would watch the electric glitter ball descend on the façade of the old Jax Brewery and the fireworks would begin, launched from the barges moored in the Mississippi.

Earlier, William had asked Giselle if she would describe the fireworks to him. She had demurred.

'How the hell can I describe them, William?' she had protested. 'It's just colours and lights and oohs and aahs, you know ...' Even though she understood his similar requests, she wanted to plead that she traded in emotions, not words.

They would stay inside instead and savour a fine cognac to go with the coffee, and their respective praline cheese cake and banana bread pudding, while the other turn-of-the-year diners watched outside, they decided. Tujague's was one of their favourite restaurants, and William swore by its traditional beef brisket, which he claimed was the most tender he had ever tasted.

Within a few weeks of her return to New Orleans with William at her side, he had fallen in love with creole food and the culinary delights the city had to offer. Giselle had never been much of a cook before, but had now acquired a handful of cookery books and was slowly improving her skills in a bid to please his healthy appetite. Never would she have thought previously that she could ever become so domesticated. And at peace with herself. She had become particularly proud of her seafood gumbo.

Sometimes, when out, they would spend almost a whole meal not even talking much to each other, savouring the food and the quality of the silence. 'Just like an old couple,' Giselle felt. They even held hands in the streets when walking, as if they had spent a whole life together. William did not use a cane, only wore dark glasses, and his step was so assured under her imperceptible guidance that few passers-by would even realise he was blind. He made Giselle proud.

The other guests began their migration to the balcony to partake in the celebrations. Giselle and William stayed put.

The young waitress in her severe black and white outfit offered them a refill. She had long, shapely thin legs inside the cocoon of her pencil skirt, her hard rump straining against the tightness of the material. Her auburn hair was held in a tight chignon. She moved with grace and Giselle was minded to ask her later if she had ever danced. She had cheekbones to die for and a small blue star tattooed on her neck. Giselle no longer ran The Place, but she had retained a connection with the club and the Network and was always alert to the prospect of new talent.

'What are you thinking?' William asked, alerted to the subtle change in her silence.

'I'll tell you later,' Giselle said, as the waitress poured the piping-hot coffee from the glass jug she was holding, her other arm folded behind her back in the grand old tradition of service. As she did so, she held Giselle's gaze.

A most definite possibility, Giselle thought. That touch of defiance would fit in well if the girl had any affinity for dancing. Or sex for that matter, which she visibly did, betrayed by her posture and the way her eyes shone. By now, Giselle was an expert in the matter.

William looked up, sensing the waitress's presence and her silent interaction with Giselle. His scowl turned into a faint smile.

A wave of applause and cries sounded from outside.

'Happy New Year,' the waitress said.

The rhythmic wave of muted explosions followed, as the fireworks were launched.

William blew Giselle a kiss over the table and its clutter of empty plates and glasses. She gripped his hand. The waitress departed before Giselle could think of passing her a business card.

A shroud of serenity swept over Giselle, as she watched the thin spider web of lines etched deep into William's face. He had trimmed his beard a few weeks ago while they visited Paris and somehow this now made him look younger and less wild and unkempt. Almost a new man, sculpted from the fires of experience and the labours of pain. Gone was his longing, to be replaced by a gentle form of acceptance, a feeling she now shared. They had buried the past and were entering the New Year in a state of mental nakedness, reborn. Together.

They had decided not to follow the Ball on its departure to the Northern wilderness, and opted to take a break from the Network's excesses for a time. William had asked if they could

briefly return to Paris before settling down as she had suggested in New Orleans. A final stroll along the Seine, walks
down the narrow streets and busy boulevards, a pilgrimage to
their sources, bone marrow and garlic snails in the restaurant
with the paisley tablecloths in Rue Guisarde where they once
were regulars, the scents of the flower market in the shadow
of Notre-Dame. It just felt, he said, like the right thing to do
before plunging headlong into what would be a new life, an
ultimate nod to the past, both its joys and its tragedies, an
exorcism. At first Giselle had been nervous at the prospect,
but he had quickly talked her round. There were no direct
flights between either Portland or Seattle across the Atlantic,
so William found a circuitous route with a stop-over in
Montreal and begged Giselle if they could stay there for forty-
eight hours, interrupting their journey. It was where he was
from, another place he wished to bid farewell to, visit his
parents' grave, climb the city's steep hills one final time, com-
mune with a share of his past she didn't know much about.

She agreed. '*Oui, Monsieur Tremblay*,' she said.

William smiled broadly. '*Merci, Mademoiselle Denoux.*' It
sounded so odd to be called Mademoiselle again. All the
dancers at The Place over the years would obediently refer
to her as Madame! She had always blamed the perennial
velvet gowns she had studiously worn in her managerial
role, but it was more than that. Her bearing, too.

To Giselle's surprise, she could barely understand the

French spoken in Quebec, a strange mix of patois and guttural accents combined with archaic expressions and turns of phrase, and felt like a stranger in a strange land, no longer William's indispensable guide, but a passenger for whom he had to interpret as he gave instructions to the taxi drivers they hailed. On the final morning of their stop-over, he took her to a small museum on Mount Royal where a permanent collection of local artists was held.

'Why?' Giselle had asked, painfully aware of his blindness and the fact that he would not be in a position to view any of the artwork on display.

He failed to answer. Muttering under his breath as she described the choice of rooms facing them. 'Unless they have changed the place's topography,' he indicated, 'it should be the room on the right.' She took his hand and guided him through.

They walked to the far wall. A half dozen assorted paintings were hung against the blankness of whitewashed stone.

Giselle's eyes ran across the display and her attention was quickly attracted to the medium-sized painting hung at the centre. She recognised the style immediately. It was unmistakable.

A painting by William she had never come across before.

Her breath stopped.

It was titled *Jeanne au Bucher*.

'Joan at the Stake.'

Winter

A hyperrealist image of Joan of Arc tied to a thick wooden pole, surrounded by a faceless crowd, flames licking her feet, the towers of Rouen a wall of stone surrounding them. Unlike in the classic imagery, Joan was buck naked. Small-breasted, open red wounds dotting her white flesh like stigmata, her bare nether regions glimpsed through a column of smoke rising from the tongues of fire already consuming her.

Giselle gulped.

'This is why I wanted you, from the very beginning. It was ordained, wasn't it?' William said, his voice a terrible hush in the solemn silence of the small museum.

Giselle's eyes were drawn to Joan's face in the picture. It was hers. And it wasn't the expected expression of pain that contorted her features, but one of pleasure. There could be no doubt about it.

Her whole body shook. As if she was right now at the stake and burning.

By the frame was a rectangular card indicating the artist's name and the year of the composition.

William Tremblay. The attribution date was a full two years before they had even met.

'You were already in my mind,' William said. 'It was my first ever sale to a gallery.'

Three days later in Paris, Giselle woke William at midnight in their hotel room close by the Luxembourg and led him to the promontory at the end of the Ile de la Cité by the Pont Neuf and in the heart of darkness, shrouded from the sight of strangers, in a cold autumnal breeze she stripped and asked William to fuck her. When she came, she screamed and the sounds of her ritual of purging flew across the river like a bird freed from its cage.

Impaled on him, she liberated once and for all her memories and her devils.

The young waitress brought their check. William searched for his credit card in the inside pocket of his jacket. While in Paris, he had signed a lucrative contract with an art gallery on the Rue du Cherche-Midi to whom he had previously submitted samples of his small, intimate sculptures, and had been given a substantial commission for a whole series of objects and larger pieces.

William guessed that the presence of the waitress intrigued Giselle.

'Let me guess ... Were you wondering what she would be like as a dancer?' he asked, once the young woman had disappeared towards the cash register.

'You have second sight,' Giselle said. 'Actually, she would also be very suitable as a model. You'd like her. She has a certain *je ne sais quoi* ...'

'Ah, but these days in order to sculpt I have to touch my inspiration, caress it, knead its material deep ...' William reminded her. 'Wouldn't that make you jealous?'

When the waitress returned with their receipt, Giselle did not pass her a business card.

'I don't know,' Giselle replied. 'The birth of beauty has its attractions. It's only art, after all. Should we put it to the test?'

They had found and acquired a small colonial-style house on the unfashionable edges of the Garden District. Giselle had managed to transplant most of the garden she had cultivated in the grounds of The Place and they had turned a shed at the back into a workshop for William. And then, there were the small jobs they still undertook for the Network and the Ball. For the first time in both their lives, the future was secure and predictable.

A new year; a new life.

It was three in the morning by the time they reached home after navigating the French Quarter crowds in full celebratory mood. Their own respective witching hour.

They undressed.

William took off his dark glasses.

'Dance for me, Giselle,' he asked.

And their waltz of forever after finally began. One note at a time.

Acknowledgements

This is our 8th volume together. We began with *Eighty Days Yellow* and the saga continues with the Pleasure Quartet.

As ever we would like to thank our agent Sarah Such, who believed in us from the beginning and has worked tirelessly on our behalf since, along with her overseas agents and our team of publishers worldwide who have made the journey so exciting and enjoyable. We've mentioned many of you before, but without you there would have been no journey to the outer reaches of desire, lust, and pleasure. Thank you, danke, merci, gracias, grazie, dziekuje, hvala, obrigado, dank je wel, sas efcharisto, tesekkur ederim, arigato, tack, tak, takk, dakujem, dekuji, aciu, paldies, vi blagodaram, and thank you again in any language not included in Google Translate . . .

We also owe a debt to all the great music that has inspired

Acknowledgements

us along the road from classical to contemporary, and the other writers who planted the seeds for our imagination to thrive on or paved the way, as well as the films and, last but not least, the men and women close and distant, known and unknown who've made our lives what they are.

About the Author

Vina Jackson is the pseudonym for two established writers working together. One is a successful author; the other a published writer who is also a financial professional in London.

THE PLEASURE QUARTET

FROM OPEN ROAD MEDIA

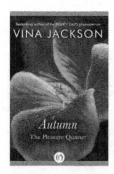
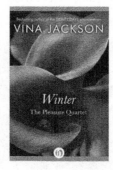

OPEN ROAD

INTEGRATED MEDIA

Open Road Integrated Media is a digital publisher and multimedia content company. Open Road creates connections between authors and their audiences by marketing its ebooks through a new proprietary online platform, which uses premium video content and social media.

CPSIA information can be obtained at www.ICGtesting.com
Printed in the USA
BVOW08s0611071015

420841BV00002B/2/P